M

W9-DBX-084

Paul Reidinger

The City Kid

Pre-publication
REVIEWS,
COMMENTARIES,
EVALUATIONS . . .

"Guy Griffith has been in San Francisco some two years, living with a female friend after his lover terminated his and Guy's ten-year relationship. Now forty, he is just becoming satisfied with being single. One day he meets sixteen-year-old Doug Whitmore near a gay beach. They talk elliptically, and when Guy discovers his bike has a flat, Doug gives him a lift. Several weeks later, Doug contacts Guy, and they fall into a mentor relationship limited by the boy's caginess and Guy's wariness. Lightning strikes when Doug's father, Ross, is arrested for public indecency, which precipitates a divorce, Ross acknowledging his homosexuality, and—almost—Doug's exploration of his sexuality with Guy. The boy flees from Guy's apartment into the night, and Guy doesn't see him again until five years later, on the beach. Reidinger's fourth novel is a welcome return to the moodier, more painful, more morally concerned atmosphere of *The Best Man* (1986) and *Intimate Evil* (1989). What's more, Ross Whitmore returns from *The Best Man* to justify that book's hero David Rice's hurt but helpless skepticism about Ross's marriage. Reidinger reflects on and generalizes from his characters' motives and actions much more than other contemporary novelists, yet his every interpretation rings true, none more than the downbeat ending's implicit endorsement of the adage, *like father, like son."*

Booklist

More pre-publication
REVIEWS, COMMENTARIES, EVALUATIONS . . .

"**T**he *City Kid* is fiction-making at its most satisfying. Elegantly written, this novel is hugely sexy and remarkably wise—a tough, clear-eyed look at the promise and treachery of human need. Confused youth and bedazzled middle age—or is it the other way around?—have seldom flirted more provocatively, or with more absorbing consequences, both bitter and sweet. Reidinger does not flinch from the difficult emotional contortions people put themselves through in their attempts to evade the truths that hurt, and he metes out his narrative justice with rueful impartiality."

Paul Russell
Author,
The Coming Storm
and *Boys of Life*

"**P**aul Reidinger's account of the relationship between a forty-ish gay man and a sexually confused sixteen-year-old boy would, in lesser hands, have devolved into sentimentality or pornography. Instead, this is a beautifully written, acutely observed coming-of-age story with one profound difference—it is the adult protagonist, Guy, who comes of age, not teenaged Doug. Guy's encounters with the troubled, erotically charged youth lead him to embrace maturity and to turn away from the puerile fantasies of gay life: he becomes a man. What Doug becomes is heartrending, but entirely convincing. This is a novel for grown-ups. Read it."

Michael Nava
Author,
The Death of Friends
and *The Burning Plain*

"**T**here is an engaging surface simplicity to *The City Kid*'s account of the not-so-unusual relationship between a middle-aged gay man and a morose teenage lad, whose paths cross at the nude beach one sunny San Francisco day, that belies this story's acute wisdom and emotional complexity. Paul Reidinger, whose writing purrs and whose thinking hums, captures other moments of contemporary queer life with invigorating honesty: the ongoing friendships of gay men and straight women who figured out on the cusp of adulthood that they weren't meant for romance with each other; the covert hypocrisy of the closet door slammed on the self; the hard-thought-through comfort of a single man aging alone who comes to trust his own worth; the tug of war between lust and common sense.

Mix those tensions with the angry, muddled yearning of a confused, sexy, sulky sixteen-year-old desperate for a father, and the result is a sagely satisfying read. And why, after all, is the relationship between a man over forty and a boy under twenty not unusual? Because many gay men do serve as mentors to younger men, and not all of those boys know whether they themselves are gay, a worrisome truth that is one of the skillful knots untangled in this tidy, intricate novel."

Richard Labonte
Book critic,
PlanetOut.com

The City Kid

HARRINGTON PARK PRESS
Southern Tier Editions
Gay Men's Fiction
Jay Quinn, Executive Editor

Love, the Magician by Brian Bouldrey

Distortion by Stephen Beachy

The City Kid by Paul Reidinger

Rebel Yell: Stories by Contemporary Southern Gay Authors edited by Jay Quinn

The City Kid

Paul Reidinger

Southern Tier Editions
Harrington Park Press®
An Imprint of The Haworth Press, Inc.
New York • London • Oxford

Published by

Southern Tier Editions, Harrington Park Press®, an imprint of The Haworth Press, Inc., 10 Alice Street, Binghamton, NY 13904-1580.

PUBLISHER'S NOTE
This is a work of fiction. Names, characters, places, and incidents either are the products of the author's imagination or are used fictitiously, and any resemblance to actual persons, living or dead, business establishments, events, or locales is entirely coincidental.

Cover design by Marylouise E. Doyle.

Library of Congress Cataloging-in-Publication Data

Reidinger, Paul.
    The city kid / Paul Reidinger.
        p. cm.
    ISBN 1-56023-168-8 (hard : alk paper)—ISBN 1-56023-169-6 (soft : alk. paper)
    1. San Francisco (Calif.)—Fiction. 2. Gay youth—Fiction. 3. Gay men—Fiction. I. Title.

PS3568.E479 C58 2001
813'.54—dc21
                                                                          00-057517

For my two little pals,
and the biggest pal of all

I do not understand my own actions.
For I do not what I want,
but I do the very thing I hate.

Romans 7:15

The gods are strange, and punish us
for what is good and humane in us
as much as for what is evil and perverse.

Wilde, *De Profundis*

Chapters

———··✄··———

Thanks to Michael Nava, Brian Bouldrey, Steven Wiesner, Liza Mundy, Charlotte Sheedy, and Michael Lowenthal

i. *The Man*

BY EARLY OCTOBER, the weather in the city turned warm and clear and erotic. It was shirtless weather, as Guy Griffith sometimes thought of it, though he could not easily bring himself to go around without his own shirt. He liked it well enough when other men took their shirts off, but his own body still faintly embarrassed him, despite years of diligent effort at a series of gyms, from temples of neon and MSNBC to seedy, smelly inner-city hulks. His body did not—and, he knew, would never—seem sufficiently iconic for public display. Even when other people were looking at his chest on those rare occasions when he bared it, he assumed they were staring in disapproval, as if to say, *How dare a man of his age parade himself like that!* In a youth culture, it was impossible not to be at least a little self-conscious about one's own ever-dwindling store of youth. To grow older was to spend down one's store of that much-prized—possibly overprized—commodity.

"There's a hole in your Spandex," Guy's roommate, Susannah, informed him as he readied himself for a Saturday afternoon bicycle odyssey to the Golden Gate Bridge. It was a trip he tried to make several times a week, even in winter, when darkness fell early and wind blew and cold rain fell often. By October, winter rains were imminent around the bay, though winter itself seemed impossible in the warm blue air. Winter seemed much more likely around the Fourth of July, when the city tended to be fogged in and frigid. San Francisco was the only city in the world whose inhabitants fled in summer so they could warm up.

"Where?"

"There," she said, pointing in the direction of his right thigh, where a seam had split, exposing a button of pale flesh.

"I know," he said. "That's been there a while."

"Sexy."

"You think?"

"I think it's time to upgrade," she said.

"These aren't that old," Guy said, examining the hole with irritated resignation. "I only got them a year or two ago."

"Yes, you were cheated," she said with a contented sigh. "Ripped off by the Man, selling his shoddy goods."

"Coming with?"

"You know I'd love to," she said. She was smoking a cigarette and drinking coffee while she glanced through the morning paper. They were together on the deck of the flat they shared. Guy kept his bike on the deck, and there she exiled herself whenever she needed to puff. It was a gesture she made for his benefit; it was her apartment, and she had taken him in when he had been a refugee from a failed union in the flat hay-scented country back East, where they'd grown up and gone to high school. Her forcing herself to smoke on the deck—she would huddle there, puffing away, even in rainstorms, like a spy nervously awaiting some rendezvous—was her way of punishing herself for persisting in a habit she knew was vile and politically problematic but could not find the will to break. It was also a kind of ritual sacrifice, an acknowledgment that Guy's presence in the apartment was not only legitimate but part of what made the place their home.

"I suppose this is one of your little sex junkets?" she wondered, face half-hidden by the pink pages.

"I beg your pardon?"

"Oh, don't think I don't know what you're up to out there, at your little Shangri-la."

"Are you impugning my innocence?"

"Oh yes, indeed," she said. She puffed her cigarette and took a sip of coffee. "Very much so."

"That's what I thought," he said.

"Not that I disapprove," she said.

"Of course not."

"I mean, someone in this household should get some occasionally, don't you think?"

"It's just a beach," Guy said. "Why don't you come along? Keep me out of trouble?"

"Well, I'd love to, I really would," she said. "But I wouldn't want to get in the way. I know how much you men like your trouble."

"I take it that's a No."

Then she smiled and shrugged her shoulders and riffled the papers, as if to say, *This is enough exercise for me, thank you very much!* In Guy's eyes she was still and always would be the vivacious eighteen-year-old he'd taken to the senior prom, the girl he'd conducted a tepid romance with, who never complained about his mysterious lack of ardor, who'd mothered him more than his own, rather self-involved mother ever had. But he could see too, as if by double vision, that time had touched her as it had touched him. She had gained weight, and acquired fine crinkles at the corners of her eyes, and her black hair was faintly frosted with gray, like a car on an icy morning. She was definitely looking a little motherly, though she wasn't even a mother, or married, or dating, or apparently much interested in any aspect of the mating game.

Guy had not yet found gray hairs on his head, nor begun to think of himself as old, though at forty he was conscious of growing older—older, at any rate, than much of the urban throng. When he had first come to the city, he had noticed how often men he met apologized for being thirty—or more—as if they had bluffed their way into some trendy gathering on a discounted student rate and, having been found out, expected immediate and scornful expulsion by the youth police, blowing furiously on their whistles.

Yet thirty seemed to Guy, in retrospect, the apogee of youth, summation of his own chaotic, sometimes ecstatic twenties. He had enjoyed being thirty. In the years since, he had noticed his face growing fuller, his beard heavier and more difficult to shave. The flesh on his cheeks was beginning to look a little leathery—a bit like fine calfskin. The boyish dew had lifted from his eyes, replaced by a glint of appraisal. One had seen and learned things, often not reassuring things, and the record of disillusionment, of time itself passing, was written on the flesh. If he didn't entirely feel like a man inside—and what man did?—he knew he no longer looked like a boy. He was no longer a sapling but a sturdy tree, an accumulation of age rings clad in coarsening bark.

He had a man's body, and a few of the attendant complaints. He had to get up often in the night to relieve himself, especially if he had drunk wine with dinner, as he and Susannah were fond of doing. (He liked white, she liked red, the latter being, in his eyes, the more adult, sophisticated preference.) He wore his glasses more often, especially in the evening, when his eyes wearied—sooner than they used to—of the contact lenses he'd worn in one version or another since high school. Most noticeable, his knees ached after he'd ridden his bicycle to the ocean, as he loved to do, especially in fine autumn weather, when the streets and parks were full of the bare-chested and recklessly cheerful young on their Rollerblades. If, as news reports ominously suggested, he might expect to live another sixty or more years, he foresaw an eventual need for knee replacements.

As a twenty-one-year-old, Guy had feared being twenty-five, could not imagine being thirty, but as he got older, the fear dissipated, the unimaginable came peacefully to pass. The incessant blare of popular culture made age out to be fearful, but getting older meant, at least in its less extreme declensions, a calming of turmoil, a settling of the dust. It was easier to dislike things instead of wasting time and energy pretending otherwise, as the energetic younger self had done. A man in his thirties knew who he was and how he'd got there; the arc of his life had become traceable. He might not like it, but he knew what it was.

Guy wasn't especially happy about his station in life, but on the other hand, he wasn't sentimental about how he'd reached it. He'd made choices and they'd counted, and there was hard comfort in knowing that they couldn't be taken back, no matter how unfortunate. He had no wish to know as little as he'd known as a younger man. Youth was ignorance, and ignorance promoted thrashing, which, under the glorified name of passion, caused all sorts of emotional and psychic injuries, especially to innocent bystanders. Passionate young people were like terrorist bombs in pretty suitcases waiting to go off in airport lounges, spraying shrapnel in every direction.

The young were desirable only to the extent that one ignored their self-serving savagery, which was something like enjoying the performance at Ford's Theater despite the presence of Mr. John Wilkes Booth. The young were best explored in private fantasy. Urban experience taught that the most alluring human vessels were often the most empty, or, if not empty, the most brimming with toxins. Knowing that—knowledge earned the hard way, through experience—made it easier to pass up the occasional opportunity that presented itself. Guy admired the young without envying them, and he was pleased not even to desire them that much (or at least not as much as he had when he'd been one of them), not even when they descended in shirtless droves on a sunny Golden Gate Park, through which he passed on his way to the bridge.

"Well, then, I'm off," he said to Susannah, who a few moments later waved to him from the deck as he pedaled by before returning to the fragrances and fumes of her late-morning weekend ritual. Guy waved, in turn, to the group of thuggy post-adolescents who lived, or congregated with those who lived, across the street in a house notable for always having a car up on blocks next to the front door.

The young thugs were all wearing black hooded sweatshirts and billowy loose-fitting jeans that exposed the waistbands, and then some, of their boxer shorts. They swarmed over the current blocked-up car, an old Chevy Nova, like ants on a rotting apple core. Guy's wave was precautionary rather than friendly, a gesture of the watchful neutrality that made it possible for wildly different sorts of people to live packed tight in cities. The young goons waved back—a gesture, Guy supposed as he pedaled around the corner and up a shallow incline, meant to suggest not amiability but that they too were watchfully neutral and disinclined, at least for the moment, to knock him off his mountain bike or throw bricks through the windows of his apartment.

* * *

Guy had fled West two years before, drawn to San Francisco partly by the presence there of his old high-school friend but more by the beckoning whorishness of the city itself. In return for cash, the old girl promised an interval of sensual distraction, and Guy, though a bit cash-poor, needed a roll in some faraway hay. When he arrived for his two-week sojourn in Susannah's guest room, he was grieving at the crack-up of his union and anxious about his unexpected future as a single man. He had lost his sense of family, and his hearth and home had been sold to become someone else's hearth and home.

He had always thought he and Philip would be together forever and never thought his expectation was in any way trite. The split felt like slipping on an unseen patch of ice. One moment he was walking along normally, the next he was suspended in space at a bizarre angle, limbs in all the wrong places. Then the shocking thud of impact, and the spread of pain.

Love was something that people built, but like all human constructions, it was far easier to wreck than it had been to assemble. Building love took effort and attention and trust. Trust was the greatest act of love. Love was trust was peace, but peace was a hard business while war was an easy one, easy to slip into. People defaulted to war, to conflict. They enjoyed it, needed it. Conflict satisfied the human hunger for drama; it was fire in the forest of human relations.

Guy thought that he and Philip had managed to trust one another. They loved one another: for a year, five, ten. The passage of time was reassuring. Time meant stability.

But time could also mean silent rot, the accumulation of resentments and secrets and unacknowledged distance until there was a sudden collapse, like a badly built tenement giving way. It was easy, and tempting, not to notice silent rot, and Guy had been tempted. He was a believer and a romantic; he had trusted. So he was devastated by Philip's announcement, one February evening after he'd come home from work, that Philip had been seeing someone else and had decided to be with him, after the new pair returned from a holiday in the Greek islands that had been explained away to Guy as as an extended business trip.

It was as if Guy had spent ten years not knowing Philip at all. The Philip he thought he knew would never have done such a thing, but then, as Guy recognized too late, the Philip he had thought he'd known was a creation of his own imagination. That was Philip as he wanted Philip to be, Philip projected from his own wants and needs, not the real Philip, the Philip who was restless and dissatisfied and deceitful and self-interested—the Philip whom, it turned out, he had never really known.

"Typical man," Susannah had said with a sigh as Guy wept out the story onto her shoulder. "Present company excepted."

"I can't believe it," Guy had said. For, among the many shames of Philip's defection was Guy's shameful thickheadedness about what was really going on. Philip might have been deceitful, but Guy had allowed himself to be deceived; he was a co-conspirator. Under the noble aegis of trust, he had submitted to being fooled. He had willingly played his role in their melodrama, because he had been unwilling to question the basis of what he took to be his—their—happiness.

Propped against Susannah's shoulder, he wanted to dispute her flippant crack about men. But he couldn't. He squirmed at the thought that she might be right: that men were inherently unreliable. Men yearned for freedom, but was freedom the great male opiate, a euphemism for reckless, pointless wandering? Would men fatally overdose on it, just as laboratory rats would take cocaine to the exclusion of all other pleasures, until they died of starvation?

It was clear Susannah thought so. He had never before considered the possibility that she might be right—just as he had never considered the possibility that he and Philip might split up. Slowly he was awakening to a world of unconsidered possibilities.

"You don't need him anyway," she murmured in his ear.

"I know," Guy mumbled back. Of course he didn't know. He had no idea how he would manage without Philip. He was an exile from a life that no longer existed, like a man in rags staggering from a town that had been bombed to rubble.

The world was made of couples, and he had been part of one—a good one, he thought, a happy one, a male one, in defiance of the endless social propaganda that men, unassisted by women, were incapable of love. But perhaps he had underestimated the corrosive power of propaganda, which drew strength and became self-fulfilling from repetition. That understanding was the basis of all successful tyranny. The same thing, said over and over again a thousand different ways, in a thousand different contexts, began to acquire the ring of truth. What man, told in every possible way by people he trusted, beginning with his mother, that male love was hopeless—and worse than hopeless: *disgraceful*—wouldn't begin to wonder?

Philip had been a decent, ordinary man, replete with the usual weaknesses, among them yearnings for acceptance and respectability, the dread of growing old, and the fear, so often swabbed with easy sex, that male love was indeed unattainable.

He needed to run away, but because he could not run away from himself, he ran away from Guy, breaking a long bond and taking up with a much younger man whom Guy regarded as dangerously self-regarding and opportunistic. For all the conventional wisdom about the vulnerability of young people, older people could be vulnerable, too. But Philip wouldn't listen, perhaps because he already knew the truth: that the real point of his new liaison was to ensure not only Guy's loneliness but his own. Being lonely was what they both deserved.

They lived their final few weeks in their jointly held house with the polite awkwardness of strangers sharing a cabin in a train. They continued to sit down to the meals Guy cooked because he couldn't imagine not cooking them, and to sleep in the same bed, even as house and home quietly slipped away around them. Guy was slowly moving his things to an apartment he'd found downtown, while Philip moved his things Guy knew not where. Wherever the boy awaited, presumably.

The disposition of some of the more valuable items—the china, a few of the paintings, some pieces of furniture—along with the most valuable item of all, the house, occasioned their few conversations. And those conversations were painful not least for their banality. Breaking up was among the most banal of human deeds. It was always different yet always horribly the same.

"I'm sorry," Philip said one night as they sat side by side on the living room floor, going through the photo albums to decide who should take what. Guy imagined himself having an out-of-body experience, drifting away from his stunned flesh toward the ceiling, from which he might gaze down on the two of them and see what he'd always seen: Two people who belonged together, who fit together like pieces of a puzzle, sitting in front of a blazing hearth on a cold winter's night seasoned with a few snow flurries. Yet this puzzle was shattering into its constituent, and useless, pieces. Philip was sorry. Guy was sorry.

"I know," Guy said, there being nothing else to say. He wondered if he should be angry at Philip's foolishness. Mainly he was sad. Theirs was an avoidable catastrophe that had not been avoided. Much later, and from far away, Guy would see things differently; he would understand that Philip was driven by forces quite beyond his control to take irreversible steps that guaranteed, among many wretchednesses, his own, and then, once it was too late, regret doing that very thing.

But even in the moment Guy could not hate Philip, nor the boy, who after all was little more than an instrument of someone else's folly, too young and hormonal to understand the storm at whose center he stood.

"I know you think I'm doing the wrong thing," Philip said. For some reason he sagged against Guy's shoulder, as he had always done, and Guy felt, as he always did, a surge of tenderness and protectiveness for this sweet, vulnerable, foolish man.

"I do," Guy said quietly.

"I can't explain it," Philip said.

"I know."

"I'll always love you."

"Don't say that," Guy said.

"You know it's true." Philip was holding Guy's hand now, kneading his fingers.

"Therefore we're splitting up."

"You'll be okay," Philip said. "You'll be fine. This is better for you. For both of us."

Guy could practically hear the pages of the script being rustled. In the most intense human situations, the range of permissible expression was at its most prescribed, and circumscribed. He glanced at

Philip's head against his shoulder and saw, as if for the first time, the markings of age: the slightly nappy blond hair going gray at the temples, hairline retreating up the forehead, skin turning rough at the nape of the neck. Philip was no longer young, and if he wasn't, Guy couldn't be, either. They had shared their youth and now, youth spent, it was time to part. That was the lesson, and it did not make sense.

"I hope you're not too mad at me," Philip continued, as if addressing the flames.

"I'm not mad," Guy said in a blank voice. He too was staring at the fire and imagining that the flames were consuming their life; in the morning, the grate would be cold and there would be nothing left, just ash and a faint sooty smell.

"I'd understand if you were," Philip said. "I am, kind of."

"What are you mad about?"

"That I'm doing this," he said. "I love this house," he said. "I loved it the minute we walked into it. Remember?"

"No," Guy said. Of course he remembered. It had been a sunny Sunday afternoon in February, more years ago than seemed possible. Everything had felt right then. But that house was not this house. This house was theirs no longer. It belonged to other people eager to install their own lives within its walls. Within a few months it would be repainted and rewallpapered and refurnished and would be unrecognizable to its old occupants. "Of course I remember," he said, his voice scratching with irritation for the first time. "I just don't want to talk about it."

"That's what you always said," Philip said.

"So naturally you went out and found yourself a twenty-five-year-old."

Philip merely sighed, leaving Guy's bit of juicy bait unrisen-to. "I don't think I was very good at it either," he said. "Talking, I mean. Getting things out. Joshua's much better at it. He's helped me be more open."

"That's nice," Guy said. He felt inexpressibly crushed; he was an emotional failure—blocked and uncommunicative. In that moment it all made sense. He and Philip didn't belong together, and Philip had recognized the fact first. He'd acted. Guy was to be succeeded by a boy named Joshua. Even his name was fresh and sexy and inevitable. "I'm sure you'll be happy," he said.

"I know we will be," Philip said. "I know you will be too."

"So you think I should find my own twenty-five-year-old."

"I know you'll find someone," Philip said. "You deserve to."

"You're very kind," Guy said. The moment had arrived either for the shattering of crockery or a farewell fuck on the living-room floor, but the moment passed, and they went back to sorting out the pictures, drifting slowly, gently apart with each snapshot.

Washing up on Susannah's shores, Guy told himself that he was through with male intimacy. He would never accept the propaganda, but he was beginning to accept that the propaganda damaged most men so much that the prophesy of male loneliness and sterility fulfilled itself. It was not a struggle he could win on his own. He would find another way, in a faraway city where people devoted their lives to finding other ways. He would learn to thrive by himself. He would cultivate his relations with Susannah, careful at all times to be realistic and honest with her. And he would stitch together a patchwork quilt of male company that did not place too heavy a burden on a single individual.

* * *

Like all visitors, Guy had been bewitched by San Francisco, bewitched not least by the fact that he would soon have to leave it and go home. Like all visitors, he hadn't worried about time or money, and he had soaked up the carnival distractions the city provided in such abundance: the food and the vistas, the men and the street life, the light and air and exotic, not-quite-American tone. The city's connections to the huge reality that lay eastward were fragile and manageable: a couple of bridges, a tunnel, some wires and satellite uplinks, scraps of language. The place was at once familiar and attractively foreign and seemed to invite fresh starts.

It was easy for Guy to imagine transposing what remained of his life to such a place, where everyone seemed to be a misfit from somewhere else. In a world of misfits, fitting in wasn't much of an issue. The physical dimension of moving didn't seem too bad, either. When Guy finally arrived in the city for good, as an immigrant rather than a visitor, his possessions amounted to a few suitcases full of clothes, and a few boxes of books and other material effluvia he'd gathered over the years. The joint effects had mostly stayed with Philip or been liquidated.

Yet marrying the city turned out to be a drastically different experience from merely visiting her, as Guy began to find out once he'd moved there. After two years, he did and did not feel at home in the city he called home. He loved the place for taking him in when he was hurt, and for swabbing his wounds in its pagan way. The city was a halfway house for wounded souls. He felt that he belonged among them, another face in a crowd of hard stories. Yet the city felt continuously strange to him. It was tiny and claustrophobic and stunningly expensive, intricately layered with strata of money and social standing, every sort of pretension and smugness and hypocrisy, a modest leavening of altruism, and failure.

Failure most of all. Failure was the city's most striking social feature, made all the more conspicuous by the general agreement not to acknowledge it. It was a city of underachievers who stayed for a while, worked temp jobs or freelance, then left when the rent spiked or the landlord evicted them on "move-in" grounds or they broke up with a lover or simply couldn't find real work or could no longer bear the sense of aimless drift, the culture of failure. Among those of independent—which was to say, generally speaking, inherited—means, there was a quiet civic pride in the city's being genteelly unaccommodating, of its ingrown webs of privilege and access that elegantly blocked outsiders. It was a stagnant place that gave every appearance of being otherwise. It was full of people whose family fortunes were invested elsewhere, hard at work creating jobs in other cities. Behind their façades of de rigueur pious liberalism, they felt entitled to do and have anything they wanted.

Unused as Guy was to big cities, he felt immediately that San Francisco would never expel him the way his town back East had done. Impoverishment, yes; expulsion, never. Big cities were made up of the indigestible elements of smaller towns elsewhere, comfortable middle-American burgs built, like cemeteries, of green lawns and conformity, with no use for irregular human pieces. Those rough and oddly shaped bits, if they were lucky, found their way into the human collages of cities where, compressed into a tight space, they recombined into an urban organism greater than the sum of its parts.

Guy had come West as a fairly rough bit, full of shame and a sense of failure, only to find the kindness of strangers who listened sympathetically to his little tale of fool's paradise, woe and exile, then responded with little tales of their own that drew him in and gave him a place. His immediate sense of belonging told him that he'd never felt he'd really belonged anywhere before. It was like smelling a lovely scent for the first time yet feeling one had known and loved the scent all one's life.

He loved the city's flair for living, the shops and cafes, clubs and restaurants. He loved its way of impersonating other cities, of seeming one moment familiar and homey and the next, around a corner, mysterious, exotic, erotic, unknowable. He loved its capacity to distract people like Guy from their troubles. But gradually reality became plain again. It was as if a shining, foamy tide had ebbed, leaving behind a beach strewn with flotsam: driftwood and garbage and knots of smelly kelp.

"Do you ever get lonely?" he asked Susannah one rainy winter night, when they were cuddled up together on her aging couch, watching cable while a duraflame flickered in the fireplace.

"Not really," she said. "I don't like people very much. I'm happier by myself. I was probably a cat in a previous life."

Guy said nothing. He was thinking that he must have been a dog in a previous life: He craved human contact; he felt cold and small when he climbed into bed at night by himself. He found himself missing Philip's warm presence, his broad back, the steadiness of his breathing. He was not meant to be alone. He needed someone. But being needy was the emotional equivalent of shark repellent, guaranteed to frighten off anyone worthy.

"Are you lonely?" she asked him.

"Not when I'm with you."

"Do you miss Philip?"

"There's a hole where he used to be."

"I'm sorry," she said, leaning over to kiss him on the forehead and hold his hand. "Maybe you'll meet someone else."

Hers was a bromide intended to soothe, but it had the opposite effect. That casual comment unsettled Guy so much that he lost the plot of whatever they'd been watching, even as she sank back into the show, unaware of how she'd disturbed him. Her remark caused distress precisely because he did want to meet someone and could not imagine how that might happen, how he might go about it.

"You think so?" Guy said during a commercial.

"I do," she said. "You don't?"

"No, I do," he said. "Philip said I would, too."

"I don't know that I'm happy being in agreement with him," she said, "but I do know you're attractive, et cetera. And there are plenty of guys here who play for your team."

That was surely true. Yet meeting people, always something of a feat for Guy, was especially so in the city, which was full of people as anonymous and isolated as he. City people kept to themselves. Of course it was possible to meet people: at the market, at parties, at clubs and sex clubs; it was possible to meet them anywhere. People were kind and seemingly accessible in the beginning, when one did not know them and strangeness was a lubricant; or, as among gay men, when meeting consisted of proffering one's penis and accepting similar proffers in return.

But once the strangeness began to dissipate, it became much harder to get to know them, to join in a mutual lowering of guard. City people who had given each other orgasms were always running off or not returning calls or saying they would call and then not calling—all serious breaches of the code of manners Guy had been raised with, but apparently survival skills in the modern metropolis. The central rule of urban romance emphasized, like good military strategy, preemption: treat other people badly before they treated you badly.

Guy had connected several times his first few months in the city, and found himself politely dumped every time. It turned out to be terribly easy to meet men who had longtime lovers and were looking for some out-of-the-house sport. Their erotic enthusiasm was matched only by the speed with which they slammed the emotional door once the play was done.

There was no feeling quite so depressing as being abandoned after sex, when two people should have been talking softly and giggling and rubbing each other's toes. The spoken-for men were friendly enough even as they cut him off; their gentle kisses and nuzzles and murmurs of goodbye said to Guy that they'd felt something. But not enough. They still fled, by bike, car, foot, back to their domestic happinesses, their hearths and homes full of warmth and love and purebred dogs. Their departures tended to be apologetic but hasty, as if Guy smelled bad.

The facts, viewed objectively, suggested that he was better off without the lightning bolt of desire and infatuation. The whole business was inconvenient and embarrassing. Its illuminations were so often, and so weirdly, false. It imperiled dignity, the quality that made loss of youth bearable.

* * *

The city, as it fell away from his feet to the north, shimmered faintly in the white autumn heat. The air was dry and fragrant, like desert air. He saw the Golden Gate Bridge, a set of rusty juts strung up with cables and framed by the shaggy dark-green head of Mount Tam rising beyond them. On the high cliffs above the bridge, lights winked from time to time: sunshine glinting from the windscreens of cars on high, twisting headlands roads. It was as if he were being beckoned onward, down the steep ski-ramp slope of Clayton, along the city streets to the sea.

At the sea, at the bridge, lay a beach full of men. It was a nude beach with an international reputation; Guy, like countless other guys around the world, had found out about it while surfing the Web in his first weeks in the city. It was one of the first such venues he'd investigated when he'd moved out, and he had made the trip with some frequency since then. He had visited when it was cold and clear, cool and foggy, windy and rainy; he'd even visited on those rare days when it was warm and sunny.

The air was still and quiet when Guy reached his favored spot, a hidden terrace of dying concrete, once a gun battery built to thwart the Japanese invasion, that lay at the end of a twisting gravel fire road. The battery was slowly being reclaimed by the wild hillside, like a temple of some lost civilization melting back into the jungle. Wild raspberry canes clambered up the cracked walls, and everywhere weeds were sprouting. It was as if the city itself had vanished, leaving Guy behind.

After locking his bike, he mounted the dying concrete steps to an intermediate level, where, in a sunny alcove, he came across a naked boy sunning himself on a towel. The boy's head was rigged with the scaffolding of a Sony Walkman, and he was reading a fat paperback novel (full of neo-Hemingway-esque bluster) Guy knew to be unreadable. The boy looked up; their eyes met, their heads nodded. Guy moved along. While he approved in theory of public nakedness, he'd never quite gotten used to it.

A rusty steel ladder led to the top level, which commanded a view of bridge, beach, strait, and, across the water, the Marin shore—an ominous mass, like some kind of humpbacked monster slouching against the sky. The beach crawled with people. A large freighter, low in the water, steamed slowly through the strait, bound for the open sea and the Orient. High overhead a 747 glinted white in the blue sky as it descended toward the airport. The world was very much with Guy, but he still felt alone, and peaceful.

He walked to the end of the battery, where a narrow trail led along the crest of the cliff into a stand of trees, where more trails branched out, some of them bearing down toward the water, others up toward the road, where tour buses plied. Amid the trees, Guy knew, was a sunny outcropping that enjoyed a wide view of beach and bridge. He liked to sit there sometimes, communing with his wilder brethren, absorbing their energy without mingling his flesh in theirs. He was a voyeur who didn't like to get too close, didn't want to see too much. The sight of human intimacy made him think of Philip, and thinking of Philip made him sad. And squeamish. He was drawn to the carnal and repelled by it, just as he'd been as a teenager. It was as if he'd completed the circle of his erotic journey and was now back at the beginning, wondering how and in what way he might begin again, if he wanted to. Wondering if he'd learned anything at all in the journey from twenty to forty.

He watched as a group of Japanese tourists, each with a Nikon slung from his neck, made their cautious way past his bike up the battery. They gawked stiffly as they passed the nude Walkman boy. Worlds collided. But the tourists' business was to photograph the bridge, and this they did, having reassembled themselves as a group at the top of the old steel ladder.

Guy, watching, heard a twig crack behind him. Immediately he snapped his head around, as if he were a rabbit alerted to the possible presence of a hungry fox. Hurrying along a nearby trail he saw a boy, naked except for a pair of white socks and hiking boots. His skin was creamy in the sunshine, and his buttocks worked like bellows as he made his way along the uneven ground. He was not approaching Guy but heading in the opposite direction.

Guy felt, simultaneously, relief and disappointment. He was about to return his gaze to the ocean when another figure appeared, as if pursuing the naked boy: A figure in green fatigues, older, with heavy black boots, a shiny brass badge, and a heavy packet hanging from his hip belt that might have been a gun. The figure, taking notice of Guy, paused briefly to evaluate. Guy felt exposed, and hugged his knees to his chest. The man in fatigues was plainly some sort of soldier or military policeman.

Guy had heard that, in rougher-and-readier days of yore, when the beach adjoined a military installation, soldier-boy types could often be found wandering the rocky acreage of the beach, looking for action or to scare people or both. Those days were gone, but here, apparently, was a leftover. Luckily Fatigues wasn't carrying a bayonet. He looked as if he were trying to think of something to say, but before he could get out the words his feet started up again, carrying him along the path in pursuit of Naked Hiking Boots.

Guy supposed that some sort of arrest or inquisition was in the offing. Public blatancy, even in an isolated spot, almost never went unremarked, or unresponded to, by officialdom. Public officials, certainly military or federal officials, could not be seen to be indifferent to a question of public morals. There would have to be the occasional patrols, the occasional busts, so that a few luckless scapegoats could be trotted out before the public as proof of tax dollars at work, of wickedness punished and public decency and military honor defended, the delicate sensibilities of God-fearing citizens protected.

The barrels most convenient for shooting this sort of fish were the places where men gathered, but to defuse charges of discrimination there were also periodic crackdowns on lovers' lanes, mainly in Golden Gate Park where teenage couples parked their cars and got down. Bored policemen would slink up in their cruisers, shine their spotlights into the suspect vehicle, and bellow through their loudspeaker, the point being more to take pleasure in inducing terror than anything else.

The naked boy's goose seemed to be all but cooked, unless he'd managed to hurry away fast enough to lose the pursuit. Guy glanced along the path he'd taken and saw to his surprise that the boy was standing at a promontory, staring out to sea as if unaware that the man in fatigues was about to reach him. And did reach him. And stopped behind him. They stood that way for a long moment, like cat and prey, breathless before the final move. Then the boy turned around. They moved closer together; their heads bobbed close. Surely they were not kissing. Guy could not see their hands. A moment later he couldn't see them at all.

He lay on his back and gazed up at the sky and was so lost in his daydream that he might not have noticed the approach of the fatigue man ten minutes or so later if the man's walkie-talkie hadn't crackled and squawked as he passed. They exchanged a glance, and a grin, and the man said, "I'm on duty and I'm late!" Tax dollars at work.

Off he went, toward the old battery, down the steel ladder, down the stairs, past Guy's bike and up the fire road, where he passed another set of figures drifting the other way: a young man and a black ball of fur that might have been a grizzly bear cub or an ewok on four legs. The pair were ambling along, in no evident hurry. Guy watched as they stopped well short of his bike and mounted another set of steps at the far end of the battery. Most likely they were oglers looking for a vantage point from which to spy on the more southerly section of the beach, where sports of both sexes played nude volleyball and the erotic energy was more heterosexual and more muted. Most likely the young man was carrying a pair of binoculars.

There was interest in watching a spy go about his work, but when this spy stood staring out to sea while his fuzzy black companion sniffed around, the tingle of vicarious prurience faded. Guy lay back again, closing his eyes and surrendering to reverie. He must have fallen asleep, because a moment later he was startled to feel something cool and damp sniffing his cheek. For an instant he thought it had to be Fatigues, stealthily returning to play, or Naked Hiking Boots with his milk-white buttocks. But when he opened his eyes he found himself face to face with a distinctly bear-like set of features: a huge square head, framed by a heavy mane, a blocky muzzle and velvet ears, triangular and upright, everything black except for the bright almond eyes, which regarded him with candid speculation.

"Chow," Guy said calmly.

The dog absorbed the word without reacting. No wagging tail, no growl or snarl, no movement of any kind. His mouth hung open slightly, revealing the grape Kool-Aid tongue and a set of unusually white, heavy teeth, like tusks. The creature stood still on his round kitty-cat feet.

"Rex!" said a voice, a voice that lacked timbre, a voice that belonged to someone who sounded as if he had a head cold. "Off!"

Reluctantly the dog swung his great head over his shoulder as his master approached, gingerly navigating his way across a small patch of mud (remnant of a rogue rainshower from the week before) and some fallen timber that had come down in a windstorm the previous winter but had yet to be cleared by the park service.

"Sorry," the reedy voice said to Guy. "He's friendly. Aren't you, Rex?"

Guy held out a hand, and the chow named Rex took a small sniff. Then, as if he had learned all he cared to know, he moved off, lifting his leg on a succession of nearby trees.

"Did he scare you?" The voice belonged to a young man who was still visibly a boy—a teenager of some sort, Guy thought uneasily. One never quite knew what to expect from them, caught as they were between worlds. Guy did not want to be fag-bashed. For the first time ever, he felt lucky that he was too shy to get naked in a public space. If this man-boy had come upon him naked, their meeting surely would have been less casually civil.

"No, not at all," Guy said. "I like dogs." He looked in Rex's direction, but the dog was entirely ignoring both of them as he went about his investigations of the little cliffside glade.

"He has a mind of his own," the boy said.

"I can see that."

"I guess there's a beach down there too," the boy said, looking over Guy's shoulder. "There's one on the other side." He motioned with his head to the far side of the battery. "Is that your bike down there?"

"Yeah," Guy said, "if it's still there."

"Yeah, it's there," the boy said. "We drove. Rex likes to look at the bridge sometimes."

If that were so, there was no evidence of it. The dog was sniffing and rooting in a patch of high grass like a pig searching out truffles. He paused only to do some tremendous wheel spinning with his stubby legs, which raised an impressive cloud of dirt and uprooted grass and an occasional pebble.

"Me too," Guy said.

The boy stepped past Guy, toward the edge of the precipice. "There are a lot of people down there."

"It's beach weather," Guy said. "You going down?"

"No," the boy said. "You?"

"I don't like the beach," Guy said. "I'm allergic to sand."

"Me too," the boy said. He gave a snorty laugh. "My name's Doug, by the way."

"Guy."

They shook hands—an oddly formal gesture in the circumstances, Guy thought, but then the boy almost certainly had no idea what the circumstances actually were, the sort of space he'd inadvertently wandered into.

"That's a cool name."

"Thanks," Guy said. "And I know Rex, of course. He introduced himself earlier."

"Where does this trail go?" Doug asked.

"It splits up over there, I think," Guy said. "One branch goes down to the water. The others go up toward the road."

"We parked on the road," Doug said. "At the top of the fire road." He was staring down at the beach as he spoke. "They look naked down there."

"Yes," Guy said.

"Is that legal?"

"I think so."

"I don't think I could ever do that," the boy said. He sounded as if he were strangling himself as he spoke.

"Take off all your clothes?"

"In public."

"Well, I don't think I could, either," Guy said, "and I'm a lot older than you."

"It looks like it's mostly men down there."

"All men, I think."

"There are some women on the other side."

"That's the mixed side," Guy said. "This is the men's side."

"Oh. I didn't know it was that official."

"I don't think it's official at all," Guy said.

The boy shuffled his feet and looked for his dog, who was trotting along one of the paths in pursuit of one of the skulking men who had emerged from the lower depths and, business apparently complete, was hurrying to his car. "Rex!" he called out. "Here! He's curious about people," he explained to Guy. "I've heard that's a gay beach. Do you think it is?"

"I think so."

"Me too."

Guy hesitated. He'd heard friends describe these sorts of encounters but had never quite believed they really happened.

"My parents have some gay friends," Doug said. He was looking down at his overlarge feet as he spoke, as if trying to figure out who they belonged to. The feet were encased in a pair of mud-spattered and no doubt fragrant sneakers. Perhaps he was as filled with wonder at them as Guy was. Doug was handsome in a soft, dough-boy way, but he was also painfully adolescent. His hands were too large, his head too small, his hair nappy; he had brushings of acne along his jaw below his ears; the timid sproutings of whiskers on his upper lip and chin looked like bits of lawn the mower missed. He wore a ragged T-shirt and a pair of dark-blue sweatpants that seemed to have been chosen for their very grunginess. He mumbled, he slurred his words, he looked away as he spoke, as if he were a guilty suspect being interrogated by the police. But every now and then he spoke clearly and looked Guy straight in the eye, as if trying on the role of man.

Guy noted no piercings—of ears, lips, eyebrows—but maybe that was just because the boy was still a little young. Or maybe he had been pierced in tenderer, less public places. Being pierced was a ritual of modern youth and, for Guy, who found it repulsive business, further proof that he was no longer quite young. He was just old enough to find the antics of younger people faintly ridiculous. The piercings, the tattoos, the streaks of lime green and raspberry in the hair, the saggy shapeless jeans worn below the hips, the incredibly expensive, ugly glasses: It was all about being like everyone else—heart of the conservative impulse, really—and defying bourgeois parents, without any recognition that defying parents' habits and expectations was a way of being shaped by them, even of being held captive by them. A pierced tongue and magenta hair did not equate to an escape from middle-class convention. Or a meaningful examination of it.

"I suppose everyone in San Francisco has some gay friends," Guy said.

"Do you?"

"Sure," Guy said. "But I haven't lived here very long, so I don't know all that many people."

"You moved here? From where?"

Guy named the town back on the prairie where he'd grown up, which of course Doug had not heard of, though he did seem to recognize the state. For native Californians, the great continent east of the High Sierra was vague and foreign, an indeterminate sea of Americana. Between the mountains and the Mississippi the country was largely empty. It was a kind of buffer zone, physical proof that California was different from the rest of the country, did not entirely belong to it or share its fate.

"Do you like it here?" Doug asked.

"Yeah, sure," Guy said. "I wouldn't be here if I didn't."

"Why did you move here?"

"I broke up with someone back East," Guy said. "I needed to get far away and start over."

"Oh," Doug said. "I just broke up with my girlfriend."

"I'm sorry."

"No big deal. Rex didn't like her. He said she was bad for me. He's usually right about that stuff."

"He does seem perceptive," Guy conceded.

"Yeah, I think we're going to go to college together," Doug said. "If we both get into the same school. I think he'll probably do better on the SAT than I will. My parents are making me take this preparation course."

Guy nodded silently. It was obvious that the boy did not want to leave and, not knowing what to say to keep the conversation going, would say practically anything. Their little dialogue was stumbling along, sputtering and coughing like a car running out of gas. There was the possibility that the boy was trying to hit on him, but that chance seemed remote. Doug was far too scruffy to generate homoerotic, or erotic, heat. He was just a sullen, eager kid who looked as if his breath smelled of milk. He was clearly in a state of uneasy excitement in Guy's presence, but it did not seem to be the same sort of unease Guy had felt when he was sixteen and painting the house of an attractive young married man whose wife was out of the house for long stretches.

That energy was missing with Doug. He was just a confused boy growing up in a strange city where heterosexual culture lacked the dominating force and certainty it exerted everywhere else. Guy felt a flush of sympathy for him. Growing up was always difficult for boys, but the time and place of Doug's emergence were especially unenviable. The culture, never too deep, had spent a couple of generations sacrificing its moral and ethical bearings to various gods—money, media, microchips—that, like all gods, had failed, were failing or would eventually fail, leaving nothing behind. How could one become a grown-up—why would one bother?—in a society that placed no real value on being grown up?

"Hey, I hope you get in," Guy said, getting to his feet. "Both of you!"

"You're leaving?"

"My roommate and I are going out for Mexican. I need to get home and take a shower. I'm all sweaty."

"You didn't say you had a roommate."

"She's an old friend from high school."

"You live with a woman?"

"Yes," Guy said.

The boy was plainly flustered. He was blushing and stammering and kicking his feet in the dirt. "Is she your girlfriend?" he finally managed to ask.

"No," Guy said. "She was a long time ago, though. When we were in high school."

"Do you have a girlfriend now?"

"I'm a single man!" Guy said. "And I really do have to take off. It's getting late."

It was past four. The air was still warm, but the autumn sun was settling rapidly now toward the Pacific, its beams growing longer and redder by the moment.

"The road's that way, right?" Doug asked, jabbing his thumb vaguely upslope.

Guy nodded. "You can't miss it. Good luck. I enjoyed talking to you." He extended a hand to the boy, who nodded in abashment but did take Guy's hand in return. His hand was soft and warm. When Guy broke their physical contact, Doug was looking at the hand, as if he'd just been stung by a jellyfish and was waiting for that lash of agony to reach his brain.

"See ya," Guy said. Gathering his things—helmet, gloves, water bottle—he set out on the path that led back to the battery, the ladder down one level, the stairs, the bike, the fire lane back to the main road. There was fairly steady traffic toward the road now, as beach hours drew to a close. Some boys would linger on the cliffside paths, looking for a little action, while others hurried along toward their cars, scarcely noticing Guy as they did.

In return Guy scarcely noticed them. He was contentedly thinking about faraway things when he heard crackling underbrush and a scrabbling on the concrete above him. He glanced up to see Doug and dog descending in his direction.

"We talked it over and decided it made more sense to go back the way we came," Doug explained. "Rex thought there might be burrs on some of those trails. He doesn't like to get burrs in his fur."

"I can understand that," Guy said. "I don't like to get them in mine! Anyway the fire lane is the easiest way back to the road."

"Do you have water in your bottle?"

"Some," Guy said. "Are you thirsty?"

"I'm fine," Doug said. "It's Rex. I thought, you know, it seems like he's been panting. It's pretty warm."

"And he's wearing a fabulous fur coat," Guy said, reaching for the bottle and handing it to the boy. "Sure. Give him a squirt. Can he take it straight from the bottle?"

But Guy hadn't even finished asking the question as Doug aimed a stream of water straight into the dog's mouth. Rex lapped eagerly. He seemed to be as interested in snapping at the glittering drops as he was in actually getting water into his mouth. But some of it went down anyway.

"There's still a little left," Doug said. He shook the bottle doubtfully. "If you need more, I've got a bottle of Calistoga in my truck. It's parked up on the road."

"I'll be all right," Guy said. He was preoccupied by a small, ochre-colored knob that protruded from one of his tires. Without thinking, he pulled it out and was rewarded with a great hissing of air that gradually subsided as the tire went flat. "Shit."

"Whoa," Doug said. "Mistake."

"Why did I do that?"

"I don't know," Doug said. "If you'd left it in it would have gone flat slower. Do you have a patch kit?"

"Yes," Guy said, "at home."

"Bummer."

"Jesus Christ," Guy said, "I'd say. I'm fucked! Maybe I can call Triple-A. Maybe my roommate's home."

Doug flinched at the obscenity, but Guy was too flustered to notice. He'd had flats before, but always fairly close to home, so he'd been able to hobble back to the apartment for repairs. But the beach was at least an hour-and-a-half walk from the apartment.

"I can give you a ride," Doug said. "It's the least I can do after you gave Rex water."

"Thanks, that's really nice of you," Guy said, "but I have this bicycle. I can't leave it here, even if I lock it up."

"You don't have to. I have a truck. It'll fit. The front wheel comes off, doesn't it?" he added, bending down to examine the quick-release toggle. "Yup. No problem."

"You're sure?" Guy said. "You don't really know me."

"You don't really know *me*. So we're even. We'll have to trust each other."

"I guess you're right," Guy said. "I owe you one."

* * *

"And how was your journey?" Susannah asked him when he got home. She appeared not to have moved at all. She was still on the deck, still smoking and drinking something from a cup and saucer, though he could see, when he approached, that she'd moved from coffee to tea, from newspapers to a magazine.

"Eventful."

"*Really,*" she said. "I've never heard one of your little expeditions described with that word. What does that mean?"

"Flat tire near the bridge."

"And you left your patch kit on your dresser."

"Of course. Otherwise the tire wouldn't have gone flat."

"I would have panicked," Susannah admitted. "Called 911."

"I suppose I would have too," Guy said, "if I'd brought my cell phone. But I didn't. And there isn't even a pay phone around there."

"You should always take your cell phone with you," she said.

"Yes, dear," he said.

"I'm serious," she said.

"I know. You're always serious when you lecture me about not leaving the house without my cell phone."

"For this very reason," she said. "It's a wonder you're here at all. Did you walk? Call a cab? You could have called me."

"I got a ride."

"Someone we know?"

"A sixteen-year-old boy."

"That's no one I know," Susannah said. "How do you know a sixteen-year-old boy? Or is that not a question I should ask?"

"He was just there," Guy said, "with his dog. This chow."

"I love chows."

"I thought they were mean."

"Some of them are!" she said excitedly.

"This one was a black chow."

"With a purple tongue."

"Yeah. So we started talking and when I found my tire was flat he offered to bring me home in his little truck."

"Things like that never happen to me," Susannah said after a moment, with surprising vehemence.

"You almost never leave the apartment. How could they?"

"I know," she whimpered. "But I like the apartment! Is he cute, this boy of yours?"

"I'm not sure," Guy said. "He's a boy. He's, you know, half-finished. Like a charcoal sketch."

"Sometimes they can be beautiful, boys."

"He's okay," Guy said.

"He must have been there to look at naked people. Like you."

"We talked."

"You were on the boy side of the beach?" Susannah had never been to either side of the beach in question, but, through Guy's reports, she knew it divided into mixed and male sections. When Guy didn't answer she continued, "And that's where he found you?"

"I think he was a little lost."

"Hmmm," she said, her tone one of complete disbelief. "Do you want some tea?"

"Love some."

"I think there's more," she said. She got up and went inside and he followed her, wanting to keep the conversation moving. He wanted to know what she thought. He needed her to help sort things out. He trusted her impartiality. They met up again at the counter next to the stove, where she had made a big pot of tea in her coffee press. She was pouring a cup for him, and another for herself.

"Well," she said, "it was sweet he brought you home. You should have asked him in."

"I did. He said no."

"Of course. That's what a sixteen-year-old boy says when he means yes, since he can't actually agree to anything."

"Was I like that?" Guy asked.

"When you were sixteen? Of course."

Guy smiled, but he was squirming inside. He did not like to be reminded of his adolescent self, that set of flimsy social masks, awkwardly deployed; every gesture he made, every step he took was like trying to open an umbrella in a windstorm. He had believed, with the blind fearful arrogance of youth, that he could control the secret of his sexuality, that if he refused to see it, no one else could, either. Michael Donofrio had seen, but Guy had never told Susannah or anyone else about him and what had happened.

Guy was not sentimental about his adolescence because he knew there was nothing romantic about it. Adolescence was a trial. It was an interval of helpless carnal thrashing, of being itchy in one's own skin, excruciatingly half-formed, scornful of the past, of parents and family, terrified of the future, unstable in the present. It was like trying to stand still on a waterbed.

For those and many other reasons, Guy had never regretted getting older. He did not go to high school reunions; he did not fantasize about reliving his teenage years, other than the occasional imagined seduction of some beautiful guy he'd had a chance with and muffed. For a teenager, being queer was largely defined by frustrations and failure: of beautiful friends one longed for but could not openly approach; of longing for someone to do the approaching, and dreading that someone might actually do just that.

Being a teenage queer meant, for men of Guy's generation, having equally tortured friends who flirted back, whose eyes told the story, but who shared the terror of making the move, breaking the barrier, being revealed, dropping the mask, however ill-fitting and uncomfortable it was. Being with those guys, late on warm summer nights, the sky aflame with blue stars and the moon like a big disc of cheese, the smell of grass and the rumble of thunder in the distance, had been like trying to love and kiss someone through a pane of glass that slowly turned foggy with hot, frustrated breath, obscuring them from one another.

"I hated being sixteen," Guy said.

"Well, then you know how he must feel. How was he about the queer thing?" she asked.

"You mean my queer thing? We didn't get into it."

She raised her eyebrows.

"He didn't ask," Guy said.

"Of course he didn't ask," she said. "That would have meant he wanted to know, which would be the last thing he'd want you to know. He couldn't possibly ask. He was waiting for you to say something."

"I couldn't just blurt it out," Guy said. "It was kind of uncomfortable. There was this big obvious thing we were pretending not to notice."

"I'm glad I wasn't there," Susannah said. "I would have had to scream."

"I doubt that would have helped."

"Here's tea," she said, handing him a cup of perfumy Earl Grey, dosed just the way he liked it with a sugar cube and a splash of whole milk. "I'm sure you were right to be discreet," she said. "No point shocking him."

"He was just a kid," Guy said. "I had no idea how to deal with him."

"Poor baby," she said.

"Him or me?"

"Both of you!" she said, not quite laughing. "Of course."

* * *

The freshly married Donofrios, Michael and Christina, were
new not just in the neighborhood but in the town in which Guy was
a frustrated adolescent. The Donofrios had moved from a similar
town an hour away earlier in the spring. They made a pretty couple—Michael with his blue-green eyes and glossy, slightly curly
black hair; Christina with her fine Nordic nose and wheat-colored
skin—and the neighborhood was glad to have them. Guy's mother
had baked them a welcome cake in her bundt pan, and Guy's father talked to Michael Donofrio about lawn mowers and oil
changes, bank CDs and real estate agents: man stuff.

Guy and Michael Donofrio, on the other hand, just stared at
each other, as if they'd been waiting all their lives for their paths to
cross but were still slightly shocked when it happened. Guy had
never been stared at like that before; the stare gave him an erection. When Michael Donofrio saw him painting the front of the
family house and asked him if he wanted to do some extra painting, Guy knew exactly what he was being offered.

"I didn't know you painted houses!" Michael Donofrio called
out from his bicycle. It was a warm summer afternoon, and a
shirtless Guy stood high on an extension ladder laying a fresh coat
of white primer on the Griffiths' rain gutters and under the eaves.
Guy's father, Alex, had commanded the work and set the rate of
payment at the federal hourly minimum wage. There had been no
negotiations. The minimum wage was the law, and the law was, in
some respects, good enough for Alex Griffith. He was man of the
house and lord of the castle, and the castle needed paint before the
onset of another winter, and a teenage son was a useful serf.

Guy descended, conscious of the few hairs that had begun to
sprout about his nipples and below his navel; a little defiant, more
than a little curious: He did and did not want this unfamiliar man to
see his body. Guy disliked his body—so inadequate and underdevel-
oped, so weedy, compared to a man's, though the nipple hairs offered hope—yet he saw that Michael Donofrio couldn't stop
looking at it. His eyes tickled Guy with small, sharp thrills as they
ranged up and down his chest and belly.

The older man straddled his bike with easy confidence. He wore only a pair of tight black shorts, white socks and hiking boots. His legs were muscular and brown; his chest was planed by muscle and shadowed with fine black hair. It had depth; it was three-dimensional, quite unlike those of Guy's peers. He could not keep from staring. Michael Donofrio noticed.

"My name's Michael," he said, though he must have known Guy already knew his name. He smiled. It was an easy, genuine smile. His teeth were straight and white. Guy had never seen a man smile quite like that. He had seen his father grin, but that was a wolf's baring of coffee- and tobacco-stained teeth, a warning of displeasure or imminent attack. He felt a strong urge to return Michael Donofrio's grin. But something held him back. He spoke instead, somberly.

"Hi," Guy said. That was as far as he could make himself go. He could not speak his own name. He had heard his parents address the man as Michael, but Michael was a man who spoke with them as an equal—a married adult, a property owner, an owner of a chest—whereas Guy had just finished the ninth grade and was trying to supplement his meager weekly allowance with housepainting gigs. Guy couldn't call him by his first name, nor could he call him Mr. Donofrio—not after the laser looks they'd exchanged, the radiant smile aimed right at him like a searchlight.

Guy's mother was inside the house, he knew. Was she peeking out through the curtains of the big living room windows? Could she see what was happening? The gross transparency of the transaction with Michael Donofrio left Guy's mouth dry, but the older man was calm and friendly and apparently oblivious to the skulking Elizabeth Griffith, and the omnipotent specter of her husband Alex.

"Are you for hire?" he asked.

"For painting?"

"Of course!" he said with a laugh.

"I guess so," Guy said. He swallowed hard and stared down. He hated himself for being solemn and standoffish and nervous, but he couldn't help it. Michael Donofrio was like the bright sun, at once alluring and unbearable. Guy wanted to throw himself into the man's arms while running far away.

"Because part of my house needs painting," he said. "A little scraping and caulking, some primer, a little inside ladder work, nothing too serious," he said. "Do you do interiors? Can you handle it? It's pretty straightforward."

Guy nodded.

"How much do you charge?"

He was treating Guy like an adult, taking the boy seriously—they were negotiating about work and money, like men—and Guy felt flattered and unprepared.

"I'd have to look at it," Guy said, with what he hoped came off as a gruff but personable authority.

"I'm just on my way home now," he said. "Can you stop by?"

"Sure, in a half-hour or so," Guy said, anxious not to seem too eager. He felt his dick continuing to stiffen in his baggy white shorts, and for a long moment they stopped talking and simply stood there facing one another. Guy swallowed. "I'm just finishing up here," he managed to say, with a gasp.

"Okay," he said. "You know where I live."

"Yeah," Guy said. "I think so."

Michael Donofrio gave his address. "Just ring the buzzer."

"Okay."

"I'll be waiting!" he said, giving Guy a last grin before pedaling off.

Guy knew that Michael Donofrio was married. But he'd also felt the ray of hot light between them, and like a phototropic plant, he was turning inexorably toward it. Twenty minutes later, on schedule, Guy rang the Donofrios' bell. His palms were sweaty and he was short of breath. The door swung open and there stood Michael Donofrio toweling his hair, dressed in a pair of loose khaki shorts.

"Hi, come on in," he said, extending a hand that Guy took and shook as firmly as he dared. Guy waited for some surreptitious signal to be exchanged through their hands: the grip held an instant too long; the rubbing of fingers. But theirs was, so far as Guy could tell, a perfectly ordinary handshake, broken at the appropriate moment. Guy felt a pang of doubt; perhaps he'd misread the signs and would now end up actually having to paint some stale little room.

"Hi," Guy said.

"It's Guy, right?"

"Right."

"I'm glad you could come. I guess it's okay with your parents that you're earning some extra money?"

"They don't know I'm here."

For a moment they looked away from one another, as if guilty.

"Yeah. So I guess we're alone then," Michael Donofrio mentioned as he led Guy through their house. "My wife's working the afternoon shift today. She won't get home until midnight."

It was a small house, appealingly bright from tall windows in the living room and kitchen. The place was sparsely furnished, but it smelled richly and strangely of domesticity, intimacy. Guy was nearly overcome as he imagined them running around naked together, if married people did that sort of thing. His own parents didn't, but Guy didn't regard them as real people. He could not imagine growing up to be an adult anything like them. Michael Donofrio was something else altogether, an older version of people Guy's own age.

Michael Donofrio led Guy along a corridor, right into the kitchen, left again toward the deck in back. "Christina," he said, spontaneously introducing the absent wife they'd both been thinking about, as if she'd been standing there at the stove. "That's my wife's name. She's a nurse."

Guy nodded. Off the kitchen was another door opening to a darkened room with a bed and chest of drawers.

"Guest bedroom," Michael Donofrio said, answering Guy's unspoken question. They had come to an emphatic stop at the entrance to this dim, close room, whose odor was pleasantly cool and impersonal, as if no one had used it in a while. "Sometimes, if we have a fight or something, one of us can sleep in here. At least that's the idea. But we haven't had to yet! We don't fight very often, Married a whole year this fall. We haven't had many guests yet, either. Maybe they don't like the bed."

There was a funny pitch in his voice as he mentioned the bed, as if his throat were tickling. Guy had never made a man nervous before. The men in his life were loud, strong, stern people—fathers and coaches and principals and police officers—who wielded authority with ease, and demanded and expected obedience.

Michael Donofrio was younger than they were, a man but not yet a father or figure of authority. The difference in their ages had evaporated, and they stood there as equals. Or perhaps not quite: Michael Donofrio might be twice Guy's age, but Guy sensed that he had the upper hand. He let his gaze drop steadily down the older man's body: past the chin, across the pulsing narrows of the neck, slowly down the chest to the hairy cleft between the nipples, past the ribs to the flat belly, cinched by a ring of muscle that showed just above the loose band of Michael Donofrio's shorts, which bulged indeterminately in front.

He watched himself perform this bold flirtation as if he were having an out-of-body experience. A brief thought of his father made him gasp, not quite without pleasure. He watched Michael Donofrio breathe and swallow and sweat with the knowledge that he had been taken prisoner by his own desire; and Guy felt his own body blush with anticipation.

The room felt terribly warm. Their eyes were locked; they did not speak. The silence had a logic of its own; it gathered strength and momentum with each second that passed. Guy leaned against the doorjamb and clasped his hands behind his head; closed his eyes and let his lips part slightly, as if his thoughts were far away. He did not know how he knew to do these things. He just did them. He did not feel like himself.

There was a very long pause, toward the end of which Guy was certain that Michael Donofrio had turned away in distaste and gone to telephone Guy's mother with the news that her sixteen-year-old son was a slutty provocateur who prowled the neighborhood offering himself to the young married men.

Then he felt something on his stomach. Something warm and soft and dry at first; then damp, hot, searching. He looked down and saw Michael Donofrio on his knees, his face pressed against his belly. Guy watched him run a finger through the now-dampened hair that descended from his navel in a svelte line, as if drawn in with a pencil. It was a trail of hair Guy was particularly proud of for its implication of virility. It was the one part of himself he liked to show off, and he was thrilled that Michael Donofrio was mesmerized by it.

A deep involuntary moan rose in Guy's gut and escaped his slack lips. He had kissed and fondled girls before, but they had not generated the sort of electrical energy Michael Donofrio was generating. As the man's tongue slithered up Guy's abdomen—over his chest and neck, toward his lips—as his hand caressed the boy's erection through his shorts, as he gently pushed Guy into the guest room toward the narrow bed, Guy was out of his mind with the joy of surrender.

"Oh yeah," he would have whispered, if Michael Donofrio's mouth hadn't closed over Guy's. The man's fingers fumbled with the button and zipper of the boy's shorts, while Guy's fingers fumbled with his. Guy felt Michael Donofrio's shorts open and fall away, as if he were unwrapping a Christmas package and finding something he'd long wanted.

* * *

"You're hot," Michael Donofrio murmured to Guy while they lay there afterward, exhausted and happy.

"You are too," Guy said, not knowing what else to say and feeling inexpressibly mortified and pleased with himself.

The man laughed. "You still want to paint?" he asked, nuzzling Guy's neck and sticking his tongue in the boy's ear. Guy's heart nearly stopped.

"Yeah, definitely."

"Good," he said. "We'll check it out and then work up a fee and schedule."

And they did. The Pavlovian pattern was set. On the days Guy was scheduled to paint, Michael Donofrio was always home alone. He would always lead Guy straight to the guest room without a word for an hour-long session. Then, after some talking, Guy would climb the ladder and Michael Donofrio would retire to some other room elsewhere in the house, reappearing now and then to inspect or chat or offer Guy food. It was as if they had two separate relationships.

It was of course the sexual relationship that figured most in Guy's feverish thoughts. He was too excited by what was happening between their bodies to wonder if what they were doing was odd, or to be troubled by the imbalances in their relationship. Secretiveness, already an enormous fact in Guy's life, added to the excitement of actual sex. Guy had told his parents that Michael Donofrio had hired him to paint, and his father had been pleased at the news that his son was earning money through work, like a man.

"He's a nice kid," Alex Griffith said in one of his typically emphatic and empty pronouncements over the dinner table. "Wife's a looker." He winked at Guy, who nodded and ate a bite of salad to conceal his panicked swallowing.

It didn't occur to Guy until years later, when he was an adult and passingly familiar with the law, that one reason Michael Donofrio might have been dry-mouthed with nervousness was because he was a man having sex with a sixteen-year-old boy. Guy could have reported him, had him prosecuted and fined or sent to prison; but of course that was the last thing he would have done to the person who was taking him so seriously and giving him so much pleasure.

Michael Donofrio had revealed to the boy the secret of the flesh, and Guy was in love with him. Alone in his room at night, he would fantasize about Michael Donofrio's somehow freeing himself from his wife and taking up with Guy, once he turned eighteen and graduated from high school. They would move in together, or buy a car and drive across America, or run off to Europe. He didn't want Michael divorcing Christina. That was too ugly and painful. It ruined the fantasy. There would have to be some as-yet unimagined, civilized turn of events to eliminate her and leave Michael and Guy guiltless and ready to make each other happy forever.

Guy believed, too, that Michael Donofrio was in love with him. He could see it in the long gazes the older man cast on him after sex; in the way he brushed the lock of hair from Guy's forehead and kissed his nose and eyes and ears and neck and murmured to him as if to a puppy. Guy loved the plush male smell of him, of his skin and hair, the musk between his legs, his sweet, heavy breath, like the perfume of fresh cream. When they were together, Guy was hard all the time, no matter what they'd just done, or how many times.

Eventually Guy finished the painting job that was officially the reason he'd spent so much time at the Donofrios', and he was paid in full. But, by an unspoken understanding, he kept coming to the house at times he knew Michael's wife would be away, and they would go at each other with an intensity that seemed to grow rather than fade with familiarity, free now of the constraint and protection of a cover story.

Guy was too young and giddy to notice the change that gradually came over Michael Donofrio—the wariness and reserve and even fear that began to twitch and flicker on his face. A fine film slipped between the two of them. Years later, Guy would understand that from the beginning Michael Donofrio had been keeping one ear cocked for the sound of an unexpected key in the lock, one eye trained against the chance of discovery. A grown man would know what the world was like; he would understand what people would think of his sleeping with an underage youth while his wife was at work. While there was a legitimate painting job to be done, the boy's presence in the house could be explained. But without the painting, their meetings were starkly reduced to their carnal and unlawful essence.

Guy began to perceive that something was changing between the two of them, but he was not old or experienced enough to see the question Michael Donofrio was obviously asking himself: How was a thirty-year-old married man supposed to dump his sixteen-year-old boyfriend? It never occurred to Guy to wonder whether Michael Donofrio was homosexual: He was a man married to a woman and could not be gay. Guy, on the other hand, knew that he was gay, despite his long and ongoing campaign against his own nature, and he assumed that what was happening in the Donofrios' guest room was his doing. He'd wanted it to happen and it had happened and he knew that somehow he'd made it happen, even if he didn't know exactly how.

One afternoon they did hear a car door slam on the street nearby, and in an instant Michael Donofrio was leaping from the bed and pulling on his clothes.

"Get up!" he hissed. "It's my wife!"

Guy was numb with panic and did what he said, but it wasn't his wife, it wasn't Guy's father with a shotgun, it wasn't a police officer, it was just a neighbor returning from the supermarket, hauling bags from the car into the house. They relaxed, but they didn't remove the clothes they'd so hurriedly donned. To Guy, it felt wrong to be other than naked with him.

"I don't think—Guy, I don't think we can do this anymore," Michael Donofrio said, stumbling slightly as he spoke, as if he'd rehearsed the line so much he couldn't deliver it naturally.

"What do you mean?" Guy said.

"I mean, we can't be this way. The way we've been."

"Don't you like me anymore?"

"Of course I like you," Michael Donofrio said. "You know I like you. You know how I feel about you."

"I don't understand."

"It's hard to explain," Michael Donofrio said. "Someday you'll understand."

"Does your wife know?" Guy asked.

"No. I don't think so. But I don't want her to find out."

"Because she'd divorce you?"

"No, she wouldn't do that," he said, sounding not at all certain. "But she wouldn't understand it, and it would hurt her. Can you see that? A lot of people wouldn't understand."

"I love you," Guy said. He saw tears in the man's eyes, and he knew that Michael Donofrio loved him too, though he could not bring himself to say so.

"Guy," he said, and he wrapped his arms around the boy and tucked his face into his hair, so he wouldn't have to say anything more, report more anguished feelings, or a sense of emptiness and loss. Guy simply loved the feeling of being in the man's arms; if that was what being dumped felt like, then he didn't mind.

"I'll always be your friend," Michael Donofrio said, straightening up and holding Guy at arm's length, a gesture of both affection and dismissal.

* * *

Those last elegiac words popped the bubble of enchantment in which Guy had lived for weeks. He had gorged himself on gory imaginings of what his father might say if he found out what was going on in the little house in the next block; the possibility of being discovered, though remote, added a definite frisson to his intimacies with Michael Donofrio.

But when the spell broke, reality intruded. For a week and more after the split, Guy would lie awake in bed at night, tense with adrenalin as he recalled the catastrophe that could easily have devoured him. He felt as if he'd barely avoided being hit by a speeding bus while stupidly jaywalking. He wondered if he were really the same boy who just a few weeks ago was routinely making hugely risky voyages into the unacceptable.

And when his father clapped him on the back and congratulated him for working hard and making money and asked after Christina Donofrio, he wondered if some sort of trap was being laid for him. He was too concerned with concealing the truth to notice the winking, approving emphasis his father, sire of a presumed wife- fucker, laid on Christina's name.

Mostly Guy was sad. He was sad about Michael Donofrio and the shipwreck of their love, the brute unfairness of a world that wouldn't, couldn't understand, a world that twisted something beautiful into something sinister. Guy believed Michael Donofrio's valediction. But he never visited their house again, nor spoke more than a few neighborly words to him. A year later the Donofrios sold their little place and moved away. According to his mother, who monitored neighborhood gossip like a wartime spy, Michael's wife was pregnant, and the couple had bought a bigger house in a new development on the south side of town.

Did Christina ever know, or suspect, about her handsome, frisky husband? At the time Guy knew nothing of marriage beyond the one he'd grown up in, and he took his parents' domestic arrangement—a stable, hostile environment, like a desert—as the standard for all marriages. During his affair with Michael Donofrio, he did not stop to consider whether Michael Donofrio was cheating on his wife, whether she knew or didn't know, would or wouldn't care, whether their marriage would survive. What sort of marriage it was. He did not know, then, that there were sorts of marriages, that people struck all sorts of emotional bargains with one another.

When he was older and had been in and out of a few affairs of various lengths and intensities, when he had become acquainted with possessiveness and jealousy and suspicion and exhaustion and boredom and the rest of the spectrum of feeling that followed upon the burning down of the erotic fireball, he found himself wondering about what the Donofrios said to each other over the dinner table after Guy had finished painting and gone home for the day, with splotches of latex drying on his T-shirt and, perhaps, a tiny droplet of Michael Donofrio's semen still clinging to the corner of his mouth. Did they kiss and make love and hold each other, and when he came inside her was he thinking of Guy, whose cream was still fresh inside *him* and who was, probably at that very moment, home jacking off to fantasies of *him?*

* * *

Soon after the crash with Michael Donofrio, Guy had forced his relationship with Susannah onto the higher, or at least more treacherous, plane of high school romance. He was too young to accept the connection, but when he was older he would come to see that many men entered heterosexual life, and marriage, as other men entered the priesthood, as seekers of refuge from their feelings for other men. He and Susannah had known each other since grade school, been friends since middle school, been confirmed together in the same church; he knew her, knew how to talk to her, knew that she had had a crush on him for some time. She would do.

If he'd been confronted with the truth of what he was do-ing—using her to protect himself from the menace of turning

queer, to prove to his father and himself that he was indeed heterosexual and a man, the two being synonymous—he would have denied it with the ferocity of someone who knew he'd been caught
out in a lie. He liked her well enough to convince himself that he
wasn't using her, and anyway she was perfectly happy to be used.
She was an attractive girl, but too smart and edgy to be popular. To
a teenager, popularity was life, and to be unpopular was to live in a
vampire world of the undead, of shadows, hopes, wounds, resentments. Guy was good-looking and accepted among the better
cliques if not exactly a central member of them; he was a modestly
successful athlete and scholar, with some standing in student government. If he wasn't a god, he certainly brought a ray of sunlight
into her life. She responded to his attentions and did not question
his motives. She liked to say that they were meant for each other,
meant to be together. When she made her little speeches along
these lines, he would be sullenly silent, resenting their implicit
pressure; years would pass before he understood that she had been
talking to herself more than to him. She was the person she was
most interested in convincing.

Together they felt, without entirely recognizing, that their bond
was the bond of wounded people—people licking at one another's
secret hurts and fears, connected at points of vulnerability. She did
not challenge him on his tepid physical interest in her, and he
made her a part of his society without making an issue of her social
marginality or suggesting that her presence at his side, at parties
and proms, was anything other than natural and expected. If the
measure of success of high school couples was the degree to which
they were accepted by everyone else, then Guy and Susannah were
the most conspicuously successful couple in their high school.
They were together from tenth grade on.

When they finally had sex, toward the end of their senior year, it
was an act almost of nostalgia. They were eighteen-year-olds soon
to meet the world, and like all eighteen-year-olds they were powerfully sentimental about themselves and each other and the world
they were leaving behind. There was even some stumbling talk of
marriage—mostly from her.

The sex, though bad and abrupt, was intense, and it intensified her feelings for him. But not his for her. He was deeply fond of and attached to Susannah. She accepted him, secrets and all. But he couldn't help feeling a little contempt for her, too. She let him use her for so long and at so little cost; she would not see what a cunning phony he was. She had played her part perfectly, and for that reason he knew he did not really love her, as their constant trading of avowals of love proved.

Their relationship ended graduation night. His idea. She shed a steady, gentle rain of tears; he shed none. The high school bubble in which they'd so contentedly floated together had popped. They were off to different colleges, and college was a place where Guy expected to live a very different sort of life, one that did not require heterosexual camouflage. He did not tell her, or anyone this, just as he had never told her, or anyone, about his countless other crushes on best friends, teammates and casual acquaintances, or his adventures in house painting. He merely held her as she wept, and they kissed and lay together on the sofa in the basement of her parents' house, while the house slumbered.

For years, a quiet bitterness lay between them. They exchanged letters and saw each other at holiday breaks, but she methodically established a distance. He thought he knew why she did this, and he accepted it. He thought that she'd finally seen through him, seen the one-sidedness of their relationship, the cold-blooded way he used her. The memory made him flush with shame. He was twenty, and too self-involved to consider the possibilities that even his shame and guilt were narcissistic, that their alienation wasn't entirely about him, that other forces might be at play in her life. Perhaps another man.

Over Christmas break junior year he came out to her, in the hope that, by explaining himself, he would help heal the cold rift. She, in turn, told him, not long after they'd graduated, that she was moving to San Francisco. She couldn't say why, exactly; her account was hazy enough to make him wonder if she might be a lesbian. But her crush on the city wasn't that specifically focused; she'd merely been a visitor with a friend and felt, as visitors so often did, that her destiny lay there, far from familiar things. He half-longed to go with her. But by then he was meeting and sleeping with men in preparation for meeting Philip, with whom he would embark on his own long journey.

Guy was suspicious of San Francisco anyway. The city managed to be farther away metaphysically even than it was physically, which was very far, perched out there, an Oz of alabaster spikes at the shaky edge of the continent. It was the place where plague had taken root; it was a place he associated with germs and obituaries. It could never be, for him, the city it promised to be for Susannah. He and Philip were constantly reassuring each other that they had no wish to move there, barely any inclination to visit.

Still, Susannah's presence in the city stimulated Guy's ongoing interest. She was like an emissary, easily accessible by mail and then e-mail: Letters rapidly became the currency of their friendship. They'd been writerish types anyway—school newspaper, yearbook—and exchanging long notes by post or Internet every few days evolved into a pleasant routine.

The Web in particular refreshed their intimacy. It was possible to confide by e-mail in a way that wasn't possible in person or over the phone; e-mail provided a level of delayed immediacy that suited them both. Guy used e-mail to tell Susannah about his split with Philip; it was easier to express the shock and humiliation by typing it out than by saying it long-distance with the meter running. But she called anyway, as soon as she'd read the note. Called to invite him to visit, to offer him shelter.

And he had accepted, partly to flee the scene of the Philip train wreck, but also to see her again, whom he'd not seen in years. He wanted to know what her life was like, what she looked like, what it would be like to be with her again, now that they'd both grown up. A tiny part of him hoped and feared that she was still in love with him. But if so, he couldn't detect it. The overwhelming first sense of their being together was surprise: surprise at finding the familiar and unfamiliar juxtaposed on the same face. They were not the people they had been twenty years before. But they recognized each other with a certain sheepish delight. And the story of his cracked-up life made it easy for her to be sympathetic.

"Have some red wine," she said, handing him a goblet. He accepted it with a tentative sniff, like a dog examining a new toy. "It's good for you," she said.

"Then I need it."

"You look good," she said. They were studying each other as they sat side by side on her couch, working their way through the bottle.

"Older, though."

"Of course. Older is better, you know."

"Up to a point."

"You're a man now," she said. "And I have crow's feet."

"No you don't."

"Oh yes, I do, just like my mother's," she said. "There are some fates you can't avoid."

"Do you think we're middle-aged?" Guy asked.

"Not quite," she said. "We're grown-ups, that's all."

"Is that what it is?" Guy said. "I like your wine."

"A friend who works for a wine magazine gave it to me," she said. "That's what people do out here—work for wine magazines. That's work."

"I thought they all ran Internet start-ups."

"Oh, them," she said. "They're the successful people."

"Do you know any?"

"I don't think so," she said. "I'm not quite sure they're real. I guess they must be. You see all these new cars." She glanced vaguely toward the street and poured herself another splash of wine.

"You're drunk!" he said.

"So are you."

"Loose woman."

"Finally!" she said. "I finally loosened up and now I'm too old for anyone to want me."

"Oh, I don't know," Guy said, surprised by the invitation he seemed to be tendering. But she merely smiled and patted his hand and went to the phone to order take-out pizza, and when they were finished with that, and another round of catching up, she gave him a long hug and a kiss on the forehead and settled him into the guest room. There he promptly fell asleep, having understood that she had indeed become a woman who knew what she wanted, and who she didn't. He had fallen into the latter category, where he'd always belonged.

* * *

"What are you thinking about?" Susannah asked him gently.

"I don't know," Guy said. "Am I thinking?"

"It looks that way."

"Am I furrowing my brow?"

"Just a little."

"I guess I'm tired," he said.

"That's what you always used to say," she said, "when you didn't want to talk to me."

They had finished their tea and were sitting on the deck watching the sun settle toward Twin Peaks.

"You're thinking about him."

"Him?" Guy said. He was startled that she could read his mind; he had never told her about him, had never told anyone.

"Your boy," she said. "From this afternoon. The beach boy. What's his name?"

"Doug," Guy said. "Doug Whitmore. And we weren't actually on the beach. I explained all this."

"Yes, yes. Whitmore," she said, rolling the name with her tongue as if she were tasting it. "It seems vaguely familiar."

"Really? Didn't ring a bell for me."

"I might have seen it in the papers or something. Isn't the mayor named Whitmore?"

"I don't think so," Guy said politely.

"Probably not," she conceded.

"Anyway, I wasn't thinking about him," Guy said. "The boy."

"It's all right if you were."

"He's just a kid," Guy said.

"So were we, once upon a time," she said, collecting the teacups and starting inside with them, leaving him to think about his remark, which amounted to a struggle to dismiss Doug as someone too young to take seriously, someone too young to matter. The struggle to dismiss Doug suggested the extent to which some countervailing force was at work, but Guy did not want to think about that force or whether or why he might be struggling against it.

"Did you know I was queer when we were in high school?" he asked as she rinsed out the tea things.

"Did you?"

"Know about myself? Sort of, I guess," he said. "I always thought you knew."

"Because you never really hit on me, you mean?" she asked.

"I did a few times, didn't I?"

"You were the perfect gentleman at all times," she said, "unfortunately. I just assumed I wasn't that attractive. Because I wasn't that attractive, as you'll recall. I just assumed you were with me because—"

She stopped.

"Because why?"

"I didn't let myself think about it," she said. "I knew you must have had your reasons. And then I was in love with you, too. Sorry, I know that's awkward to bring up."

"Not really," he said. "I knew you were. I loved you for it. I mean—"

"Yes," she said.

"I wish I'd been more honest with you."

"Oh, I don't think so!" she said. "I don't think I would have reacted terribly well. I didn't react all that well when you did tell me, and that was quite a while later, wasn't it, when we hadn't even seen each other in several years."

"I wish I'd handled it better, is all," Guy said. "I get red in the face when I think about myself in those days."

"So do I," she said. "So do we all, or most of us. So grant your boy some leniency."

"Oh, I'm sure I won't see him again," Guy said. "It was a chance thing, that's all."

She hummed to herself with pleasant skepticism, as if she perceived some greater design Guy couldn't see. That had always been one of the differences between them: Her fondness for certain elements of mysticism, his for the rational. In this case he was certain he was right: There was no reason to think that the little drama of Doug would feature an Act II. Their crossing of paths, after all, had ended in a knot of anticlimax. After unloading Guy's disabled bike from the back of the truck, the two of them had chatted awkwardly for a few moments and shaken hands. Guy had offered the dog more water from the hose bib at the side of the building. Then Doug had driven off, back to wherever it was he belonged in the city—the clubby world of native sons that had nothing to do with Guy.

"I think I'll take a shower," Guy said as Susannah finished tidying up the kitchen.

"Yes, do," she said. "You're a little ripe."

"Ten years ago, that would have been a compliment," he said.

He went off to take a shower, to rinse away the ripeness and, with any luck, the lingering tingle of the boy.

ii. *The Boy*

A FTER JOTTING DOWN Guy's address on a scrap of aging milkshake cup from McDonald's, Doug ran his fingers through his hair, hopefully examined his mustache in the rearview mirror for signs of thickening, and took his pager from his front pocket to see who was trying to reach him. It had vibrated while he was saying goodbye to Guy. He hoped it was his best friend Adam, mostly because Adam was not Teresa, his recently dumped ex. But the page was from Teresa. Luckily he'd left his cell phone at home to recharge. He turned the pager off, started the engine, and lurched off down the street.

The truck had been a gift from his parents for his sixteenth birthday. They'd wanted to give him a small BMW or a shiny new Honda: something sleek and modern and reliable; something they could imagine driving without feeling foolish or old or of limited means; something that would remind him that they had given it to him, that they loved him, that they were important.

"You don't want to have to worry about what's going to happen when you turn the key," his father had admonished him.

But Doug hadn't wanted a BMW or a Honda or anything else shiny or remotely new. Instead, by scanning the classifieds in the paper, he'd located an eight-year-old Suzuki Samurai. The little truck was a little battered, but it made a better fit in his life. He didn't even try to explain to his parents the downmarket prestige of the truck's grubbiness. He pointed out, instead, that it offered four-wheel drive, for his occasional forays to hike the wilderness and ski the snowy Sierra. And, for the transport of a furry and ever-shedding dog who smelled when wet, it was far more suitable than any of the glossy vehicles his parents had proposed. On that point Ross and Katherine Whitmore conceded.

Part of Doug hadn't wanted a car at all—or anything—for his sixteenth birthday. He did not like his parents to spend money on him. Taking their money and accepting their gifts meant having to answer their nosy questions about his life. He didn't want them to know anything about his life. He wanted to be independent; he wanted to decide what kind of car he should drive, what kind of shoes he should wear, whether he had enough jeans or socks or cash in his pocket. He wanted to handle those matters himself, and if that meant doing without, or with much less, then he was prepared to do that. He did not like to be thought of as a rich kid, or one with a huge sense of entitlement, though he knew he was both.

Still, a car was a possession in a class by itself. And a shabby little sport utility truck with a balky transmission and ripped seat covers became, in the hands of a teenager like Doug—ashamed of his privileged circumstances and determined to camouflage them, though not of course give them up—a center of social gravity. Almost as soon as Doug took the keys to the car, his phone began ringing. People who hadn't been his friends before suddenly formed a gang around him. He was invited to parties. He met girls. He met Teresa and let her throw herself at him.

He was thinking about calling her back as he bounded up the steps of the house he'd called home all his life. Rex bounded before him, having waited patiently at the door, square muzzle pointed skyward like an antiaircraft battery, as Doug worked the key in the lock. He looked forward to some distraction from his earlier encounter at the beach, though before getting out of the truck he'd carefully torn Guy's address free from the rest of the cup and stuffed it in the front pocket of his sweatpants.

Just as he came in, he heard the emphatic closing of a door upstairs. A moment later his father appeared, descending the staircase with a heavy tread and an even heavier look on his smooth, fleshy face. It was a CEO's face, bland and hard at the same time, its middle-aged skin having retained an unnatural, almost baby-like softness from the diligent use of a battery of pricey cosmetics.

"Where have you been?" Ross Whitmore asked, without preface. It was the sort of question a colonel might ask of a wayward corporal whose uniform had wrinkles.

"At the beach."

"What beach?"

"Ocean," Doug lied smoothly.

His father grunted and turned toward the kitchen.

"Where's Mom?"

"Upstairs," Ross Whitmore said. "Oh, and Teresa called," he added over his shoulder, scarcely bothering to turn his head, his feet thudding on the polished oak floors of the gallery that ran the length of the house, front to back, as he rushed away from whatever it was he was rushing away from. "She wants you to call her right back. Do you have her number?"

"Of course I have her number."

"She left it. I wrote it down. It's on the pad by the phone," Ross said, his baritone now muffled by being in another room. Doug nodded to himself and gingerly started upstairs, toward his own room, aware, as he passed his parents', of its tightly closed door, and the tight silence beyond.

Once in his room, he did not call Teresa back. He knew that he didn't have to; he knew that, sooner or later, she would call again. His dumping her had vastly increased his power over her; his unpredictability and remoteness stimulated her. Since they'd broken up, she had taken the position that she wanted to be friends with him, which, he understood, was her way of saying that she hoped for an eventual reunion, the pot of gold at the end of a rainbow that began with conciliatory phone calls.

Doug claimed not to want to be friends with her and he professed to Adam and others that her persistence annoyed him, but the truth was that he found it flattering. It was a new experience for Doug to be desired and pursued. He liked it. He bathed in the warm flow of energy she poured on him: her attention, her barely concealed lust, her determination to undo losing him. He felt secure with her; he knew where he stood. She wanted him more than he wanted her. She was always interested in what he had to say. She listened, was sympathetic, took his side. She paid attention to him. She made him feel special, and he had never felt special before. Her energy was like a strong, steady wind that filled his sails

when he wanted them filled. When he didn't, he simply struck
them and let the wind keep blowing.

The girl had, during her tenure as Doug's official girlfriend,
made a particularly strong impression on Doug's father, who let it
be known how much he approved of her, and of their being a couple. Fatherly approval made Doug flush with pride and relief and,
simultaneously, fear that the approval might be withdrawn if he
broke up with Teresa—an inevitability that had been on his mind
almost from the moment they'd gotten together. He understood
that her neediness, while useful, was not only unattractive but
somehow toxic. He knew that she was bringing out the worst in
him, and he could see that he was doing the same to her.

The light and heat of erotic desire, and the thrill of experimenta-
tion, had briefly chased those shadows. But he didn't respect her
enough to allow himself to be really turned on by her, and as lust
faded, as the novelty of her body and her busy lips became ordinary, he found himself longing to be free of her.

He became impatient with her conversation. When they were
together he began to sulk. For solace she turned to the television,
which always had something to offer the bored and the lonely, and
while the screen flickered he would get up and leave the room. It
was as if they were two people locked in a prison of bad marriage.
He longed to shout out his frustration, but when he shouted at her
for some petty offense she simply burst into tears and threw her
arms around him, as if animal contact would cure their misery, not
merely mask and prolong it.

His parents, when told that he'd dumped her, took the news with
surprising calm. His mother reassured him that he would soon find
another girl and asked if he had anyone in mind. His father suggested that it was a good thing to have a wide range of experiences
in youth. Neither inquired closely as to the details of how Doug
and Teresa had hit the rocks; they expressed their anguish in the
discreet Anglo-Saxon way, by simply not mentioning the painful
subject. But when Teresa began to call again, and leave messages,
and talk to them about Doug, their elation was not at all discreet in
the Anglo-Saxon way.

* * *

There was a knock on Doug's half-open door, and his mother appeared, poking her head in sheepishly while he fiddled with his CD player. She had long been a practitioner of the pop-in, with its veneer of casual friendliness—as if a mother, or a father for that matter, could be a friend. Doug felt embarrassed for them when either of them tried to strike the comradely note, and he found it difficult to play along. Parents weren't meant to be friendly. They were arbiters and rulers, necessary and awesome to the child, exasperating obstacles to the adolescent. Why his own parents failed to recognize and abide by this principle he did not understand. He braced himself for a round of chat and glanced at his mother. She did not look good. Her face resembled a half-squashed wedding cake; her hair was dry and disorderly, like autumn chaparral waiting to catch fire in the hillsides.

"Have you seen your father?" she asked.

"Yeah, about ten minutes ago," he mumbled, glancing away from her, back to the CD player. "He was going to the kitchen."

"I looked there," she said. "I've looked everywhere."

"Maybe he went out."

"He was out all afternoon!" she said.

"Maybe he's busy."

"Maybe," she said.

"Is Dad making dinner?" Doug mumbled almost inaudibly.

"I don't know," she said. "If he doesn't, we'll do something fun, how's that? We'll order a pizza or something. Just the two of us. How does that sound?"

"Fine, I guess," Doug said.

"Oh, and Teresa called," Katherine said, as if it were some bit of trivia she'd just remembered.

"Yeah?"

"She tried to get you on your cellular."

"I didn't have it with me."

"Where were you?"

"At the beach with Rex and my friend Guy."

"I didn't know you had a friend Guy."

"You haven't met him," Doug said.

"Is he in your class?"

"No."

Katherine waited for her son to say more, but he didn't.

"Anyway, Teresa wants you to call her. I told her she should page you. Is your pager on?"

"She probably forgot the number."

"I gave it to her," Katherine said, "so I don't think that was the problem. How is she?"

"Fine, I guess," Doug said, examining his shoes, within which his feet restlessly paddled the floor.

"I always liked her."

"We broke up, Mom, okay?" Doug reminded her. He raised his head with a snap and glared at her. "You and Dad went out to dinner so I could have the house to myself so I could tell her, remember?"

"Of course I remember," Katherine said. "You don't have to shout."

"I'm not shouting."

"I think she still likes you," Katherine said. "She keeps calling. She likes to talk about you."

"Great. Did Dad send you in here to tell me that?"

"Of course not."

"He told me not to break up with her. He told me we were a good couple. Like it was any of his business."

"Maybe you mentioned something and he thought you might like his advice. He is your father."

"I didn't ask for any advice!" Doug said. "I just said, you know, I needed the house so I could break up with her the right way, and he gives me this big speech about what a great girl she is and how important it is that I'm going out with this great girl and all this other stuff. He didn't tell you all that?"

"He might have told me something," she admitted. "I know he he thought she was good for you. We both thought so. It's not a conspiracy for parents to look out for the well-being of their son, you know. We care about you."

"So you think I shouldn't have broken up with her."

"I didn't say that."

"It's my life!" Doug said. "I don't have to explain it to you or him or anybody else."

"I know that," Katherine said. "Please don't shout. I have a headache."

"You don't look good."

She absorbed this shot without comment. "You know I would never tell you what to do," she said. "Neither would your father. We would never interfere in your private life. I'm just telling you she called and she wants you to call her."

"I'll call her right now, then," Doug said, turning away to dismiss her.

"I'll be downstairs," Katherine said. "Let me know what you want to do about dinner."

Doug listened to her steps retreating downstairs. After a suitable interval, in which a telephone conversation between a high school guy and his pining ex might have taken place, he followed his mother downstairs, and found her sitting in the front parlor. Rex lay on the Turkish rug at her feet.

"She wants to get together," Doug announced.

"That's nice," Katherine said. "When?"

"Right now."

"Oh," she said, trying to keep her face from falling, like a camper trying to hold up a collapsing tent. "So I assume you won't be needing dinner."

"I think she's got something there," Doug said, half-apologetically. "Sorry."

"That's all right," Katherine said. "I'll be fine. Who knows? Maybe your father will even turn up and make me something."

"I'm pretty sure there's leftover pasta in the refrigerator."

"I'm not that hungry," Katherine said. "Right, Rex?"

The dog looked up, wagging his tail slowly, as if not quite sure whether he was the topic of conversation.

"I'll be back, then," Doug said, and he went out the door with a wave over his shoulder while she got up and went into the kitchen and opened a bottle of white wine.

* * *

The house through which Doug hurried had been, as his parents had hoped and intended, the only home he'd ever known. It was the house they had bought and restored so they would have a place to raise the family they each wanted, for different reasons they did not share with each other or with Doug.

Like most Victorians, it had been originally a big house of little rooms, a poorly lit maze, a warren. And, like most old houses (which was to say, most houses in San Francisco, where the difficulty of building a new house was exceeded only by the difficulty of making room for it by tearing down an old one), it had undergone seasons of neglect and rejuvenation. Dry rot here, a new foundation there, grade faults, warped window frames, cracked and patched plaster everywhere, the aftermath of earthquakes great and small. It asked for attention. And attention was what it got.

Mr. and Mrs. Whitmore had strong architectural and aesthetic views and were passionate about Victoriana. They subscribed to home design magazines; they spent many a Sunday afternoon wandering the neighborhood's open houses, looking not just for a place of their own to buy but ideas on what they might do once they found the property they were looking for. Once moved in, and having completed their own renovation, they became the sort of people who telephoned the planning commission if they believed that a neighbor was tinkering with his façade or plotting an addition in a way that disturbed the "character" of the neighborhood. When they'd gotten what they'd wanted, their interest in the status quo became proprietary, and fierce.

The Whitmores made, in their middle thirties, when they'd acquired the house, a handsome couple. They looked like an advertisement for a certain sort of urban marriage, or one of those preppy-hip clothing stores that came and went and came again, under new and equally fanciful names, in the blocks around Union Square. They had discreet good looks, money, education, social position, Swiss watches and two late-model European cars (one with four-wheel drive, to escape chain controls in the snowy mountains where they skiied, and to haul bags of groceries and, later, Doug's puppy).

They traveled frequently to fashionable locations, stayed in fashionable hotels, ate in the au courant restaurants they'd read about in *Gourmet,* then discussed it all when they returned, with friends who'd been to the same, or very nearly the same, places—friends who were just like them. They saw themselves as belonging to the city's aristocracy, though they never would have used that distasteful word. They were the chosen people; their sense of entitlement was decorous and unshakable.

The purchase and renovation of their house was occasioned by the birth of their first—and, as it turned out, only—child, Timothy Douglas. Before the escrow had closed, they had commissioned men in moon suits, licensed by the state, to remove from the façade the blight of asbestos shingles, a failed utopian innovation of the 1940s. They commissioned other men to restore the original gingerbread millwork, and still more men to repaint the whole house, so that it looked better than it ever had in its century of life.

Inside, they blew out the hodgepodge of closets, pantries, chambers and corridors. They replaced the wiring and the plumbing; they expanded bathrooms into temples of marble and chrome. They installed skylights, and a sumptuous kitchen (Ross liked to cook) with Italian granite countertops, a black restaurant range with six burners and an oversized, stainless steel commercial refrigerator that could not be put into place until the subfloor had been strengthened. An adjoining great room and solarium gave through French doors onto the deck and garden, where Ross grew his cilantro and leeks and the rest of his cold-weather, fog-tolerant crops and where Rex, when he arrived as an eight-week-old puppy on Doug's tenth birthday, would come to exercise sovereignty through the sprinkling of urine: a little monarch of black fuzz, with a rear leg for a sceptre.

Even before Doug was born, the Whitmores appeared to have everything—each other most of all—and they seemed to be content. Their life together since their wedding on a hot June afternoon at Stanford's Memorial Church, followed by a Mediterranean honeymoon through the Aegean that included nearly a week on

Mykonos, had been serene and unremarkable. Ross ascended the career ladder toward partnership in his big, politically connected Montgomery Street law firm, while Katherine juggled various ad-agency gigs with domestic and social responsibilities—and with Doug, when he arrived in her thirtieth year.

The idea of having a child had been, though mutual, more Ross's than Katherine's.

"It's why we got married, wasn't it?" he would say when she raised her vague reservations. "To have a family?" She was happy enough with things as they were and did not burningly aspire to be a mother, but she could not say exactly why. She had trouble defending her diffuse doubts against Ross's mild, relentless determination. It was hard to argue against family. It wasn't enough to be uneasy, or unenthusiastic; those were feelings, not arguments. And Ross was nothing if not a rational arguer.

It occurred to her that if he had been less enthusiastic about starting a family, she would have been more so. That sort of balancing was characteristic of their dynamic; they tended to differ, but seldom vigorously. Their disagreements were innumerable and polite. She had no strong feelings about parenthood, other than supposing it was inevitable and being suspicious about his enthusiasm, which was not typical of the men she'd known. Her college frat boyfriends had often been skittish about second dates. But of course they had been mere boys, while Ross, when she met him, had been a sober law student, an adult. She supposed he'd always been that way: responsible, rational. She felt ashamed for being suspicious when there was no reason to suspect him of anything other than wanting to be a father. Men and women got married and made babies. That was the story of the race. That was the point of it all. And it was to be, apparently, the point of Katherine and Ross Whitmore, happily married couple.

She didn't like to think that she had accepted his proposal of marriage because he'd asked her at a time when she was feeling pressure from her family about the direction of her life. Of course that was exactly what had happened. Her shame at having doubts about her husband and her marriage alternated with flashes of confidence that doubts were normal. Doubts were natural. In the long run, they were strengthening. That which did not split them up brought them closer. Ross *was* attractive—good-looking in a sandy, fine-cut way; he had a trim, strong body; was educated, well-spoken, gentle, suitably employed, with bright prospects, considerate if determined to prevail in disputes great and small.

Their sex life was mild. They had sex often enough in the beginning, but he never insisted on it, and if she said no or lost interest, he never argued. Sometimes she would even suggest sex and he would turn her down. He was always hard in the morning and came easily when she blew him, and he did not complain when she pulled her mouth away at the last minute, or spit his spunk onto his belly, or the sheets. He ate her out with an energy that struck her as the professional energy of a gigolo. He was determined and skilled and unenthusiastic; he made it seem like a question of manners. She couldn't help thinking of a well-bred dinner guest determined to finish his steamed turnips.

When she asked, he would say how much he liked and was turned on by the taste of her, but he never spontaneously offered such flattery, and after a while she stopped asking because she felt she was overreaching. She supposed that most men felt this way. She had heard that men joked about the horrors of eating cunt, although in college she'd had a brief affair with a frat rat who grazed lovingly down there for what seemed like hours, getting her off time after time until she could hardly find the energy to get up from the bed to get a glass of water for a throat parched from endless moaning and groaning.

Of course everyone knew that marriage ruined sex. The dousing of desire in the still pools of domestic ritual was part of the price one paid for stability. Life was a succession of trades and barter. But secretly she felt that the failing was hers: She wasn't pretty enough, her hips were already too wide, spreading like rising bread dough, breasts too soft and floppy, she didn't turn him on enough. She was starting, unmistakably, to resemble her mother.

"I'm pregnant," she told Ross one winter night as they were getting ready for bed. She'd been to the doctor only that morning, after several weeks of inexplicable sensations and growing suspicions. After work they'd gone to dinner at a trattoria in the financial district, and she'd sat there waiting for him to read the news on her face. She could not quite imagine that he was not experiencing the feeling she was, that he did not feel the rising of another life as she did. Instead they ate tagliatelle and osso buco with tiramisu for dessert, then went home to floss their teeth and get ready for bed so as to be able to rise with the dawn the following morning for another day of toil.

Ross was in mid-floss in the bathroom, in his boxers, as she spoke the words from the bedroom. Her father had always worn boxers, but Ross's were young-man boxers, and they reminded her of her college boyfriends, and even her college friend David Rice, whom she'd seen in—but never out of—them. Ross seemed young in his boxers, not like a father at all.

"I'm sorry?" he said, though he must have heard perfectly well. The door was wide open and she'd spoken clearly.

"I went to the doctor today," she said. "He told me I'm going to have a baby. We're going to have, I mean. A baby."

A moment later Ross materialized in the door, toothbrush hanging loosely from his hand.

"We're going to have a baby?"

She nodded.

"When?"

"Sometime this summer, the doctor thought," she said.

"Why didn't you tell me this before?" he asked.

"I didn't know before."

"But you went to the doctor."

"Yes, I'd been feeling kind of strange."

"You didn't tell me that."

"I didn't think it was important."

"Didn't think it was important!" he said. Then he came up and threw his arms around her in a vigorous, sincere, mechanical hug, as if he were a sensitive droid from a sci-fi film. She didn't take the awkwardness personally; it was at least as much about his own body as about hers. "Of course it was important!" he said, laughing a little. "We're going to have a baby! We're going to be parents!"

"Yes."

"You should have said something at dinner! We could have had a bottle of champagne! We had a celebratory dinner, and I didn't even know it!"

"I won't be drinking any champagne for a while," she said.

"I'll drink enough for both of us," he said. He was capering now, and smiling, as if preparing to pass out cigars to strangers. "Does he think it'll be a boy or a girl?" he continued.

"The doctor?" Katherine said. "She doesn't know. I don't, either."

"I have a feeling it'll be a boy," he said.

"Would you prefer a boy?"

"Either way!" he said. "I'm very happy." He returned to her and planted a kiss on her lips. "We'll have to think of names," he said, "I want him to have a good name."

"Are you done in there?" she said, indicating the bathroom.

"Not yet," he said, "but yes! Sure. Of course. Go ahead. I'm too excited to brush right now anyway. You go ahead!"

She did.

* * *

It was through Doug that Katherine became reconciled to David Rice, the college friend with whom her passionate friendship had never quite bloomed into romance. They'd been inseparable in college and shared an apartment in the city after graduation, but although David had attended the wedding, things between them had not been the same after she'd met Ross.

David had given them a wedding gift, an earthenware pasta bowl, hand-painted in Italy, but she never managed to serve him any pasta from it. They continued to live in the same city, but their paths diverged throughout their twenties. Katherine's was the gilded path. She graduated from shopping at Crate&Barrel to Williams-Sonoma and Gump's; she was a wife who became a mother with her name on a deed and a raft of title-insurance papers safely stowed in a safe-deposit box at the bank.

David, meanwhile, moved from apartment to apartment, telephone number to telephone number, job to job, boyfriend to boyfriend, until his boyfriends and ex-boyfriends started to die and, for all she knew, he might as well have been living on Mars. She could not imagine what it felt like, what it meant, to have one's life disappear piece by piece, one beloved person after another, any more than she could have imagined what it would have been like to live in Nazi-occupied Europe. Because they did not speak and their paths did not cross, she developed a fear of talking to him, a fear that their paths eventually *would* cross. She felt guilty that her own life was untouched by woe; she felt untested. She was ashamed of her good fortune. But she did not forget him. And she never stopped being a little in love with him, across the gulf between their stories.

On the occasion of Doug's birth she'd sent him an announcement at his last known address, mostly as a matter of form and a gesture to the past. She did not expect to hear from him, and, for months, she didn't. They no longer had a life in common, and David had been inexplicably hostile to Ross, who was indifferent in return.

So David's call to her, one June morning when she was nursing the baby, was a classic thunderbolt from a blue sky. She didn't even recognize his voice at first, and then she guessed wrong.

"It's David," he'd corrected her gently. "You were in my freshman English class."

"David!"

"You *do* remember."

"Where have you been?"

"Well, you know," he said briskly. "Here, there and everywhere. Mostly here. So the word now is that you're a mommy."

"You got the card? I sent it ages ago."

"I have a little gift," he said. "I thought I might present it in person."

He appeared on her doorstep in the middle of a warm autumn afternoon, bearing a wrapped package tied with a bright blue bow.

"I wrapped it myself," he whispered in her ear as they embraced in a lingering hug.

"I can see that," she said, examining the package. "I've missed you. I thought we'd have tea. In the garden. It's so lovely out today."

"Let's see this baby of yours first."

They peeked in the nursery, where Doug was napping content-edly, his little pink fingers clamped around nothing. He gurgled in his sleep and leaked a bit of drool onto his chin, but David did not seem to notice these small indelicacies. He stood over the cradle, holding one of Doug's tiny hands in his own.

"He's adorable," he said to Katherine, and set the package on the dresser next to the cradle.

"Do you think so?"

"He looks just like you."

"I think he looks like Ross," she said.

"Oh no!" he said. "Like you."

Just then the baby awoke briefly and stared at David with his round blue eyes. He smiled, gave a squawk of distress, burped and went back to sleep. Taking their cue, they left the room, closing the door gently behind them.

A pot of Earl Grey tea on the sunny deck. They spread French preserves on little brioches Ross had spent half of Sunday making; by the time he'd finished, the kitchen was spattered with butter, eggs and flour, as if some kind of pastry bomb had exploded. It felt as if years had not gone by since they'd last sat like this, as if they had not been estranged, were not tentative with one another. She commented to this effect, and he nodded.

"I've missed you," he said simply.

"It's Ross, isn't it?" she said. "You don't like him, do you? You never have. I never understood why."

"I don't know him," he said.

"But you don't like him. You never did. You didn't think I should marry him. That was obvious."

"I didn't think you should marry anyone," he said, "to be fair. 'Cause I knew I'd be left behind."

"That's not very noble," she said gently.

"No, it's not. It's just true," he said. "I'm not very noble. Hate to disappoint you."

"Just another self-centered prick, then?"

"Check."

"Did you ever find anyone?" she asked, searching for a gentle way to phrase the question.

"Oh yes, scads!" he said, and she almost smiled with him, until he added, "One after the other. Then they started to, you know, die or whatever. There's been a lot of that going around."

"David, I'm so sorry."

He nodded and patted her hand. She wondered if he were full of rage—the sort she'd seen on television. She wondered if he hated the bourgeois accoutrements of her life: the Wüsthof knives and the custom-made Roman shades in the nursery, the house, the medical insurance, the elaborate baby stroller, the organic Earl Grey tea she'd bought that morning at the Real Food Company, the fussiness about everything. She wondered if he hated her merely for being untouched and complacent.

She found it hard to believe that David would hate her things, or her for having them. He'd always had champagne tastes, and he didn't seem bitter. In fact he looked better than ever—skin ruddy, hair neatly barbered, clothes of quiet quality; he'd grown up into a civilized man, and she ached for him a little—but she knew that his world, unlike hers, had been turned upside down, as if it were a war zone. In his life, there were no longer any safe assumptions. The basic certainties were, for him, uncertain.

"Yes," he said. "I'm a bit numb these days. You don't have to look embarrassed!" he added. "I can't tell you how glad I am to be sitting here with you, in a part of the world that hasn't been ruined. I suppose I should be really pissed. Most people I know are. I can't say I blame them. Sometimes I wish I were that way. Rage seems purifying, at least for a while. But I'm not that way. I get sad instead of angry. I guess that makes me ineffective." He looked out at the garden and briefly motioned with his arm. "All that is Ross's doing?" he asked.

"Mostly," she said. "I water sometimes."

"*Do* you," he said with a smile. "I always knew you were the watering type. Well, it's beautiful. Tell him I said so. You must look at it a lot." He spoke with the enthusiasm of a man whose garden consisted of a few fist-sized pots of anemic basil above the kitchen sink, and a ficus plant shedding its leaves on the floor next to the television in the living room. He did not look poor, but he had never had serious career ambitions and, she supposed, had never embarked on a serious career. The last job she knew he'd held was as a slinger of truffles and slices of cheesecake at a Haight Street dessert shop. And that was nearly ten years ago. The shop had long since folded and been transformed into something else, then something else again.

David too, had presumably moved on, though to what she could not guess. It seemed impolite to ask, raising as it did the specter of failure. And not just his. They had been brought up and educated to do something with their lives, to matter. She had answered the call by marrying the first man who'd asked her, and he by working in a dessert shop before disappearing into what was quickly becoming a plague city.

"Do you like being married?" he asked, gazing at a rosebush whose pale lavender blooms she was especially fond of.

"I don't know if 'like' is the word," she said. "It's a fact I've gotten used to, I guess. We get along. I have a son, and all this, the house and everything." She gestured limply toward the house, a huge and ponderous edifice full of items that needed looking after, many of which she no longer wanted and had banished to the basement to keep company with the water heater and the furnace and the mildew and an army of spiders. The basement was a purgatory of possessions that had outlived their usefulness but not their purchase on their owners' imaginations.

A life of possessions meant maintenance: The furnace filter needed to be changed. The roof leaked in the living room and had damaged the plaster; it would have to be repaired, the entire room repainted. Rotate the cars' tires; change the oil. Buy dishwasher detergent. Set out the recycling bin, and the grocery sacks full of newspapers. Speak to the neighbors about their wayward cats, who howled in the night. David wouldn't be interested in any of this nonsense, she thought with embarrassment.

"Do you love him?" David asked—almost shyly, she thought.

She did not answer immediately. She could not. She could feel him staring at her, interpreting her hesitation. Love, she was thinking, was a word used only by people who had no idea what they were talking about; it was essentially a religious word, unanchored to fact. She and Ross were married and living together, raising a family; those were facts, and theirs was a subtle and complex mission far beyond the pop culture meaning of love.

Yet whatever love did or didn't mean, she believed that she loved Ross. She was certainly devoted to him. He had fathered her son; he came home to her (almost) every night. Like all couples of long duration, they had woven a fabric of shorthand between them: jokes, references, history, memory. She knew him better than she had ever known anyone—even David—and she knew that he knew her better than anyone else ever had.

No one had ever told her that knowing someone intimately was not the same thing as falling in love with him or sleeping with him or accepting his proposal of marriage. She had discovered that truth on her own. Intimate knowledge of another person was a journey, not a destination, and, like all long journeys, it consisted of roughly equal parts of surprise and displeasure, amusement and comfort, interest and boredom. And effort. Most of the value one extracted from life resulted from unglamorous effort.

Only she knew, for instance, how much Ross talked to himself, or how insanely particular he was about his Picardie juice glasses, which he had meticulously organized into groups that were not to be meddled with. Only she knew how conflicted his feelings were about his parents, who, he told her, had starved him for love as part of their long guerrilla war against each other. He had, he said, been a POW in his own family.

And only he knew how much she disliked her body, her large breasts and thighs ("Christmas hams," she would call them in desperation at bedtime, slapping them and watching the flesh jiggle), which scarcely shrank even under the most drastic regimes of diet and exercise. Only he knew how much she feared her own mother, smiling mistress of the indirect cut and the genteel snub. Husband and wife were joined not least in their emotional waifdom, in unresolved resentments and hurts from their childhoods. The strongest human bonds so often grew from two people revealing their wounds to each other. People who bled together, stayed together.

"I guess that means you don't," David said, when her long moment of pondering her answer seemed to have become the answer.

"Sure, I love him, yes," she said. "It's just—I don't know, it's not a yes-or-no question."

He nodded. "I guess it's none of my business," he said. "It's not like I've ever been married."

"But you've been in love."

"Maybe once or twice," he said dismissively. "I don't think I'm really cut out for love. It's been a relief to figure that out, finally. Love isn't for everybody! One less thing to worry about."

"What do you mean, love isn't for everybody?" she asked.

"Some people can make it work," he said with a shrug. "Look at you. And some can't."

"And you can't?"

"I think my record speaks for itself," he said. He wasn't at all self-pitying as he spoke, just matter-of-fact.

"I don't believe that at all," she said. But after he'd gone home, she sat with the tepid dregs of her tea and asked herself if in fact she did believe it, and whether, more to the point, she was cut out for love. She had certainly wanted to be in love with Ross when they'd first met, and maybe she had been, maybe not. It was hard to be sure; feelings made slippery memories.

David's re-entry into her life was gentle but persistent. Also discreet. He always succeeded in calling when Ross was not home, and they always seemed to meet when there was no possibility of Ross's joining them—and so, she concluded, no need for David to do the awkward dance of disinviting him.

She did not tell Ross that she had revived her friendship with David, not even when she began leaving Doug in David's care so that she could play tennis or have lunch with a friend down the Peninsula. She trusted David and saw, with a mother's eyes, the connection that rose immediately between her toddler son and her old friend from college, whom she now saw as a kind of brother, for whom she felt only faint fugitive longings.

Ross, she believed, would not approve of Doug's being left in David's care. He would not want his son looked after by a homosexual. Ross was becoming that sort of man. For that reason alone, she was determined to continue the arrangement. David and Doug plainly adored each other, and she liked the idea of subverting Ross's genteel, Montgomery Street homophobia. Educated liberals always made the worst homophobes, because they were never honest about their small-mindedness. They were practiced at thinking well of themselves, of congratulating themselves for being tolerant, and of convincing others that they were something quite other than what they in fact were. Intelligent, educated people's self-portraits were the ones most often at dramatic odds with reality, most full of will and contrivance.

Naturally it was Doug who let the cat out of the bag one night at dinner, when Ross asked him what he'd done that afternoon.

"Played airplanes at Uncle David's!" he'd replied excitedly.

Ross looked up sharply from his plate of cavatappi, as if he'd caught the squeal of a smoke detector in one of the bedrooms upstairs. He glanced at Katherine, who did not look away.

"Who's Uncle David?" he asked her.

"He lives on Hartford Street!" Doug announced.

"David Rice," she said. "From college. You remember."

"I remember," Ross said. He sipped chardonnay to conceal his incipient scowl. "And Uncle David has airplanes?" he asked his son.

"He has a 747!" Doug said.

"A real one?"

"A toy one," Doug said. "He lets me fly it."

"I played tennis with Leslie today," Katherine explained. "We're in a tournament down in Burlingame."

"I didn't know David had re-entered our lives," Ross said pleasantly. He dropped the subject in favor of dessert—a raspberry tart he'd made earlier in the week, with scoops of vanilla gelato on the side—until Doug was safely in bed and it was just the two of them in their room with the television on, going about the business of retiring.

"So," he said. "David."

"David."

"*Uncle* David?"

"That's what Doug calls him."

"Were you planning on telling me this?"

"I don't think so," she said.

"Don't you think I have a right to know who's looking after my son? Don't you think you should tell me that?"

"Our son," she said. "You don't trust David?"

"I haven't seen the man in years," Ross said, "and even then, I hardly knew him."

"I know him," she said, "and I trust him."

"And you're sure he's a good influence on our boy."

"Yes," she said. "I'm sure. Despite the fact that he's gay."

"You said that," Ross said, "not me."

"You certainly implied it."

"Is he, you know, all right?" Ross asked.

"I haven't asked."

There was a heavy pause. This was not the sort of thing one enjoyed discussing at bedtime. Or ever.

"I think it's a legitimate question," Ross said mildly, "if he's looking after our son. I'll ask him, if you like. It is a relevant question, I'm sure you'll agree."

"I'll handle it, then," she said. "I'd rather you didn't reintroduce yourself to him with a cross-examination."

"He doesn't want to see me?" Ross asked.

"I said I'd deal with it," she said. "But I don't think it's a question that needs to be asked."

He grunted. "Has he discussed it with you?"

"No."

"Hmmm," he said, making it clear that he regarded David's silence on the question of his health as utterly damning, much as he would an obviously guilty suspect's unwillingness to testify. He resumed cleaning his teeth. While he rinsed and gargled, she lay flat on her back, eyes closed, thinking about things David had said about his dying friends. She could not picture him dying. She could not picture him, in fact, as anything other than the tall, self-effacing nineteen-year-old she had fallen in love with. Even the featherings of premature gray above his ears hadn't made him seem older in her eyes. Certainly he didn't seem mortal. None of them were mortal, not yet.

She squeezed her eyes more tightly shut as Ross settled himself into the bed beside her. She waited for him to return to the subject of David and their son. She was not worried about David's looking after Doug. She had seen for herself the look of simple affection in David's eyes when Doug sat in his lap asking questions about the moon or wheedling to be taken out for ice cream. She saw the same look in Doug's eyes, because he had made a friend, a friend who was innocent and not beleaguered.

Even if David were infected—and of course he wasn't—he could not possibly pass the infection to Doug. She was sure of it. Even if David kissed Doug goodbye on the forehead or cheek, as she had seen him do, there was no danger. The virus didn't lurk in saliva; she had called one of the hotlines, and they had reassured her. It was a disease transmitted by sex and blood transfusions and shared needles, the helpful young man said.

None of those things was part of David's relation to Doug. Doug was a small, trusting child. Of course she had read lurid newspaper accounts of sinister Cub Scout masters and tortured priests and back-rubbing soccer coaches ending up in the dock. But David was none of those things. She was sure of him. She trusted him, in part because she could see that Doug trusted him.

"So Doug likes David," Ross said, his voice deep in the darkness. "Uncle David."

"They're friends."

Ross made a grunt that might have been a mirthless laugh. "I don't know many thirty-five-year-old men who are friends with little boys who haven't even started kindergarten," he said. "Or vice versa."

"They're friends," she repeated. "And he's thirty-three."

"I don't like it," Ross said after a pause in which she had almost allowed herself to believe that he was dropping the subject.

"I can see that," she said. "I'm not surprised."

"You're not surprised," he said, "because you know as well as I do that it's a bad idea."

"No," she said, "I'm not surprised because I know you're a homophobe. That's what this is all about."

"I am not a homophobe!" he said, his voice rising as if involuntarily. "And that has nothing to do with what we're talking about, anyway."

"It has everything to do with what we're talking about."

"David is not Doug's uncle," Ross said. "It's wrong to let him think otherwise. It's wrong to let David think the connection is more than it is. Or ever can be."

"It's so nice of you to take David's feelings into account."

"We're not talking about David's feelings, we're talking about the well-being of our son. And I do not think that his well-being is well served by letting this man pose as his uncle."

"He isn't posing!" she burst out. "It's a figure of speech, for God's sake. Stop making a mountain out of a molehill and just admit that you're uncomfortable with this whole thing because David's gay and you think he's going to molest Doug."

"I can't believe you would even suggest that," Ross said after a moment. "That thought never crossed my mind."

"Bullshit."

"Now you're losing your temper," he said.

"Of course I'm losing my temper," she said. "I'm losing it because you're being a complete asshole."

Her use of coarse language threw him, as she knew it would. He could never quite stop being a prig.

"I'm sorry," he succeeded in saying at last, "but you wouldn't be so angry if you didn't know I was right."

"I'm sorry," she said, "but that's a crock. You're not right. You're not always right, whatever you might believe."

"I never said I was always right."

"We both know," she said, with surgical calmness, "that that's exactly what you think."

"He's my son."

"He's my son too," Katherine said.

* * *

David entered the hospital for the last time a few weeks before Doug's sixteenth birthday. The boy rode his bicycle to Davies to see him. He was young, but he had grown up in the plague city, and he had understood from the first what his mother meant when she told him four years earlier that David had AIDS and had gone to the hospital: She was announcing his eventual death.

Cycling through a cool May evening, the blue air sprinkled with blue stars, Doug did not have to be told that David's death had ripened from eventual to imminent. He knew he would never see David again. They held hands but didn't talk much. David was thin and sleepy, and his lips were parched and cracked; he was like a dried-out leaf at the end of autumn, waiting to be blown from the tree by a chilly gust of wind. Doug cycled home from the hospital in time for dinner, after which he took his basketball and his dog, Rex (David had suggested the name: "It means king," he had said, "and he looks lordly") down to the park.

Ross found him there under late moonlight, still shooting layups against the ghostly backboard while Rex reclined like a sphinx at midcourt, obstructing any unseemly fast breaks. Ross took a rebound and dropped it gently through the hoop, and from that beginning father and son segued into a wordless bout of one-on-one.

"I'm sorry about your friend," Ross said during a breather.

"You mean David."

"Yes."

"He's going to die."

"I know."

"I thought he was your friend too."

"I knew him a long time ago."

"Mom likes him."

"Yes. They were best friends in college."

"She was in love with him," Doug said.

There was a pause.

"I suppose that's true," Ross said.

"Were you ever jealous of him?"

"She married me," Ross said.

"She had to," Doug said. "David was gay. She couldn't marry him. It would have been a mess."

"It wouldn't have made any sense," Ross agreed.

"He's lonely," Doug reported. "He doesn't have anyone. Most of his friends have died. Except me."

"I'm glad you went to see him," Ross said.

"He's really skinny," Doug said in a guarded voice, "and he kept coughing. His hair is funny. Like, hay or whatever."

Ross patted his son on the shoulder. It was an uncomfortable gesture. He had never been good at touching people. He had never been especially at ease with his own son, and now that his son was on the verge of adulthood, he was particularly ill at ease with him. The boy was no longer cuddly but gangly, and already he showed signs of male wariness about other men, rivals and competitors who were not to be trusted. Men were always testing one another, always probing for—and concealing—weakness. Fathers and sons were not exempt. He and Doug had never been close, and despite Ross's clumsy efforts they weren't getting closer.

"He asked about you," Doug said after a moment and a successful layup. "Do you care?"

"Of course I care."

"He's sorry you're not friends any more."

"Doug, please," Ross said. "People don't stay friends forever. We never had that much in common. We had less as we got older. I don't really know David anymore."

"I know him," Doug said. "I think he wants you to go see him. He'd like to see you."

"I can't."

"Why not?"

"It wouldn't be appropriate," Ross said.

"It's because he's gay."

"It's not that."

"You're homophobic."

"That is not true," Ross said.

"And because he's dying of AIDS."

"It's not that," Ross said. "I don't really have anything to say to him. That's why."

"You don't have to say anything," Doug said. "I didn't say much. He was just glad I was there. He just wants to see you."

"I'll think about it."

"You'd better not take too long."

"Let's go in," Ross said finally. "I'm cold. Your mother must be wondering where we are."

Rex led the way.

* * *

Ross didn't visit David in the hospital, and he didn't attend David's memorial several weeks later, on a Sunday afternoon at the end of June. The service culminated in a release of white balloons from a glade atop Buena Vista Park. But he did send a check in David's memory to one of the local HIV relief organizations, which delivered hot meals to the afflicted and had provided sustenance to David in his last months at home.

Katherine did attend the memorial, holding Doug's hand. For the first time she felt strength flowing from him to her; for the first time she caught a glimpse of the man her son might—she hoped would—become. Strong, gentle, empathetic, honest, sure enough of himself to be vulnerable. She wondered what Ross had been like as a sixteen-year-old, whether he would have attended the memorial of an older gay friend who had died of AIDS. She concluded that the sixteen-year-old Ross would never have made friends with a gay man because he would be frightened of how it would look. Ross, she knew, had been born risk-averse and highly sensitive to external forces. He wanted to be approved of.

They stood there hand in hand, mother and son in the breezy sun amid a small throng of young men, several of whom leaned on canes or walkers as the wind blew their wispy, lifeless hair. Hair died first in people with AIDS. The group listened to reminiscences and studied David's aged parents, who had driven in from their home in the Central Valley. They looked lost and out of place, too stunned and disoriented to grieve publicly.

After Katherine said her little bit—about all David had meant to her in college, about how they had drifted apart and then reconciled, about how he had befriended her son—she went over to David's parents and gave his mother a buss on the cheek and put her arms around his father, although she hadn't seen either of them since the hot June day she'd graduated from college with their boy. Then she whispered to them. Doug stood beside her, as if at attention. The balloons sailed up erratically, and dispersed. They walked back down the hill and got into the car and drove home.

It was the same home they had left just hours before. Sunlight filled the front room, and Rex greeted them at the door, wagging his featherbrush tail in excited circles. Ross wasn't home; his note, too perfunctory to qualify even as cryptic, explained that he'd gone into the office to see after his mail and review some paperwork. He might as well have said that he was flying to the moon. But then, it had long been his habit simply to disappear from time to time on weekend afternoons and reappear at dinnertime. He had never failed to appear to cook a meal. It was a small but important bastion of reliability.

Katherine went upstairs to rest. For a long time Doug sat in the front parlor, staring out the window at nothing. Rex sat with him.

* * *

For Doug's tenth birthday, his parents gave him a chow puppy. It was a type of dog the boy had long been fascinated with, having been convinced, as a small child, that the black woolly versions of the breed were in fact some sort of bear. On the morning of Doug's birthday, the three of them drove to Sonoma County, where a breeder had a litter of yipping, squirming eight-week-old pups from which Doug was given his choice. The puppy actually did the choosing, bounding to the boy across the dry grass, wagging his spike of a tail and licking Doug's face when it was offered to him. Doug laughed, and the puppy gave a sharp little bark before running around in a circle, squatting briefly to urinate, then returning to his new master.

"He didn't lift his leg," Doug noted. "Why didn't he lift his leg? Is he a he?"

They picked up the little creature and examined him to make sure. He was. Meantime, he licked Doug's face again, inducing more laughter and cementing the bond between them.

"He's probably just young," Ross said.

"He's just a baby, remember," Katherine said. "We're taking him away from his mother."

"Oh," Doug said.

The mother struck a leonine pose in another pen, watching the proceedings with inscrutable calm. She showed no sign of distress that her offspring were being touched, assessed and, in one case, taken from her, but all the same her calm was somehow not reassuring, and none of the Whitmores was unhappy when she passed through a dog door into a building.

The family happy about its new canine member had been a family divided, at least in its upmost echelon, until virtually the moment they'd gotten in the car for the drive to Sonoma. Ross, who'd been denied dogs in his youth, felt strongly that a boy should have a dog as an introduction, among other things, to the world of responsibility. Katherine, too, saw the question as one of responsibility but feared it would devolve on her shoulders; she was afraid that once the shine of puppyhood had worn off, Doug would lose interest and it would fall to her to care for the creature—to become, in effect, its mother.

But Doug turned out to be conscientious and loving with the dog. He fed Rex, walked him in the park every morning before school and every afternoon after school, picked up after him without complaint. The puppy slept in Doug's room and followed him wherever he went. He grew, and went to obedience school, where he learned to sit and stay and heel.

But even though he stopped looking like a puppy, he remained one at heart. One warm May evening when Doug was walking him off-leash on Twin Peaks, the dog saw something—a feral cat, a squirrel: the boy never saw what, exactly—and bolted into the twilight. Doug's reedy wails weren't enough to bring him back, and soon after, having melted to tears, he came stumbling miserably down the hill to the family house, where his father sat reading the evening paper in the front room.

"Stop crying!" Ross immediately commanded.

"It's Rex!"

"What about Rex?"

"He ran away," Doug managed to say, before a sob overtook him.

"Crying won't bring him back!" Ross nearly shouted. "Douglas, that's enough crying!"

"What's going on?" Katherine said, rushing in from her little office to investigate the commotion.

"Your son has lost control of himself," Ross said, settling back on the couch with the paper. "Tell him that if he hopes to be a man, he'd better learn to stop crying like a girl."

Doug, meantime, had run to his mother and thrown his arms around her. She soothed him and smoothed his hair, and slowly, as his tears subsided, he managed to explain to her what had happened.

"It's all right," she murmured to him, "it's all right, baby. We'll find him. He can't have gone far. He's probably looking for us right now. He's just a puppy. He won't go far."

"You think so?" Doug said.

"I know so," she said. "We'll get the car and drive up there and find him. Don't worry. Ross, are you coming with us?" she asked her husband, knowing what the answer would be. He shook his head.

"You shouldn't coddle him like that," Ross said to her, just as they were leaving. "We don't want him to be a sissy."

"He's not a sissy," Katherine said. "He's our son."

"I don't want him to be a sissy," Ross said, but she went out the door as he spoke. "I didn't raise him to be a sissy."

"That's enough!" Katherine said. "He's upset, that's all."

Ross grunted dismissively, but too late: She was already out the door.

Rex turned up at about the point where he'd run off. He was sniffing at something and did not seem surprised to see them. Doug wept again, and the brief drive home had the faint flavor of a triumphal procession. Ross was waiting for them, but after a perfunctory greeting under a veneer of civility he marched Doug up to his room for what he called "a talk."

The boy sat on the edge of his bed, trying not to sniffle and averting his reddened eyes. He didn't want to talk or be talked to.

He wanted to pet his dog. The puppy, exhausted by his wayward-
ness but otherwise clear of conscience, rested at, and on, Doug's
feet. They made a sweet picture—a recruitment photograph for the
family-values satisfactions men were supposed to find when they
undertook the duties of fatherhood. Becoming a father meant having a son, a small replica of oneself, to be raised in one's image
and to carry on one's manly legacy; it meant having a son with a
dog, without which no boyhood could be complete.

"Dog looks okay," Ross said, his tone gruff but faintly approving. The truth was that he was just as attached to Rex as Doug was,
and he admired Rex's male verve in running off. That was what
males were supposed to do: assert themselves, explore the world.
He leaned down to pet the dog between his ears, upright velvet tri-
angles that swivelled like satellite dishes. Rex gave an enormous
yawn, licked his chops with his grape Kool-Aid tongue, and settled his leonine head on his forepaws.

"Yeah," Doug said.

"He was just waiting there for you."

Doug nodded.

"I knew he wouldn't go far," Ross said. "Dogs generally don't
do that. They stick close to their masters."

"I guess."

"Your mother says he was glad to see you."

"He licked my face," Doug said in a hoarse whisper.

"I knew he'd be okay," Ross said.

"So did I." Doug's voice was barely audible.

"No," Ross said, "you panicked."

The boy hung his head, though his father's tone was more matter-of-fact than accusatory. The accusations would come later,
when Doug had lowered his guard.

"You lost control," Ross continued. He had clasped his hands
behind his back and paced the room slowly, as if he were giving a
closing argument. "You didn't keep your head. It's important to
keep your head in a crisis."

"I know."

"You say you know," Ross said. "But it's not enough to say you
know what you're supposed to do. You have to do it. That's the

test. What if your mother and I hadn't been here to help you? What could you have done, crying like that? You couldn't see, you couldn't think. You were useless. Rex would still be out there somewhere, wondering what had happened to you."

"I couldn't help it," Doug said. "I was scared."

"Of course you were scared!" Ross said. "But that's the whole point. Everyone's in control when they're not agitated. That kind of self-control is meaningless. The self-control that counts is when something's on the line, when it's easy to panic. Do you understand?"

"I think so."

"All right, then," Ross said. "Next time, keep your wits about you. Take a deep breath. Don't let the panic take over. Don't let yourself cry. Once you start crying, it's all over."

"Okay," Doug managed to say. He held off crying again until his father had patted him on the head and marched from the room.

"What did you say to him?" Katherine asked her husband later, when they were alone in the TV room. She was half-watching; he was reading a memo. It was the sort of casual time they shared increasingly less of. And even though they were physically together, they were far apart. Still, that was so often the way of marriage. And they had the house to themselves for a while. Doug had pulled himself together enough to go out and play with a friend.

"I said what had to be said," Ross said, stirring from his work as if from a troubling dream.

"I hope you weren't too hard on him."

"Not at all. I just told him the importance of a man's keeping his cool in a crisis."

"He's not a man, Ross."

"Not yet, no."

"I don't want him growing up too fast."

"He cries too much," Ross said. Abruptly, like a hawk stooping from the skies upon a hapless rabbit, he alighted on his issue, and he was forceful about it.

"That's not true," Katherine said, raising her voice.

"It is true!" Ross said, raising his even more. "His dog runs off for a couple of minutes and he's bawling his eyes out. He had snot all over his face!"

"That's what Kleenex are for," Katherine said.

"This isn't about Kleenex!" Ross said. "It's about self-discipline and self-respect."

"He's ten. Did you cry when you were ten?"

"No."

"Then I feel sorry for you," she said.

"You don't need to feel sorry for me," Ross said, "I'm fine. It's our son I'm concerned about. I hope we're together on this."

"I hope so too," Katherine said.

* * *

Doug left Teresa's with a pounding heart and a strange sense of jubilation and incompleteness. In the midst of their emotional jousting they'd started making out, and, as if daring one another, they went pretty far—farther than they'd ever gone when they were officially going out.

Then, it had been necessary for Doug to do some inflating and imagining, some spin control, when he discussed Teresa with his buddies. Since the buddies did the same sort of spinning when talking about their own girlfriends, they were naturally suspicious of Doug's tales—and at the same time eagerly credulous. Very young men, whose interest in sex was fantastically disproportionate to their experience, were hormonally inclined to believe in their peers' stories of erotic adventure. By believing that their friend had actually done the thing of which he bragged, they gave themselves hope that they too might soon do that very thing. Yet the fact that they were all liars and exaggerators gave them a heightened perceptiveness to the tall tales of their friends.

Dumping Teresa was something Doug had done for a variety of reasons whose deep roots he didn't care to examine, but its principal side effect was turning out to be a release of sexual energy he never guessed she had. When they were boyfriend-girlfriend, she was passive and soft; he had to make all the moves and suggestions. Now that they were exs, she was all over him, full of fire and filthy propositions, willing to do things he'd been afraid to suggest. She even hinted about going all the way, something he'd never done, and never admitted he'd never done.

They hadn't yet gone quite that far, but they'd finally gotten all their clothes off and done just about everything else. He wondered if his buddies would believe him, now that the truth so wildly exceeded the leering half-truths of his earlier huffings and puffings. To be believed, he would have to omit some of the juiciest pertinent facts. Adam might be the exception: He'd been Doug's best friend since eighth grade, and each had an acute sense of when the other was lying. Of all Doug's friends, Adam was the one whose mouth was most likely to twist into a smirk when Doug launched into one of his girl chronicles. But, ironically, he was the friend most likely to accept the new truth: that sex was better after breaking up with a girl, at least for a while. Adam was the only friend Doug would consider telling the whole truth to, on the question of Teresa or any other matter of consequence.

For the first time, Teresa had seemed intent on getting Doug to ejaculate. In their boyfriend-girlfriend encounters, she had seemed reluctant to touch him at all, and on those few occasions when he'd gotten off in spite of her inept stroking, she acted as if he'd splashed her with dirty dishwater. She made him wipe her up, and she looked away the entire time, like someone averting her eyes from a syringe about to be plunged into her forearm.

So it came as a considerable surprise to him when she not only stroked it but took it in her mouth, touched his balls, asked him to stroke himself so she could see how he did it. He'd never discussed with her what he did in private, locked in his room or in the bathroom, and if he'd been less aroused he might have allowed himself the pleasure of becoming indignant at her assumption that she knew about his solitary practices—that there *were* solitary practices. As it was, he kept his mouth shut and showed her. Moments later, she was reproducing the effect with surprising skill, and when he popped for the first time, her face was just inches away, eyes wide as if observing some spectacular experiment in biology class. He couldn't help but feel proud that he and his body were so mesmerizing.

He'd felt an immediate urge to get up and leave. But she wouldn't let him; she lay on top of him, nuzzling his neck and pressing her breasts into his chest. He liked her breasts. They were tight and firm, they fit nicely into his hands, and he liked the groaning sound she made when he licked and sucked at the rubbery nipples. When he'd stopped, she'd moaned for him to go on, which, after a dramatic pause, he had.

"That was really nice," she whispered in his ear as she nuzzled. "Next time I want to swallow it."

He was, instantaneously, hard again, and she shifted around atop him so that he began slipping inside her. He pushed his hips up, without thinking—without thinking, among other things, of rolling on one of the rubbers he had carried around in his wallet for the past two years, the rubbers his father had taken him down to Walgreen's to buy when he turned fourteen. He'd interpreted that event as a prod and even a bit of a threat. It was clear, perhaps too clear, what his father expected of him, what sort of man his father expected him to be. And here he was, with his dick pointed like a missile at his ex-girlfriend's ravenous cunt.

She smiled and kissed him and twisted her hips so that the head slipped just wide of the mark. It bounced against his belly with a little spank of frustration.

"Not yet," she whispered. "Not until you love me."

"You know I do," he heard himself saying. He was just barely aware that he was saying it because it was what she wanted to hear; it was the incantation, like abracadabra, that would open the magic portal but, like all gibberish, had no other use or meaning.

"I'm not sure we should yet," she whispered, but she was smiling as she spoke. "I don't know if we're ready."

"I'm ready," Doug said.

"Have you ever done it before?"

"No," Doug heard himself saying with unthinkable candor. "Have you?"

She was nodding.

"With Graham?" He was her boyfriend from last winter and was now the starting shortstop on the JV team.

She kept nodding.

"Wow."

"His isn't as big as yours."

He couldn't help groaning with pleasure at that revelation. He'd always been intimidated by Graham. But being hung was worth a hundred double plays—five hundred. He put his hands on her hips and pulled her belly against his and started thrusting.

"God," she said.

"Mmmm," he said. He was getting close when she pulled away, breaking the frictive spell.

"So where are we?" she asked.

"We're right here," he murmured, eyes closed, fingers running over the silky skin of her back.

"I mean . . . you know what I mean. I'm talking about you and me. I'm talking about our relationship. I mean, here we are. We've never gone this far before. It's obvious how we feel about each other. Isn't it?"

"It is," Doug agreed.

"I mean, I want to, so bad," she went on. "I love you so much. But I have to know you love me. I have to know you're committed. It has to mean something."

"You know it does," he said, "you know it means something." He was maneuvering her hips again, trying to find his way back in. She went along for a moment, and he felt a pleasurable slipping. Then she shifted, slightly, but just enough so that he flopped out.

"Doug," she said.

"I'm right here."

"Tell me what you're thinking."

"You know how I feel about you."

"I don't know how you feel," she said. She was sitting upright now. "You don't tell me."

"I do too tell you."

"No, you don't. I tell you. I need to know how you feel. I need to know where we're going, if we're going to . . . you know."

Doug did indeed know. He was groaning silently with the urge to go there immediately, to that place he'd never been, not quite, but almost in the last half-hour. All he had to do was tell her what she wanted to hear. All he had to do was agree to be her boyfriend, to reunite. Things would be better than they'd been the first time, she was assuring him; they were older, they'd grown up and learned, they wouldn't make the same mistakes again.

The word "mistakes," piercing the fog of lust like a searchlight, startled him. Had they made mistakes the first time, or had the mistake been their getting together at all? He'd liked and wanted and pined after her while she was going out with—and apparently putting out for—Graham, but once she and Graham had broken up and she'd drifted into the range of possibility, her glitter seemed to diminish slightly, though he hadn't been able to admit that to himself at the time.

Once they were actually going out, once he'd gotten what he thought he'd wanted, he found he didn't want it that much any more. He disliked her fawning, her gossiping, the way she would kittenishly submit to his advances after they'd fought because she was afraid of losing him. It was convenient and distasteful at the same time. It also meant that they'd fought a lot, about nothing in particular. Fighting primed the pump of desire; it was their way of being together, the engine of their closeness. But he wasn't ready to admit that he didn't like her, didn't respect her, and that he was turned on by his contempt for her.

Their breakup took the shape of an amicable splitting of ways, and for a few days he was relieved. Then he saw her with another guy at a classmate's party (parents out of town for two weeks, traveling in Europe), and he was jealous. He told himself he missed her and had to have her back, and he could tell by the way she looked at him that she felt the same way. She was using the other guy to agitate him; her eyes brimmed with yearning and frustration. He knew he didn't have to do anything; she would call, she would make the overture, she would take the risk of abasing herself. And she did.

"I guess so," he heard himself say incoherently.

"You do?"

"Sure."

"I need to hear you say it."

"I said it."

"No," she said, "you've never actually said it. You've never actually said 'I love you.' You have to say it. You have to say those words. I've said them to you. I love you, Doug."

"I have too said it."

"I'd remember if you had. And you haven't. Say it."

"Don't boss me."

"Maybe you don't, then," she said. She shifted above him, as if she were a gymnast preparing to dismount from the parallel bars. Tears pooled behind her eyes. "You can't even say it. Maybe it was better that we broke up. I love you and you don't love me. You never did. Admit it."

"Don't say that," he said. "You know it isn't true." As he spoke he gently placed his hands on her hips, to keep her in place. Of course it was exactly true, or else he wouldn't have said it wasn't.

"I'm tired," she said.

"You are?"

"I don't feel like talking any more."

He didn't particularly feel like talking, either, but he still had a full erection, love or no love. He was uncomfortable.

"You should go home."

"Like this?"

"Put your clothes on," she said. "Here." She handed him his boxer shorts and rolled away from him. A moment later she'd slipped on her panties and was pulling on her T-shirt.

"You're throwing me out?"

"We both need to think," she said.

"Okay," he said reluctantly.

"I'm just not sure where this is going."

"Do you want me to call you?"

"I'll see you in chem on Monday morning."

"Yeah," he said.

She kissed him on the cheek before he slipped from her house, and he drove home angry and frustrated that he'd gotten so close, achieved so much, only to fall three syllables short of the much-desired goal. He couldn't stop squirming, could hardly wait to get home and, with a few quick strokes, put himself out of misery.

* * *

He returned from Teresa's to find the house bathed in dark and quiet. Rex lay just inside the front door, dozing like a lazy sentinel. He wagged his tail when Doug appeared, but did not get up to follow his master.

Both cars were in the garage; Doug had checked before coming inside. That meant his parents were home, and presumably together, one way or another, behind the closed door of their bedroom. At the foot of the staircase he paused briefly to listen for some sound of them, but he heard nothing—just the night sounds of the house: the sigh of the breeze in the window frames, the hum of the distant refrigerator, the ticking of the grandfather clock in the upstairs hallway. Doug concluded that they must be asleep, which meant they must have gone to bed some time before, which meant that wherever Ross had gone earlier in the evening, he hadn't stayed late. Doug liked to think that they had somehow reconciled, if in fact they'd fought. He didn't like to think about their fighting, but trying to ignore the evidence was like trying to stay dry in a rainstorm.

He stopped in the kitchen for a glass of water from the chilled carafe in the refrigerator. As he stood in the dark, drinking, a voice issued unexpectedly from the TV room. Doug couldn't help but jump.

"Is that you?" a deep voice was saying. The voice was full of command, and Doug responded automatically.

"Yeah," he said, moving toward the source of the voice.

Of course it was his father's voice. Ross Whitmore was sitting in an easy chair in front of the TV. He was wearing jeans and a button-down and a pair of hiking boots flecked with dirt, as if he'd just come home from a road-construction job.

"Your mother's upstairs," he explained to his son. "She wasn't feeling well. Where have you been?"

"At my friend Guy's."

"Who's he?"

"Just a friend."

"I don't know him."

"No, you don't," Doug said. "Is Mom okay?"

"Just a little under the weather, I think."

"Were you working in the garden?" Doug asked his father.

"No."

"I guess it's too dark."

"Hungry?" his father said. "I was thinking about going out for burritos. But it's probably too late now. Almost midnight."

"I had pizza at Guy's."

"He live around here?"

"Not too far."

"I thought tomorrow night I'd cook something," Ross said. "Maybe some beef on the grill, some gratin potatoes. Simple things. You'll be around?"

"Sure."

"Your mother told you Teresa called?"

"Yeah," Doug said. "She told me."

"Everything all right there?"

"Everything's fine, Dad. I'm kind of tired."

"I guess I am too," Ross said, though he didn't sound as if he meant it. He seemed wide awake, almost fidgety—almost anxious, if men as poised and determined and successful as Ross Whitmore felt anxiety. "Your mother and I were surprised you broke up with her," he continued. "She seems like a nice girl."

"We've been through this."

"I know we have," Ross conceded. "It's just that I've never really understood what went wrong."

"I don't want to talk about it!" Doug said.

"Fine," Ross said. "Whatever. I just thought you might like to get some things off your chest. Now that it's just you and me."

"I don't have anything I want to get off my chest."

"That's good," Ross said. "That's the way you want it to be."

"I'd better go to bed," Doug said. "I'm tired. Are you coming up soon?"

"Soon," Ross said. He was staring at the empty TV screen.

"Good night then," Doug said.

"Good night."

Doug paused at the door, then spoke over his shoulder. "Guy says she was bad for me," he said, as if offering an inoffensive afterthought, most likely of little interest.

"Wait a minute, wait a minute," Ross said, looking up from the TV. "He says that, this Guy? What does he know?"

"He knows a lot."

"So he told you to break up with her and you did?"

"No!" Doug said. "I just met him the other day."

"You broke up with her a couple of months ago."

"I know."

"So I don't see what he has to do with it."

"He's helped me see that I did the right thing."

"Hmmm," Ross said. "Who did you say he is, this Guy?"

"I told you," Doug said. "He's a friend of mine. What is this, Twenty Questions?"

"We like to know who your friends are."

"I told you who he is," Doug said. "His name is Guy. He's a friend of mine. What's the big deal?"

"I didn't say there was a big deal. How do you know him? Is he in your class? You say you just met him?"

"Met him walking the dog."

"And the next thing you know, you're telling him the story of your life? Even though he's practically a complete stranger?"

"He's not a complete stranger, he's a friend. He wanted to know. He was curious. Besides, Rex liked him."

"I'm sure he did," Ross said. "I'm sure he's a good guy. You know we trust you, your mother and I. It's just that I don't like it when I can't put a face to the name. What school does he go to?"

"He lives in the Mission with some woman."

"He's older than you?"

"Um, yeah," Doug said.

"How much older?"

"Way older," Doug said.

"Doug."

"Not as old as you. I didn't ask him his age. I don't see why it matters. Or that it's any of your business."

"We're your parents," Ross said. "Of course it's our business. We're responsible for you."

"Sorry I can't tell you more," Doug said sarcastically.

"This woman he lives with is his girlfriend?"

"I guess," Doug said. "They live together. Doesn't she have to be? I mean, it would be weird if she wasn't."

"There are a lot of strange people in this town," Ross said. "You need to be careful."

"Check," Doug said. "I'm really tired."

"All right then," Ross said grudgingly. "Go on."

"Does that mean I'm dismissed?"

"It's not a joking matter," Ross said.

"Should I leave the light on for you?" Doug called softly from the foot of the staircase.

"Yes, please," Ross said. "I'll be up soon." But he continued sitting there in the shadows as his son performed his nightly toilet—flossing and brushing his teeth, scrubbing and swabbing the mutinous skin of his face—and climbed into bed. Doug, after his swift and violent orgasm, fell asleep so quickly that he did not hear the slow, heavy footfalls of his father ascending, around the time the grandfather clock struck midnight.

iii. *The Duet*

VALENTINE'S DAY was a bad day to be alone, so Guy spent as much of it as he could in the communal fleshpot that was the YMCA. There he ran into his friend Will, an attractive mid-thirties fellow—stocky like a wrestler, reddish-blond hair clipped Marine-short—with whom he'd shared a steam room romance in the early days of his membership. Only later had he discovered that Will was co-landlord, with his longtime companion Dennis, of the building in which Guy and Susannah lived. Guy had the sort of ongoing crush on Will that depended on Will's being only slightly available—ambiguity being, after indifference, the greatest aphrodisiac.

The Y was not the place Guy would have expected to find Will late on a Valentine's Day afternoon, but there he was in the showers, soaping himself up with great fervor, to the delight of his elderly audience, who gathered beneath the showerheads like elephants cleansing themselves under African waterfalls. Will shot Guy a smile as Guy entered the shower chamber, and he gave his soapy, half-hard dick a loving stroke. Guy smiled back; inside he felt a pleasurable shiver.

"Hey, Handsome," Will said as, a few minutes later, towels in hand, they stood together in the antechamber of the steam room, watching people scuttling in and out with the fierce concentration of people trying to force their way onto crowded commuter trains.

"Me?"

"You see anyone else handsome here?"

"I was hoping," Guy said.

Will laughed.

"Don't say it," Guy said. "I get the picture."

"Well," Will said with a grin, "at least we have each other."

"Yeah," Guy said. He'd been glancing at Will's crotch, and suddenly he felt abashed. Like most unattainable crushes, Guy's on Will was self-sustaining, a beguiling mirage always shimmering on the horizon, reinforced by an occasional glancing encounter, always at the Y. That had to do with the nature of the Y itself, which had come as something of a revelation to Guy when he'd first joined, in one of his first civic acts after moving to the city. Desire beat through the place like throbbing drums in the African bush.

But the candid presence of lust only briefly obscured a deep civilization. The Y was a universe of male bonding, fraternal physicality, play, laughter, conversation, reinforcement. It was a male culture that had achieved a kind of completion. It was a place where men talked to one another about everything from the NASDAQ to pastry cream, then sucked each other to orgasm in the far corner of the shower chamber before going out for vegetarian burritos.

It was a kind of womb for grown men that Guy, once he'd worked out his erotic fascinations (on various stages that included the steam room, sauna, showers, locker room, racquetball courts, roof garden, and several of the stairwells), found himself not wanting to leave. When he did leave, he thought about the place and looked forward to going back. He met other people, and through them still more people, so that in a matter of a few months he had spun a social web sturdy enough to support the weight of his being single. The Y gave him a sense of belonging he'd never felt before, along with bigger pecs and tighter glutes. He found it was possible to like other men, not merely desire them.

Sometimes, as in the case of Will, one did both, and that could be difficult. If Will had ever actually become available, if they'd ever gone home together and actually gone to bed in a real bed and fucked each other, the whole thing would have disintegrated. That was one reason Guy did not want Will becoming any more available: He needed the fantasy of Will more than the reality. Another was that Will's becoming genuinely available would mean a broken home of one kind or another, and Guy did not see himself as a homewrecker; he did not want that charge posted to his account.

Still, fantasizing about Will was a pleasant distraction, particularly on Valentine's Day. Being unattached on Valentine's Day was something like being Jewish at Christmas, Guy supposed. Everyone on the street, everyone in restaurants and shops and passing cars, seemed to be locking arms with a beloved, or aspiring to find a beloved, or fleeing the wreckage of a union gone sour. On Valentine's Day, it was impossible to escape the many symbols of love, good and bad. For some reason all the symbolism had him thinking of Doug, whom he'd not seen or heard from in weeks—or was it months? Will and his smile and his body, round and hard with muscles, made a nice change of subject.

"Sir?" Will said, holding open the steam room door with one hand and gesturing with the other. "After you."

"Thank you, sir," Guy said, and felt Will's hand on his ass as he passed into the swirling white murk. They drifted to the split-level benches at the rear, where the more sporting types gathered. It was considered bad form to talk in such a setting, male lust being for the most part a sullen and silent business, but for some reason Guy could not keep his lip buttoned.

Will had always been a good listener, but his interest in Guy's obscure encounters with a teenage boy ran far beyond the bounds of polite interest. He asked questions, sought the tiniest details (whether, for instance, Doug had hair on his knuckles; answer: a little), interpreted and speculated freely. But he continued to be a good listener and to give Guy the chance to relieve some of the pressure that had been building up inside. And, when Guy had finished talking, he offered some advice.

"Stay away."

"Stay away?" Guy said. "That's what you'd do? You've practically been salivating."

"I know," Will said. "I'm afraid I wouldn't stay away. Dennis fears for me, you know. He's afraid that someday I'll meet some kid like this kid of yours, and he'll have to come down to the jail with a Platinum Visa card to bail me out."

"You wouldn't really do anything."

"I wouldn't trust myself," Will said. "Maybe you're stronger than I am," he added doubtfully.

"I don't see why I have to avoid him altogether," Guy said.

"That's why," Will said. "Because you don't see. You can't really see him. You don't really know what he's like. All you know is that he's playing games with you."

"I think that's a little harsh," Guy said, but he couldn't mask his hesitancy. "He's just a kid."

"Just be careful, that's all I'm saying. Keep your wits about you," Will said, laying a hand across his shoulder and massaging his neck, which gave Guy an erection. A group of elderly men immediately gathered to see if anything more was going to happen. They peered, like wolves at the edge of a campfire, eyes glossy with anticipation. "Don't underestimate. What were you like as a kid? You never plotted trouble?"

"Well," Guy said. He hadn't discussed Michael Donofrio with Will. "You know. Every kid is looking for some kind of adventure, isn't he? Isn't that what it means to be a kid? Anyway, I don't see what you're getting at."

"He's up to something," Will said. "He's not innocent."

But he looks innocent! Guy protested in his heart. *And aren't people always what they seem to be?*

"He doesn't even know who he is," Will continued. "He's not finished. Do you want to have sex with him?"

"Of course not," Guy said.

"Ah."

"He's sixteen!"

The elderly wolves edged in closer, as if, by some queer bit of magic, the adolescent in question were about to be conjured.

"Yes?" Will said. "And sixteen-year-olds aren't interested in sex, is that your position?"

"I'm sure they're interested," Guy said. "That's not the question. Whether they're ready, that's the question. And I'm just slightly older than he is."

"There is that," Will conceded. "An experience with an older man could really help him. Or not."

"I'm concerned about the not."

"There you go," Will said. "It makes no sense. It's not wise. That's the rational view. What he wants doesn't matter. He's not old enough to know. It's your responsibility, really. You have to be old enough for both of you."

"I didn't know you were wise," Guy said.

"It's easy to be wise when you're talking about someone else's problems!" Will said with a little laugh. "I'm not sure Dennis thinks I'm wise. Sometimes I'm not even sure he likes me."

"But you have such sweet-smelling sweat!"

"I'll remind him of that tonight when he comes home," Will said, "and chastises me for fucking up the laundry or something."

"You fuck up the laundry?"

"You can't imagine," Will said.

"I'd chastise you too," Guy said. "Rub my toes." It was easy to think when one's toes were being rubbed, easier to absorb Will's blunt advice. *Stay away.* Guy knew he should, and knew he wouldn't. He knew that eventually, sooner or later and more likely sooner than later, he and Doug would meet again, in charged circumstances. It would be dark, it would be lonely: They would meet in a park, say, late-ish, and the city would not intrude.

For a moment, in the steam, Will became Doug, and it was Doug going down on him, Doug's lips on his mouth, Doug's dick between his lips, Doug's chest he was shooting on, to the delight of the geriatric wolves. Except Guy was certain Doug didn't yet have hair on his chest. That was a Will characteristic. Will was smiling, tousling Guy's hair with one hand while dragging the fingers of the other through the pearly beads on his pecs.

"Feel better?"

"Yes," Guy said with a deep exhalation. Ejaculating in steam rooms surely was not a recommended activity for men forty or older. "Aren't you going to?"

Will laughed. "I'm saving myself for marriage!" he said. "I've got a date tonight with the boss."

Guy nodded, but the thought depressed him: not that Will and Dennis would be together, but that he would be alone. There were only a few nights of the year when Guy found it difficult to be alone; Valentine's Day was one of them.

They parted ways with a nuzzle. Will had had enough; he was off to the showers to make himself presentable at home. Guy, meantime, lingered in the steam, glad of the warmth and the sense of satiation and even the simple animal comfort of the old wolves, who sustained their air of watchful expectancy just as the younger—but alas far too scarce—men they adored sustained erections. Soon a dark-haired, goateed, creamy-skinned twenty-six-year-old boy Guy knew to be named Pete burst through the door and came to the back of the chamber wrapped in a dark tense cloud of desire. Guy liked Pete for his correct use of the word, "sycophantic" in a bit of shower conversation they'd exchanged a few weeks before, after jacking each other off. And for being so frankly and unapologetically horny.

But while Pete, hands folded suggestively in his lap, was now glancing fervently in Guy's direction, Guy lacked the energy to respond. He was spent, like a drained car battery in need of a nice long easy drive to recharge. He got up, went over to Pete, kissed him (giving the boy a huge and instant hard-on), then whispered that he was just leaving. Then he left.

He was aware, as he dressed, of how insistently his thoughts had turned to Doug all day long. Will and Pete in succession had provided some distraction, but as soon as he ceased to be with them, they faded from consciousness, like lights being switched off, and he was back to Doug, whom he hadn't seen since before Christmas. He had trouble remembering exactly what Doug looked like. The boy had made a vivid impression on Guy in the autumn, but like the Cheshire cat vanishing except for his grin, he had mostly disappeared from Guy's thoughts except as a memory of magnetic sulkiness.

He supposed he defaulted to Doug because there was no one else to obsess about. He was like one of those old generals whose battle plans reflected the last war rather than the next one. Obsessive natures tended to look back.

By the time he got home it had begun to rain. Susannah was nowhere to be found; the answering machine was silent, its baleful, unblinking red eye staring back at him until he looked away. All day he'd had a feeling, and on his way home he felt certain that the machine would hold a message, a signal from Doug that he wanted to resume their conversation, suspended for no apparent reason for week upon week.

* * *

Guy had come home on a similar evening late in November, take-out burrito in hand, to find the machine's red eye patiently blinking. There was a message. He played it as he loosened his tie and took off his blazer and khakis. The voice was unfamiliar and slightly garbled and he nearly deleted the message without making any sense of what was being said. Answering machines around the city were cluttered with drug-deal messages left at wrong numbers, or by automated mass-market messages touting term life insurance or especially worthy political candidates, or by hawkers of credit cards and car loans whose automatic dialers didn't hang up fast enough when Guy's machine answered.

This voice was vague and nasal—not at all professional, Guy thought with annoyance as he pulled on jeans and a sweatshirt emblazoned with the name of a winery he'd never heard of; it had been a gift from Susannah. The first part of the message kept dropping out because the machine's digital technology did not handle soft-voiced speakers well. But toward the end the communicator pumped up his volume, and Guy quite clearly heard the words, ". . . please call me. It's Doug. 'bye, Guy. Oh yeah, my number." He gave the number. Then some clumsy rustlings, and a click.

Guy played the message again. The voice began to sound familiar; Guy began to see a face, a shuffle, a pair of dilapidated sneakers. The message played out; the caller again recited his number, which Guy wrote down. He played the message again, to make sure. Then he opened a beer and ate his burrito, which had been stuffed with shreds of roast pork. Meat, he was discovering, tasted far better in a city full of reproachful vegetarians.

He was staring at the telephone, wondering if he should return the call, when the device rang. It rang four times before the machine picked up. Guy's outgoing message played. The beep. The barest pause at the other end, before the rustling sounds of the handset being returned to the cradle. Someone he or Susannah knew? Friends generally left messages. Telemarketing technology had evolved, if that was the word, to the point where automatic dialers recognized answering machines and hung up on them before they'd finished issuing their outgoing statements. Guy picked up the handset and dialed *69 and waited as the phone started ringing.

"Hello?" said a sullen voice, the voice of someone who'd been awakened, of someone with a head cold.

"This is Guy Griffith," Guy said. "Who is this, please?"

"Who?"

Guy repeated his name.

"How did you get this number?"

Guy explained his feat of telephonic wizardry.

"Oh," the voice said, sounding faintly chastened. "I've heard of that. My number's listed, anyway. You probably don't remember me. It's Doug. Doug Whitmore. From that day out at the bridge. The Golden Gate. You got a flat tire on your bike. You pulled out that thorn or something."

"Of course I remember," Guy said. "Doug. I thought you'd vanished."

"I didn't vanish," Doug said. "I've been busy."

"Yes, of course," Guy said. "How did you get my number?"

"I looked it up," Doug said. "It's listed, too. You told me your name." He sounded defensive, as if he'd come into possession of information he wasn't supposed to have.

"Yes, I remember," Guy said. "So we're both listed."

"Yeah, I guess. I know where you live, too," he added, not at all threateningly. "I dropped you off."

"When you say you know where I live," Guy said, "you're assuming I haven't moved."

"Have you?" Doug asked. "Moved?"

"No."

"That's good."

"Why is it good?"

"I don't know," the boy said, lapsing into mumble. Guy could picture Doug's chin caving into his chest, as if his neck were made of melting wax. "It must be hard to move and everything. I've never moved. Well, once, when I was little. I don't remember it."

"I was surprised to hear from you."

"I told you, I just looked up the number in the phone book," Doug said, a little peevishly.

"Yes, I understand that," Guy said. "That was very kind of you."

"Thanks," Doug said.

"What I mean," Guy said, both amused and exasperated, "is that I'm not sure *why* you looked my number up in the phone book. I wasn't expecting to hear from you. Is something wrong?"

"No, nothing's wrong," Doug said. "Does something have to be wrong? I enjoyed talking to you, that's all. We had a good conversation. Did you enjoy talking to me?"

"As a matter of fact, I did," Guy said.

"Oh," the boy said, but he sounded utterly pleased. "Are you still living with that woman?" he asked.

"You mean my oldest and dearest friend?" Guy said. "Yes. You have a good memory. Why did you hang up on my answering machine?"

"I didn't," Doug said. "I left a message."

"I mean just now."

"I didn't want to leave another one," Doug said. "Use up all the tape or whatever. I hate when people do that. I hate it when they keep leaving messages, like they're desperate or something. Or they don't trust you. I don't like to be like that."

"My machine's digital," Guy noted benignly. "It doesn't run out of tape."

"Oh," Doug said. "That's cool. I didn't have anything else to say, though, so there was no point leaving a message."

"You didn't give me a chance to call you back," Guy said.

"Were you going to?" Doug said. There was a flicker of eagerness, quickly extinguished, in his words.

"I was thinking about it," Guy said. "I was going to, actually. It sounded like you wanted to talk to me."

"I did want to talk to you," Doug said. "I mean, I do."

"Well," Guy said, "here I am."

"Yeah," Doug said. "Um, it's, I don't know. It's kind of hard to talk about on the phone."

"Are you all right?" Guy asked.

"Yeah, sure," Doug said, but his voice was guarded and low. Guy pictured him hunched over the phone, glancing furtively over his shoulder to make sure no one was listening in. "I'm fine, yeah. I was wondering if we might . . . I don't know. Because I can't really . . . I'm just . . . it's just weird here right now."

"You want to meet?"

"Yeah!" Doug said, exhaling a huge gust of relief that Guy had spoken the necessary words. "Can we?"

"Sure," Guy said.

"You're not busy or anything?"

"I was just going to have a little dinner," Guy said. "That's all. It shouldn't take me too long. Where do you want to meet?"

"I don't know," Doug said. "I have wheels."

"I remember. Some place near my place, then?"

"Okay," Doug said. "Where?"

"Well, let's think about that," Guy said, letting his mind wander across the neighborhood's assortment of coffee bars, restaurants, cafés, bars, and bookstores.

"Maybe I should just come there and we could decide then," Doug suggested. "I could park there and we could walk somewhere."

"Yeah, that's fine," Guy said slowly, "that'll work."

"I can be there in ten minutes."

"Give me a half hour," Guy said. "I need to eat something. Have you eaten dinner?"

"Yeah, I ate a while ago," Doug said. "Half an hour. That's seven-thirty. That's okay?"

"Perfect," Guy said. "You remember where I live?"

Doug recited the address, with cross street.

"That's it!" Guy said. "You have a good memory."

"See ya," the boy said. He rang off abruptly, leaving Guy in the dark, half-dressed and bemused. And hungry.

* * *

From the beginning, Guy had been aware of an odd energy emanating from Doug. The boy mumbled; he shifted self-consciously on his feet; his eyes darted; he behaved like a guilty suspect failing a polygraph. Even in the course of a brief telephone conversation, he managed to communicate unease. He seemed simultaneously to crave approval and to suspect anyone who might be able to provide it.

But Guy supposed that these peculiar vibrations were nothing more than some sort of obscure erotics. He had been sexually attracted to the boy at once, and it was very likely the boy, at some level of consciousness, perceived that attraction, and felt something similar in return, since being attracted to someone was in itself an attractive quality.

Wasn't it one of the great unacknowledged truths of the human story that men and youths were erotically drawn to each other? It was an attraction that had nothing to do with individual tastes. Men were drawn to youth and saw, in younger men, younger versions of themselves, passing through a phase in life many of them had misplayed or squandered. What man wouldn't want to be a youth again—provided he could take back with him all the knowledge and experience he'd gained in becoming a man, so that he might make good on all those chances he'd muffed the first time around?

Youths were drawn to that very knowledge and experience. They sensed that men knew how to make things happen. They admired men's bodies, so much heavier and better-developed than their own inadequate and scrawny vessels, whose slender beauty they could not see. They wanted to be men, and because, being youths, all their wants were touched with Eros, they desired men, at the same time fearing that the desire for men meant they could never be men.

Guy had only the vaguest grasp of that delicate, troublesome mechanism. His own adolescent experience with a man had been notably smooth, perhaps because it did not cause a crisis of identity for Guy: He already knew who he was and what he wanted when he happened to get a taste of it. But he'd fallen easily enough into relations with people his own age, and as he grew up and older, he did not find himself gazing at boys' high school soccer teams practicing on broad green fields. He had no wish to reenact the Michael Donofrio story, cast this time with Guy in the role of the older man, the teacher and guide.

He avoided eye contact with teenage boys on the street, even when he could feel them staring at him, with their special laser heat of attraction and doubt and fear. He knew that some of them wanted him to try to make it happen, so that they could turn him down. A young man was never so confident of his heterosexuality as when rejecting a homosexual advance he had gone out of his way to encourage. And young men needed to build up their heterosexuality; it wasn't something any of them took for granted, in themselves or their peers. Young men needed queers to be interested in them, just as dictators needed conspirators and traitors to make examples of. But Guy wouldn't play that game.

Despite the golden erotic haze that hung about beautiful youths like morning mist, Guy suspected them of being, more often than not, forgettable sex. Beautiful people, for one thing, expected to be oohed and aahed over and to have everything done to and for them; they were an aesthetic experience best enjoyed from a distance. And boys knew nothing; were stiff and unsure of themselves, were blindly eager and clumsy, came too fast, then were apt to leave abruptly, in shame and contrition and anger, a confusion of feelings that would soon reform itself into a desire to do it again.

These sublime monsters had occasionally crossed Guy's path during his infrequent adventures in cruising. Boys out looking for male sex were usually just savvy enough to know not to declare themselves underage; if they claimed to be twenty, they were seventeen, and if they said they were eighteen, they were probably fifteen. Yet backpacks were a rather massive giveaway, as was girlishly soft skin, pubic hair like puppy fur, a capacity for near-instantaneous ejaculation, and a corollary capacity for staying hard and doing it again without even a token breather. Boys might be bad sex, but they tended to be indefatigable.

Guy was gentle with them, kissing and nuzzling and touching, on the theory that gentleness was one of the hardest things to teach a young man. The making of a man was a brutal and disorienting process, and quite different from the making of a true grown-up of either sex. Guy was pleased, in his small way, when opportunity presented, to disrupt the flow of clichés and propaganda to tender ears. Gentleness did not have to mean weakness; it could—should—flow from strength.

Still, boys didn't turn up that often, which was just as well. Much of their appeal attached to the violation of taboo—not to say the law—and the rest to their insatiable, nervous enthusiasm. It was new to them, and they were somehow, without being aware of it, able to transmit their sense of wonder and freshness to partners who had made the inevitable trade of innocence for experience. To play with someone very young made possible the fantasy of being young again oneself. The fantasy didn't last long; it was the equivalent of being briefly weightless in one of those crazily flown airplanes NASA used to train astronauts. But it was real while it lasted.

And when it was over, Guy would go back with a flush of relief and pleasure to muscles and whiskers and hairy chests: to guys who had managed to yoke boyish lusts to the more serious purposes of adult pleasure. It was possible to be wild with a man, and also, paradoxically, to relax with him. A man was an equal; he did not need to be taught or kept from fleeing or from imploding in guilt and fury. A man could give energy as well as take it. A man made possible a genuine exchange, however brief.

The problem with men was that most exchanges *were* brief. That was their power and their attraction. In the city, it was always possible to find someone else, someone new and exciting slipping into the steam room, or reading a book on Muni, or standing at the ATM machine. Men tended constantly to be on the lookout for their next chance, even as they walked arm in arm down Castro Street with their current chance. Men met, exchanged deep ecstasy, often revealed themselves afterward without self-consciousness, agreed to call and get together again to see what might develop. But they didn't call, didn't get together again, nothing developed. The city's bureau drawers were full of napkins and scraps of paper on which names and numbers of dimly recalled men had been recorded: an archive of unrealized possibility.

It struck Guy as curious that his own name and number and address were part of that archive—recorded, perhaps, on a scrap of tablet paper left over from third-period calculus—hoarded in the drawer of a strange high school boy named Doug Whitmore, whom Guy had met once, and only barely. Judging by the urgency in the boy's voice, he was in some kind of need and believed Guy might be able to help him. Guy was a friendly stranger, from a chance meeting weeks ago. It was odd; people were always crying out for help, and it was almost never possible truly to help them. But the alternative was saying no, and no was hard to say.

* * *

The doorbell rang and Guy pressed the buzzer that unlocked the steel gate at the street. He opened the apartment's door and stood in the gap, listening to a set of fast, heavy footsteps take the stairs two at a time. He actually smelled Doug before he saw him; like a springtime storm, the boy was preceded by a fresh scent, in his case, the mingled perfumes of Tide and Pantene and, vaguely, milk, with an even vaguer, contrapuntal stench of overripe sneakers wrapped around toenails in need of a good clipping.

Doug was bigger and heavier and better developed than Guy remembered. It might have been the dim light in the hallway, or perhaps he really had grown up that much. Guy had no meaningful experience of teenagers by which to judge this teenager. He knew they ate a great deal and were constantly outgrowing their clothes. Hence the shabbiness. He offered his hand in greeting, and the boy, after hesitating, shook it.

"I hope I'm not disturbing you or anything," he said to Guy once they were inside the apartment. The place seemed suddenly smaller with Doug in it. There was something sinister about the coziness. Guy switched on the table lamps at either end of the sofa. In their friendly yellow glow the boy seemed to shrink a bit. But he was still taller than Guy, who had begun to wonder why he had agreed to let this stranger into his apartment.

"Not at all," he said.

"Did you eat?"

"Burrito."

"Cool," Doug said. He was looking at his feet, as if they were deeply interesting. Guy glanced and saw only a pair of ragged Nikes. The boy's clothes were a collage of scruffiness, from the shoes to the dark-blue sweatpants with a hole at the knee to the dark-blue slicker with an athletic insignia to the blue knit skullcap he'd neglected to remove after coming inside. The ensemble was a perfect declaration of Doug's bourgeois origins and the beginnings of his half-hearted effort to deny them. The children of the bourgeoisie prized grubbiness as proof of their morally superior indifference to the material world in which their parents scrambled, and to which they had been born. But it was all for show: Doug's straight, white teeth were a small monument to expensive orthodonture. And underneath the carefully assembled, street-thug sloppiness, Guy was fairly sure, lay a pair of expensive boxer shorts, possibly of silk.

That thought, of silk boxers on pale skin flushed with rose, like the flesh of a white peach, gave him a sharp illicit thrill, and he forced himself to pay attention to their conversation, so far a balky affair. The boy, having hurried to Guy's, seemed to be as uncomfortable as Guy was at their softly lit seclusion.

"Can I get you something to drink?" Guy said. "There's Calistoga, Evian, some kind of Snapple, a beer? I think there's a bottle of white wine open in there somewhere."

"Beer?" Doug said.

"You want a beer?"

"Do you?"

"I'm not sure I want anything," Guy said. "I had a beer for dinner. But have what you want."

"My parents let me have wine sometimes with dinner," Doug said in that guarded, slightly strangled voice of his. He spoke as if someone were tightening a clamp around his neck.

"That's a wise policy," Guy said. "Wine belongs with food."

"When we go out or whatever," Doug continued, as if he hadn't heard. "Not that we go out that much. Usually we stay home. Usually we don't even eat together," he said, sounding clearer.

"My dad's a good cook, though. He does the cooking when we all eat together. We still do, sometimes."

"I think I will have a beer," Guy said, starting for the kitchen. Doug followed.

"Me too," he said.

"Your parents let you drink beer?"

"They know I do drink it," Doug said with a little smile. "I don't really like the taste, do you?"

"As a matter of fact, I do."

"Is your roommate here?" Doug asked. They'd twisted off their caps and taken swigs. "That woman."

"Susannah? No, she's out on a date."

"Oh yeah!" Doug said. "I thought she didn't go on dates."

"Did I tell you that?" Guy said. "Well, let's say she doesn't make a habit of it. But sometimes lightning does strike."

Doug shrugged. "I don't know anything about lightning," he said. "So, you don't have a date or whatever?"

Guy couldn't help laughing.

"Nope," he said, "not even whatever."

"Oh," Doug said.

"And don't you? Have a date?"

"Nah," Doug said. "I'm single."

"Well, here's to being single," Guy said. He clinked his bottle against Doug's in a small toast.

"Yeah," Doug said uneasily. He was looking around the kitchen as if casing it, but really he was just trying to conceal a nervousness he was making more apparent through his efforts at distraction. Guy wondered, with horror, if he had been so transparent at that age, such an obvious bundle of motives and insecurities and inept cunning. He wondered what Doug wanted.

"I like your place," Doug said.

"Thanks," Guy said. "It's Susannah's more than mine. She got here first." After a pause he added, "I can give you the tour, if you'd like. It takes about thirty seconds."

"Yeah, okay," Doug said.

They walked from the kitchen to the glass doors that opened onto the deck, which overlooked the garden, domain of the neighborhood's many cats; then on, past the dining table and the living area with its sofa and wide-screen television, to the bathroom and toilet and, at the end of a short corridor, the two bedrooms, side by side and overlooking the street.

"Two bedrooms," Doug noted stonily.

"One for her, one for me." Guy threw on the light in his room. He'd tidied up a bit before Doug arrived.

"That's your bed," Doug said, in the same flat voice.

"That's it," Guy said.

"It's big."

"I'm a big sleeper," Guy said.

"Do you snore?"

"Is that what you came here to ask me?"

"No," Doug said, once again inspecting—or possibly sniffing—his sneakers. Without a word Guy led the way back to the living room, where he took a seat in one of the easy chairs. Doug sat on the sofa, perpendicular to him. They worked their beers a bit.

"You haven't said why you needed to see me," Guy said pleasantly. "It sounded urgent."

"Did it?" Doug said. "It is, sort of. Not really."

"Sort of urgent, but not really. I see."

"You said," Doug began—pausing for a sip of beer—"back when we met, in October . . . do you remember?"

"I remember our meeting, yes, of course I do."

"You said"—beer—"when you pulled that thorn out of your bike tire and it went flat—the tire—and I gave you a ride home that if I ever needed anything I should call you."

"I owed you one, I said," Guy said. "Did your tire go flat?"

"No!" Doug said with a laugh.

"Good!" Guy said. "Because I'm not good with tires."

"My tires are okay," Doug said. "But I thought you might be able to . . . I could sort of use some help with something."

"Okay," Guy said. "Let's hear it."

The boy sat silent.

"You're okay, aren't you? You're not in trouble or anything."

"I'm fine," Doug said. "It's my friend Adam."

"Adam."

"He's my best friend. Since eighth grade."

"So Adam's in some kind of trouble?"

"Not really," Doug said. "It's his parents. They're splitting up. His dad's moved into this apartment, and Adam's going to be living with him part-time."

"I'm sorry," Guy said.

"It's cool," Doug said. "He likes his dad."

"I'm not quite sure where we fit in."

"It's his bike," Doug explained. "I'm supposed to take it over to his dad's new place."

"And this bike is too heavy for you to manage by yourself?"

"No," Doug said. "I've got it in the back of my truck, actually. The front wheel comes off. But I don't know how to get it back on. I thought, you know about bikes and all . . . "

"Sounds like a job for Adam."

"He and his dad went up to Yosemite for the weekend."

"And you want to get this bike out of the back of your truck and be done with your errand."

"Right!" Doug said. "Exactly. I'll buy you a doughnut," he added. "As a reward or whatever."

"You're tempting me," Guy said. "I choose the doughnut?"

"Sure, if you want, yeah."

"I think we have a deal."

"Thanks," Doug said. "I really appreciate this."

* * *

Doug's Suzuki Samurai jerked and shuddered as they made their way along winding hillside streets toward wherever they were going. The boy was plainly making his best effort to conceal the fact that he and the manual transmission of the obstinate truck were not on altogether easy terms. From somewhere under the floorboards emanated an arrhythmia of squeaks, groans and rattles, like the efforts of a drunken percussion section.

After ten jolting minutes (like a really awful commuter flight, Guy thought, in one of those little prop planes that were always crashing into cornfields or mountainsides), they ended up in front of a newish, faux-Edwardian building of flats on one of the side streets off Roosevelt Way. Eureka Valley opened below them, a cozy, shallow canyon of human habitation, a carpet of glittering lights laid on the black and undulating earth.

"This is it," Doug said.

Without much effort they hoisted Adam's mountain bike and its detached front wheel from the back of the truck and hauled them up one flight of harshly-lighted stairs to Adam's father's apartment. Doug produced a set of keys and, after a bit of fumbling, got the door open. They stepped inside. Guy was feeling several degrees of separation: He scarcely knew Doug, Adam was only a name, Adam's father and his shattered marriage were mere whispers. Yet now he was standing in the man's apartment in the company of an adolescent, both of them scented with beer. Surely the vice squad would burst in at any moment.

The place smelled empty even before Doug switched on the lights. There was a cold, slightly stale odor of bare walls pocked with nail holes, and of weary carpeting. Unread junk mail and old newspapers had accumulated on a side table. A half pot of undrunk coffee had turned cold and acrid in the carafe on the kitchen counter, as if the person or persons living there had been called away at short notice, with no time to make arrangements.

The apartments of transient college students and post-grad city dwellers at least glowed with chaotic energy. In the apartments of Guy's own youth, there were posters tacked to the wall, stacks of milk cartons full of books, magazines on the floor, piles of clothes waiting to be washed, and, in the air, the mingled scents of pot and pizza and beer and sex—of life. Adam's father's apartment smelled middle-aged and hopeless and dead.

The overhead lights cast a stark, punitive glare into what was, in largest outline, a big, open room that felt even bigger and more open because of the wall of glass doors that gave onto a deck and a view of the Castro, the Mission beyond, and, to the left, a few teeth in the skyline's ragged grin. The twinkle of the downtown towers' lights was dimmed by the mist.

Someone with design sense might have done a lot with the apartment, but Adam's father, whoever he might be, had been exercising his heterosexual male privilege to do nothing at all with it. Heterosexual men made it a point of pride not to have a sense of style. If they suffered the misfortune of having one, they concealed it. The big room was devoid of furnishings, except for an undersized Pier 1 bistro table with two taverna chairs in the dining nook near the kitchen, and a lonely sofa (upholstered in very 1970s black leather: plainly salvage from basement purgatory, or from one of the sidewalk estate liquidations with which so many of a generation of city lives had been prematurely concluded) gazed out the glass doors over the view.

"He hasn't lived here that long," Doug explained, "just a few weeks. Let's take the bike into Adam's bedroom."

"Let's put the tire on first," Guy said. "I want to earn my doughnut." He had the tire in place and the brakes reconnected before Doug could ask whether he needed help. They rolled the bike through an open door into a small corridor that ended in a squat U of three doors. One opened onto a narrow, dark bedroom with a futon; the second, into a bathroom; and the third, into a suite that seemed to be, thus far, the only occupied region of the apartment.

The suite's main room held a large bed in a frame, with pillows; a plush leather reading chair with ottoman and chrome pharmacist's lamp; and, opposite the bed, a television in a stand, crowned by a VCR eternally blinking 12:00.

"This is Adam's room," Doug said, indicating the smaller bedroom with the futon, "when he stays here."

They rolled the bike into the darkened room and leaned it against one of the bare walls. Then they crossed the hall.

"He's got cable in here," Doug said, poking his head into the master suite. He threw himself on the bed like a big hound and, picking up the remote-control box from the nightstand, switched on the television, surfed, paused at FX. "I hate TV," he said, setting down the remote, "even cable."

"I don't," Guy said, for lack of anything better to say. It didn't matter what he said, so long as he said something that would fill the space between the two of them, which otherwise seemed to be evaporating. The apartment was making Guy nervous and un-happy. It was a warren of Sheetrock boxes arranged around a B+ view, like the better sort of Triple-A-approved motel. The huge bed was full of implication. He wanted to leave, and he wanted to say so, but that would have sounded too much like asking for per-mission, as if Doug were in control—which, as keeper of the car keys, he was.

Guy could walk home, but it would be a wearying forty-five-minute hike, and at night perhaps not entirely safe. The crime page of the neighborhood newspapers increasingly con-tained reports of lone single men being mugged and robbed late at night on quiet side streets lined by expensively restored Victorian houses within whose state-of-the-art security systems people were safely asleep. The paper did not describe these incidents as fag-bashings, and possibly it could not be proved, but the subtext was plain.

"I think Adam's bi," Doug announced. He was lying on his back, knees flexed and arms folded behind his head, as if he were Huck Finn watching the river flow by.

"Your buddy Adam?" Guy said.

"Yeah."

"Bisexual?"

"Yeah."

"Why do you think that?"

"They have this sauna at their house," Doug reported. "Adam's dad built it in their basement. It's cool."

"You've seen the sauna."

"Oh yeah, I've been in it," Doug said, the words seeming to scrape in his throat. He dropped his voice: "I've been in it."

"With Adam."

Doug nodded. "I kept my underwear on," he said. "He didn't. I was sleeping over that night. This was a couple of years ago," he finished, rolling the episode into the safe and sanitary past as if he were pushing an unwanted car with a couple of incriminating corpses off a cliff into the rocky sea.

Guy nearly burst out laughing. "He sounds more like an exhibi-tionist than a bisexual."

"Do you believe in bisexuals?"

"What a question," Guy said. "I've never thought about it."

"Why were you at that gay beach that day?" Doug said, his voice suddenly full of challenge.

"That day we met? Up on the cliff? I wasn't on the beach."

"There were guys all over the place," Doug said. "I saw them. I could tell they were gay."

"How could you tell?"

"I could just tell!" he said. "I know what they look like."

"So they look a certain way? Gay men?"

"I could just tell," Doug murmured. He thrashed on the bed, covering his face with his arm.

"Did I look like one?"

"You were biking," Doug said.

"And bikers aren't gay?"

"I don't know," Doug said. "You tell me."

"If you're asking me if I'm gay," Guy said, "the answer is yes. Are you gay?"

"No!" Doug said. He sat bolt upright. "How can you even ask me that question!"

"You asked me," Guy pointed out.

"That's different."

"I don't see how."

"I can't understand how two men—" Doug began, "—can, you know, feel that way about each other. I mean, I know they do. I guess it's okay. I mean, I don't feel it."

"You can't picture it."

"Oh, I can picture it," he said in a throaty voice keen with feeling. "I just . . . I don't want to. Are you hornier when you're drunk?" he asked Guy suddenly.

"I'm even nicer than I usually am."

"I think I'm less inhibited," Doug said, "and less horny. Does that make sense? Like I'm more willing to do things, but I don't want to do them as much."

"It's getting late," Guy suggested.

Doug paid no attention. "Be right back," he said, vaulting to his feet and into the toilet, where he peed without closing the door.

Guy listened to the steady, heavy splash of water, the extended, satisfied sigh, the long pause that preceded a flush that didn't come. Guy knew he was standing in there. The light from the bathroom flowed out the open door, and Guy felt like a moth, instinctively drawn to it. He was being summoned and tested; Doug was applying pressure.

Then, at last, the flush, and the gurgle of water in the pipes in the flimsy Sheetrock walls. Guy tensed for his return, but Doug passed quickly into the hall, calling, "Be right back!" as he went.

Guy looked at his watch. He wished he were safe in bed at home, teeth flossed and brushed, contacts cleaned and stowed for the night, a few pages of some novel read. He did not want to be held hostage in a stranger's barren and frightening apartment by the stranger's son's unpredictable friend, who had some kind of fever on the brain.

Where had the boy gone? Guy heard faint sounds elsewhere in the apartment and was disquieted by them. Even ordinary noises were scarily amplified by the bare walls and empty rooms. It was like being on the set of a snuff film. He felt an insane fear that the power would fail and they would be trapped together in the dark. He was working out the question of whether to abandon his dignity and bolt for the street when the boy returned, holding a can of beer in each hand. He was drinking from one and offered the other to Guy.

"Sorry, no burritos!" he announced. "We could order out for pizza. If you're hungry. I am, sort of," he added, cutting off Guy's reply. "Actually, I already phoned for one. That's okay, isn't it? We can get doughnuts afterward."

Guy stood dumbstruck.

"I hope you like pepperoni," Doug added. "It's my favorite."

"Did you even think about asking me?" Guy said.

"It was an impulse thing," Doug said with a shrug. "I'm an impulsive guy. I like to do things on the spur of the moment."

"Whose beer is this?"

"What do you care? This one's for you," Doug said, waggling the beer—it was Miller—in Guy's direction and smiling.

"No thanks," Guy said. "I'll be up all night peeing."

"But I already opened it," Doug said. "Well, okay, if you don't want it, I'll just have to drink it."

"This is your friend's father's beer?"

"Actually it's Adam's," Doug said. "And he owes me, so it's really sort of mine, if you see what I mean."

The can was indeed open. Since letting Doug drink both beers was out of the question, Guy reluctantly accepted the can and took a tentative sip. Then a bigger one. The beer was friendly; it warmed him and thinned the cloud of anxiety about being with Doug—drinking beer with Doug—that had been gathering around his brow. He took another sip and felt his anxieties continuing to dissipate. Drinking the beer no longer seemed reckless. It seemed fine. Doug said it was okay; it was Doug's beer. He'd somehow provided it. Doug was fine.

Guy didn't hear the door buzzer, though Doug did: He jumped up to answer. Presumably the caller was the pizza delivery boy. Guy had once rented a porn film that featured a popular pizza delivery boy. While Doug was away, the telephone rang. Surely one of the banes of modern life was the simultaneous shrieking of various bells, all demanding attention. It was like having a squalling baby in every room, and all of them discovering they were wet and hungry at the same moment.

"Can you get that?" Doug called from some other room.

Guy, after hesitating, picked up the handset cautiously, as if it were a hot iron, and said, "Hello?"

There was a difficult pause, and Guy assumed it was a wrong number—most likely a drug dealer who'd misread the number on his pager. Then an irascible voice said: "Who is this?"

It was a man's voice, smooth, educated and assured despite his annoyance. Guy glanced down guiltily at the beer in his hand. The man sounded like a parent, and Guy felt like an adolescent caught out in a bit of foolish mischief.

"Sorry, wrong number," Guy murmured, and carefully returned the phone to its cradle, as if, gently handled, it would return to its silent slumber, like a tired puppy inadvertently roused.

A moment later, Doug returned with a flat cardboard box full of pizza.

"Who was it?" he asked.

"Some man."

"Probably my dad," Doug said.

"Your dad?"

"I told him we'd be here."

"We?"

"He knows we're friends," Doug said.

"Oh."

"What did he want?"

"I'm not sure," Guy said.

"Did he say he's coming over?" Doug asked.

"I hung up on him."

"Wow!"

"I didn't know he was your father!"

"He's probably on his way over right now!" Doug said. Was he exultant or horrified? Guy couldn't tell. Guy was simply horrified, though he had nothing to hide. It was more a matter of appearances, of propriety.

"Maybe it wasn't him."

"I'm sure it was," Doug said. "Do you want to meet him?"

"Am I going to have a choice?"

"We could leave," Doug said. "If you wanted to."

"What about your pizza?"

"We could eat it at your place," Doug suggested. "I think we should get out of here. I don't really want to see him. Did he sound pissed or anything?"

"He didn't sound pleased."

"Yeah, that's him," Doug said. "He never sounds pleased. He'll really be pissed if he finds us here drinking beer."

"I helped you move a bike."

"Yeah, but you're gay," Doug said as he replaced the top of the pizza box and gingerly picked it up.

"How does he know that?"

Doug shrugged. "He's good at figuring things out."

"You didn't tell him."

"How could I tell him?" Doug said. "You only told me tonight. But I knew. I figured it out. I figure he has, too."

"What does your dad do again?" Guy asked. He was trying to picture protective, paternal, homophobic anger: the cold blazing eyes, jabbing finger, controlled, harsh, threatening words; perhaps a fist raised.

"He's a lawyer," Doug said. He named the firm, a Montgomery Street behemoth full of suits.

"He doesn't like gay people?"

Doug shook his head. "He thinks they're evil."

"Is he religious? A Christian or something?"

"No," Doug said. "Just homophobic. He'll flip if he finds us here alone together and everything. He knows you're older than I am. How old are you?"

Guy told the truth. There was no reason not to.

"Jesus!" Doug said with pleasure. "You don't look that old."

"Thanks."

"You ready?" Doug said. "Let's go."

He led the way from the apartment, stopping briefly in the kitchen to hoist the balance of the six-pack of beer cans from the refrigerator. "Pizza goes better with beer," he said.

If they hadn't been leaving, Guy might have objected. But he did not wish to slow their exit from the apartment. As they stepped into the dark, quiet street, Guy flinched, as if he expected Doug's father to open up with automatic-weapons fire from his sniper's nest in the neighbor's hedge, or from the fire escape across the street. But the night was quiet, except for the occasional whoosh of tires on nearby pavement, rising and falling, like surf.

They climbed into the mulish little Suzuki, Guy with a vast sense of relief. The boy could do what he liked with his pizza and his partly depleted stock of beer. In a few short minutes, after a few perfunctory pleasantries, he would be safely behind his door, deadbolt thrown; he would be flossing his teeth and brushing them and settling into his big bed, alone and quite content.

Then Doug took an unexpected turn, and they were headed onto Upper Market, which wound like a mountain highway along the shoulders of the hills, while the city opened out behind them, a twinkling silhouette of points and peaks.

"I live over there," Guy said, motioning vaguely in the direction of his neighborhood.

"I know," Doug said. "I thought we could eat this pizza first. You know. And drink the beer."

"Where are we going?"

"Just up here," Doug said. "There's this turnout. It's close, just around the curve."

"Doug," Guy said, but it was too late, and pointless to argue; they were already making a U-turn. A moment later Doug had pulled the truck into the turnout, a lookout post from which to gaze over the luminous city. The few cars around them seemed to be empty, though the windows of a Firebird parked at the far end were entirely and suggestively fogged up.

Doug took no notice. He had retrieved the pizza and the beer from the back seat and was tucking in as if to a feast. "I'm hungry!" he said. "Dig in. Have a beer."

"I think I'll pass," Guy said, as if somehow his declining a second beer would exonerate him should the police pay a call. Yes, he was a fortyish gay man alone in a truck at a dark, lonely turnout with a teenage boy and several cans of beer, but it was all innocent! *It was all about the pizza, Officer.*

"You're passing?" Doug said.

"I've had enough for tonight. But thanks."

"I hate to drink alone," he said.

"Me too," Guy said. "It's not a good idea."

"Yeah, it's kind of pathetic," Doug agreed. He set down the beer on the truck's floor.

They dug into the pizza, Doug from sheer adolescent ravenousness, Guy in the fragile hope that the sooner the pizza was gone, the sooner Doug would take him home. He disliked the feeling of being held hostage. He could get out and walk. He could speak sharply to the boy, exercise his adult authority. He could be a man. But if he felt uncomfortable, he did not feel threatened. He perceived a great bursting fullness in the boy's heart, and a struggle to bring forth the things he was holding inside himself. Who, after all, didn't want to hear confession?

Guy was a stranger, but a friendly stranger, and often friendly strangers were the easiest people to confess to. They had no expectations; they might never be seen again. They were blank slates on which the truth could be written. The boy so plainly wanted and needed to talk, and it would cost Guy very little to listen. Listening was a gift he could give; he could let the boy's voice be heard. That was all most people wanted, in an overcrowded and noisy world: to be heard, paid attention to, just for a moment.

The air in the little truck grew pleasantly warm and close. It smelled of garlic and sausage and yeast. The city lay silent below them even as it bustled with unknown lives: people going out to dinner or to clubs, getting together, breaking up. Susannah was out there somewhere in that web of light. He did not envy her. He sat shoulder to shoulder with Doug, wordlessly, aware of the mingling of body heat and scents, of their sagging slightly toward one another, as if to kiss.

"When did you figure out you were gay?" Doug asked suddenly, in between slices of pizza. He would not eat the crusts and was throwing them, like watermelon rinds, back into the box.

"I always knew, in a way," Guy said. "But I suppose I didn't really think I might be until I was fourteen or so."

"Did it bother you?"

"Sure," Guy said. "It's isolating. At least it was when I was growing up. But that was a different place and time."

"There are a couple of gay guys in my class," Doug said. He spoke carefully, as if the truck were surrounded by eavesdroppers.

"You don't have to whisper," Guy said. "We're alone."

"I know," Doug said. "We are, aren't we. Totally alone."

"I mean, it's not as if there's anything wrong with your classmates being gay anyway, is there?" Guy said. Suddenly he did not want the conversation to change course. "It's not something people of your generation have to whisper about, I hope. Not these days. Not here."

Doug's answer was a long silence.

"So what kinds of guys do you like?" the boy asked when he spoke again. The pizza sat in its cardboard husk between their seats, like a little table with no legs.

"What kinds are there?"

"You tell me," Doug said. "You're the expert."

"I like guys," Guy said, "not kinds of guys."

"Have you ever had sex with anyone younger than you?"

"Um, sure, sometimes," Guy said. "The older you get, the easier it gets. It's a statistical thing, I guess."

"You like younger guys?"

"I've liked guys who are younger," Guy said, "but I've liked guys who are older, too. It depends."

"Yeah," he said, reaching for more pizza, "that's true. It depends. I've been thinking maybe I should find an older woman. Girls my age are really immature."

He burped, as if to emphasize the point. "I'm tired!" he announced, and tilted toward Guy, folding an arm under his head like a pillow. "Maybe we should just spend the night here."

"Won't your parents worry when you don't come home?"

Doug made contented wheezing noises in reply, and Guy was alarmed to think that he would go to sleep then and there, propped against the steering wheel. The boy's face was alarmingly close to his own. His lips looked full in the dim light.

"Did someone teach you about sex?" Doug asked. His eyes were closed but his voice was crystalline.

"Yes," Guy heard himself saying.

"Who?"

"An older neighbor."

"A man?"

"Yes."

"Was he gay?"

"He was married. I painted part of his house for him."

"So," Doug said, "were you, like, in love with him, or what?"

"I was sixteen," Guy said.

"Is that a yes or a no?"

"I think it's a yes."

"And what about him?"

"We never talked about it."

"I'll bet he did," Doug said. "Love you."

"It was a long time ago."

"Yeah," Doug murmured. "Did you hit on him?" he asked suddenly. His eyes were still closed.

"Um," Guy said, "We sort of . . . I guess it was mutual. It was kind of clear what was going to happen."

"Wild," Doug said.

"I'm not comfortable talking about this."

"Did his wife find out?"

"She never caught us, if that's what you mean. I doubt he told her. She was always nice to me."

"Did you tell anyone?"

"No," Guy said, "never. Who was I going to tell?"

"Your parents would have been pissed?"

Guy felt a twinge of the dread he hadn't felt in twenty years: that his father would somehow find out, come bursting into his room with a face purpled by rage, would beat him or scream at him or just wordlessly glare at him with the contempt he reserved for the truly loathsome, for a son revealed to be a husband fucker instead of a wife fucker. He felt sixteen all over again. He would be disowned, too ashamed ever to leave his room, unless it was to be packed off to some military boys' school where he'd have manhood pounded into him like a big nail.

"Yes," he said, "they would have been pissed."

"What happened to the guy? You know, the one you got together with or whatever."

"They moved. I think they had a baby."

"God," Doug said.

Guy felt a wave of fatigue sweep over him, and he could not stifle a yawn. He was tired, but alert, like a soldier expecting an attack from the shapeless dark around him.

"When you yawn it makes me sleepy," Doug said. He yawned too.

"We should go," Guy said.

"I don't want to. I'm comfortable right here." He sighed happily and closed his eyes.

"Doug."

Doug snored a little.

"Maybe I should just walk home," Guy said. "It's not far."

"No way," Doug said. "I don't strand my buddies." He struggled to roll down his window. "I don't feel so good."

"You're going to be sick?"

"I don't think so," he said, leaning his head into the cool night mist. "It's the pizza," he said. He burped again. "Better."

"Ready to roll?"

"Ready," he said. He turned the key in the ignition, and the engine came to life with a cough. Moments later they were jolting along. "This thing's such a piece of shit," he said. "It's going to make me barf. I wish somebody'd steal it so I could get the insurance money. I leave it unlocked. But even the car thieves don't want it, that's how big a piece of shit it is."

"Right at the light," Guy said.

"Right."

The rest of the drive home was uneventful. Doug parked in the driveway, and they sat there for an awkward moment.

"Do you want me to tuck you in?" Doug asked.

"I'll be fine," Guy said, "but thanks."

"'Cause it's no problem."

"Don't forget," Guy said with a smile, "I'm forty!"

"No way I'll forget that! " Doug said. "Thanks for your help with the bike and everything. I still owe you a doughnut."

"Yes, you do. Good night," Guy said.

"'Bye," Doug said.

Guy clambered from the car as if from an especially wild amusement park ride, half expecting his knees to buckle, or Doug to follow him up the stairs on some pretext. But Doug didn't. He just sat there in his truck. He was still sitting there five minutes later, as Guy went around the apartment dousing the lights and closing the blinds for the night. Guy didn't hear him drive off. But he assumed Doug did eventually leave, while Guy tossed and turned, as if he'd been wounded and couldn't get comfortable.

* * *

It seemed slightly pathetic to be cruising the Internet on Valentine's Day—or night—but then possibly there was always something pathetic about it. It was less a question of voyeurism—and
Guy was nothing if not a fully self-actualized voyeur—than of
cool remoteness and disembodiment. Disembodiment was especially unattractive on a day that was all about, or supposed to be all
about, embodiment, the mingling of bodies. Of course Will at the
Y and his little blowjob had been lovely. But that had been a while
ago, and Will was now safely at home with Dennis and a bottle of
Opus One, while Guy was sitting before a glowing monitor in a
badly heated apartment, skulking in and out of chatrooms and occasionally clicking over to a Web site that gave the lowdown on
public sex spaces worldwide.

Friends of Guy's did report the occasional hookup with people
they'd met in chat rooms, but it was not a step Guy had taken. He
had no objection in principle to the idea, though the likelihood of
deceit online seemed higher than in face-to-face venues. When sex
was at stake, most people would say anything, but at least in a bar
or club, you could see what you were getting, no matter what fanciful self-promotion you were hearing. You could have some pre-
liminary tactile experience of the object of your desire before
actually agreeing to anything.

Photographs exchanged online, on the other hand, while often
excitingly explicit, were unverifiable. Better just to download
some porn, skip the exhausting maneuvers, the revealing and concealing and misleading, required when dealing with other people.
At some point, well beyond one's twenties, when the insane, blind
hunger for joining one's body to those of others had subsided to an
intermittent mania, the idea of other people began to compete in
appeal with the reality of them; flirtatious chat became a satisfying
end in itself. The Internet was a perfect mechanism for scratching
that itch. It was a window, it gave as long a glimpse as one desired,
and its action figures, no matter how lively, made no demands in
return that could not be evaded simply by logging off.

For a while—a while that stretched into an interval, in which he lost track of time—he stared at a photo, downloaded from one of the newsgroups, of a cute boy, evidently with some gymnastic background, sucking his own dick. The boy looked like someone he had had a crush on in high school. The photo was of course undated, so there was no way to be certain it *wasn't* the same boy. Was this what that kid had been up to after school, while everyone else was at band practice or football practice or smoking dope at the far end of the parking lot? Had he been making a little extra cash posing for some seedy old pornmeister at the back of a tavern downtown? Guy felt an odd pang of jealousy: of having been excluded from a lively bit of knowledge, of having been left out.

Just then there was an elegant tingling sound that startled him, as if the dream police were bursting in on his little private party. Then a small box appeared on his screen, announcing the user name MREX, a tag that for a moment meant nothing to him.

Hi! said MREX in the little box.

Hi, Guy typed back, a little hesitantly. He scrolled and clicked to the member directory, where he searched out MREX's profile. Its information was skimpy, and unhelpful in a puerile way; for Sex, the user had added Yes! The only other relevant tidbit was that MREX lived in San Francisco.

It's me!

Who?

Doug! It's me. Hi, Guy.

Wait! Don't go so fast. How did you find me?

Okay, sorry. I read your profile.

How did you know I use AOL?

Everybody does. How are you?

OK.

Haven't seen you in a while.

That's true.

Rex is bugging me for a walk.

Well then, you'd better go.

Isn't there a park kind of near your place?

Yeah, there's one not too far.

*It's sort of between our neighborhoods. I think that's where
we'll go. Rex likes to keep an eye on his parks.*
I understand.
*Maybe you can meet us. If you want. It's not that big a deal.
We'll be there in half an hour. My mom's calling me now. I have to
go, bye!*

. . . and he logged off before Guy could respond. The exchange
had been uncomfortably abrupt. Guy liked e-mail, but not, he
thought, online chat. It would have been easier to telephone.

"Where are you going?" Susannah asked him as he put on his
coat and started for the door. She had been in the kitchen, whipping something up, and she wore a chef's apron spattered with to-
mato sauce. She looked as if she'd just committed a multiple
axe—or chef's knife—murder.

"Out for a little walk."

"Oh," she said.

"I'd ask you to come along," Guy said, "but I can see you're
cooking and everything."

"Oh, this!" she said. "This is nothing."

"It's all right," he said. "I'd prefer to go alone anyway."

"Are you going to a sex club or something?" she asked him.
"No!"

"I know you go," she said. "You don't have to keep it a secret."
It was her way of asking to be told the lurid details.

"How do you know I go?"

"Just a feeling," she said with a sly smile, having outbluffed
him. "I'm very intuitive, you know."

"Well, anyway, I'll be back," he said, and slipped out the door
before she could say anything more.

The night was cool, smelled fresh, was full of bright blue stars
that twinkled above the orange mercury-lamp haze of the city. At
every corner he looked both ways, expecting to see something unexpected. That was the appeal and terror of urban life. But he saw
nothing except the usual traffic, people with dinner reservations
crawling along in the cars they had no place to park.

He would have felt no pity for them even if he had had time to
feel pity. But he had been summoned, and he was hurrying to

a rendezvous with someone he couldn't resist meeting, because there was no countervailing force. Doug had been casual—entirely too casual—in proposing that they meet, in some park Guy was barely aware of. It was as if Doug had no doubt that Guy would come when called. And here he was, hurrying along so as not to be late, like a man going to a job interview. As he walked along he talked to himself, debating the question of whether he was doing something against his better judgment.

The park, lacking lights, was a zone of ink streaked with shadows as, a few minutes later, Guy gingerly entered from the lit street, passing through a wrought-iron gate and drifting along an asphalt walkway toward the sound of a basketball being dribbled. On the court a lone figure moved, filling the air with a scent Guy immediately recognized.

"Is that you?" Guy asked.

"I wasn't sure you'd come," Doug said.

"You logged off before I could say I would."

"Yeah, I had to log off," Doug said. "My mom wanted something and she doesn't like it when I'm online."

"Does she think you're up to no good?"

Doug's grin glowed in the dark. "Sometimes I am up to no good!" he said. "She's right about that. There's a lot of good stuff on the Internet."

"I just like e-mail," Guy said.

"I e-mailed you," Doug said, "right before I came down here. Did you read it?"

Guy shook his head. "I logged off right after you did."

"Did your roommate make you?"

"Susannah? No, she didn't make me."

"Is she your age?"

"I'm three weeks older."

"It must be cool to live like that."

"With a woman three weeks younger than I am?"

"To have your own place and everything."

Suddenly he was off, racing toward the basket and laying the ball up and through the hoop. Guy followed, grabbed the rebound, pivoted and fired a jumper that bounced with a heavy dull clang from the front of the rim.

"You're rusty!" Doug shouted from across the court. He launched a three-point attempt that quickly became an airball.

"I'm rusty?" Guy said.

"It's dark," Doug said. "It's hard to see."

"At least I hit the rim."

"You were closer."

They fell into a game of one-on-one that involved a fair amount of shoving and rubbing. Doug didn't back away from the contact. He defended Guy vigorously, constantly pressing against his back and shoulders, reaching around for the ball.

"You'd have fouled out by now," Guy pointed out, "about three times over."

"Hey, I know how to play defense," Doug said.

"I'm practically giving you a piggyback ride."

"You're not strong enough to do that," Doug said laughingly. "You're too old!"

"I'm not that old," Guy said.

"I think you're pretty old!" Doug said. His jeer was friendly, even a little nervous. "No way can you do it."

It turned out that Guy could do it. Doug whooped and prodded from his perch on Guy's shoulders, but all Guy was aware of was the heat of the boy's thighs around his neck, the pleasant weight of him, his engulfing sweet scent. Quickly he set Doug down.

"That's it?" Doug said. "You tired?"

"Do I look tired?"

"I can't tell, it's so dark in here. I'll lift you," he suggested abruptly, squatting so Guy could mount him.

"I don't like heights."

"Come on."

With reluctance and something else, Guy spread his legs around the boy's neck and permitted himself to be lifted. Doug wasn't husky, but he was surprisingly strong, and once he had Guy secured on his wide shoulders, he ran around the basketball court with a series of yelps.

"You're heavier than you look!" he said, breathing noticeably, when he set Guy down. "Are you fat?"

"Muscle is heavier than fat."

"You lift at some gym?"

Guy nodded.

"Which one?"

"The Y."

"Which Y?"

"The one downtown."

"There are a bunch of them downtown."

"The slummy one."

"I've never been to that one," Doug said.

Guy was silent.

"What's it like?"

"Slummy."

"Who goes there?"

"Members," Guy said.

"Slummy ones?"

"All kinds."

"Are you slummy?"

"Thanks for asking," Guy said.

"Is it gay?"

"Well," Guy said, "you could say that."

"I thought maybe that's what you meant by slummy."

"Mostly I meant it smells bad."

"I don't think I could handle that," Doug said. He drew his shoulders together, as if shivering in a cold breeze.

"A stinky gym?"

"A gay gym."

"It's just a gym. Just a plain old Y."

"I lift sometimes," Doug said. "You want to take a walk or something? This park smells like dog piss."

"Slummy."

"Yeah," Doug said with a little laugh.

"Where is your dog, by the way?"

"Oh, he decided he didn't want to come. Sometimes he does that. He just sits there and won't budge."

They drifted out of the park, up an adjoining street. Televisions flashed dimly in the bay windows of refurbished Victorian homes, doing the important work of holding the republic together with sit-coms and commercials. Guy had no idea where they were walking to, but Doug plainly did.

At the end of the block the street tipped sharply upward, and the sidewalks became long flights of steps, climbing toward the Market Street viaduct. Another set of steps, this in the shape of a helix, led to an overpass, on the far side of which lay apartment build-ings, on quieter streets that grew steadily narrower. They passed a pair of men in blue jeans and black leather jackets headed down-hill; Guy reflexively looked back, over his shoulder, and found one of the pair looking back at him with a smile that was, in classic queer style, at once polite and suggestive. If Doug noticed this bit of signaling, he did not let on.

Soon the pavement ended at a low retaining wall of rough rocks. A footpath disappeared into the gorse, running uphill toward Twin Peaks, the distinctive set of round, treeless hills that sat like a pair of upturned tits in the center of the city.

"Where are we going?" Guy asked anyway.

"The top of the hill," Doug said. "It's a beautiful view."

They climbed in the dark for a while before reaching the asphalt roadway that made a figure eight as it wound around the two hills just below their summits. It was to those summits Doug was lead-ing them. They crossed the road and climbed a twisty rocky path to the top, where they found a lonely park bench. They sat side by side, close but not too close.

The twinkling star map of the city unfolded below their knees, which occasionally touched. Doug did not flinch from the contact; he seemed actually to have spread his legs a bit, making the brushes more likely. The smell of him made Guy woozy. It was cold and breezy on the mountaintop, and they couldn't help lean-ing together slightly for warmth.

"I like it up here," Doug pronounced.

"It is freezing," Guy agreed, "if you like that sort of thing. And windy."

"There's my house."

He was pointing down and to the left.

"See it?"

Guy peered.

"My dad keeps a telescope on the deck," he confided. "He's probably looking up here right now. I told him we'd probably come up here later. He knows I like to."

"We?"

"Yeah," Doug said. "I told him I was meeting you. I don't like to keep secrets from my parents."

"He couldn't see anything anyway," Guy reassured them both. The illicit pleasure of being alone with the boy on a dark, lonely peak quickly turned to apprehension about the very illicitness of things, though nothing illicit was going on. How it looked was all that mattered, and it would look strange to a parent, especially a father, especially a father with a telescope, especially one who didn't care for queers. Guy imagined that if he were a father, the scene would not look terribly different to him, and his instinct would be to protect. He imagined parenting to be largely an exercise in instinct.

"We should kiss," Doug said, turning away as he said it. "That would really rock his world."

"He'd call the police," Guy said. "I'd go to prison."

"Really?" Doug said. "You think so?"

"He's your father," Guy said. "Do you think he wants you going around kissing forty-year-old men?"

"Yeah, he'd think you're too old for me," Doug said. "He'd say I could do better."

"I don't know if I'd go quite that far," Guy said.

"You don't look like you're forty," Doug said. "You're almost as old as my dad. He looks a lot older than you do."

"He's a dad."

"You'd really get sent to prison? For, you know, kissing me or whatever?"

"It wouldn't look good."

"But you said no one could see us up here."

"I'm not sure," Guy said. "There are people around. Look at all those tour buses."

"I hate tour buses," Doug said. "You don't think I'd really kiss you, do you?"

"We hardly know each other."

"Even as a joke."

"Kissing isn't a joke," Guy said. "It's intimate."

"You think I'm homophobic," Doug said. "You think I'm afraid of you because you're gay."

"If I thought that," Guy said, "then why would I be here?"

"I'm just curious," Doug said, "that's all. I've never known a gay guy before. It's kind of new to me."

"Is there something you want to tell me?" Guy said gently. "Something on your mind it might help to talk about?"

"No!" Doug said. "What makes you think that?"

"You seem preoccupied."

"I've been thinking about Rex," Doug said.

"Your dog?"

"He has to go to the vet tomorrow to have his teeth cleaned. They knock him out for like two hours."

"That's what you're worried about?"

"Yeah," Doug said. He was smiling strangely, not quite in Guy's direction. "You thought it was something else?"

"I didn't know," Guy said. "I don't read minds."

"I'm comfortable with your being gay," Doug said. "I'm not homophobic at all. I don't have any problem with your lifestyle."

"I have a life," Guy said, "not a lifestyle."

"Whatever. Tell that to my dad."

"What does your dad think?"

"That being gay is a choice."

"That's silly," Guy said. "Who would choose it?"

"That's what I told him," Doug said in a low voice. "He said some people just do, because they're perverse and have no self-control and they're weak and evil."

"I think it's just the opposite," Guy said. "It takes strength and courage to come out and acknowledge who you really are. It takes courage. Denial is easier."

"That's what I said."

"You argue with your father about homosexuality?"

"I argue with him about a lot of things," Doug said. "He's this big conservative guy and everything."

"What about your mom?"

Doug shrugged. "She's a liberal, but she doesn't say much. I think they argued more about it when they were younger."

"Now they don't argue?"

"They argue about other things," Doug said, barely audibly.

"I'm sorry."

"It's not that bad," Doug said. "All married people argue."

"I suppose."

"Did you ever want to get married?"

"To a woman?"

"To anyone."

"I lived with a man for a long time," Guy said. "Before I moved out here."

"Did he die?" Doug asked in a whisper.

"No, nothing that dramatic," Guy said. "We just split up."

"How come?"

"I'm not sure," Guy said.

"Did you love him?"

"I probably still do," Guy said. "I just don't like to admit it to myself, you know."

"I'm sorry," Doug said.

"Don't be," Guy said. "It's over. He met someone else."

"How long were you with him?"

"Ten years."

Doug whistled.

"I know it must sound like a long time to you," Guy said.

"I'd say," Doug said.

"You'll have a long relationship like that, a good one," Guy said. "And it won't end the way mine did."

"How do you know?"

"I just do," Guy said.

"Do you think you'll ever meet anyone else?" Doug asked.

"I doubt it," Guy said. "I'm not sure if I even really want it any more, though sometimes I think I do."

"Maybe you just need to meet the right person," Doug said.

Guy smiled into the windy darkness. "Young people think there's a right person," he said.

"You don't?"

"Love is mostly circumstantial, you know. It belongs to a certain time and place. A certain environment two people create at a moment in their lives. But you can't hold all those pieces in the same position indefinitely. Time flies. Everything changes. We change. That's life, everything changing, becoming something else. People aren't the same at thirty-five as they are at twenty-five. They can grow apart. They can become strangers to each other. And love isn't always adaptable. It rarely is. That's part of its charm, that it's fragile and breakable."

Doug was silent.

"I don't mean to depress you!" Guy said. "Sure it matters who the other person is. I'm just saying it's not all that matters. And people have to believe that love is possible. It's like faith. You just have to have it, you can't reason through it."

"I have it," Doug said. "I believe."

"I know you do."

"How do you know?"

"I can just tell," Guy said. "I just feel it in you."

"I broke up with Teresa again," Doug said.

"Again?"

"We sort of got back together," Doug said sheepishly. "Right around the time I met you, that day at the beach. It was, you know, mostly a lot of fooling around and stuff. That stuff was a lot better after we broke up, isn't that weird? But, I don't know, I couldn't handle it or something."

"You didn't tell me this the last time we saw each other."

"I know," Doug said. He was squirming. "I wasn't proud of it. I was afraid you would say I was stupid or something."

"No stupider than most people," Guy said, "including me."

"You've been stupid about, you know, love stuff?"

"Constantly," Guy said. "That's part of the fun of it. Just being a total blockhead in love."

"Yeah!" Doug said.

"You seem sad about Teresa."

Doug emitted a long deep sigh. "I just never really liked her that much," he said. "I was just trying to see how far I could go."

"How does she feel about you?"

"She's in love with me," Doug said. "She always has been. She keeps saying so. It bugs me. We fight about it. That's why I had to dump her again. I just couldn't deal with it."

"Better to move on, then," Guy said.

"That's what I think," Doug said. "Someone else will come along. Maybe someone older. I'm ready."

"You'll know you're ready," Guy said, "when you don't even stop to wonder whether you're ready."

"Are you cold?" Doug asked. "I'm cold. My hands are freezing." He wedged them under his thighs.

"Maybe we should head back," Guy suggested.

Doug agreed, and a few moments later they were stumbling down the rough track, back to the road, over the retaining wall, down the dark slope toward the glowing houses below.

"Teresa and I used to make out up here," Doug said, when they paused for a breather. Odd that going downhill should be so much more exhausting than going up. Yet it was. Gravity was a troublesome, if powerful, friend. Doug had stopped suddenly to issue his observation, and Guy, who was bouncing down the path like a truck with failed brakes, careened into him.

"Sorry!"

"It's okay," Doug said. "At least you're warm."

"This doesn't seem like much of a make-out spot."

"It's not great," Doug admitted. "It's better over there, on those steps we came up."

And by which they were about to return: a narrow public stairway, running between an apartment house and a bit of steep ground handsomely landscaped with Princess flower trees, whose droopy branches formed a canopy over the steps.

"It's pretty quiet along here at night," Doug said as they descended, he slowly leading. He paused briefly and for no apparent reason, well before the steps ended at the street. He turned toward Guy, his eyes wide, his lips poised with some comment he couldn't quite bring forth. Then, without a word, he resumed the descent.

They didn't talk on the way back to the park. There they found Doug's basketball on one of the benches courtside, right where he'd left it. The breeze shook and sighed in the tree branches overhead; the city hummed and murmured in the distance: a train whistle, an ambulance siren, the ceaseless white noise of traffic, like the roar of the sea. But all that was far away. They were alone, in the dark, facing one another in a failure of words.

"It was good to see you," Guy said at last.

"Yeah." Doug was staring at his feet.

"I'm glad you found me."

"Yeah?"

"Yeah."

"I'd seen you online before," Doug admitted. "I just, I don't know, I just didn't send you an instant message or whatever. Not before tonight. I wasn't sure you wanted me to."

"Well, now you know otherwise."

"I'm glad you came," Doug said. "To the park and everything. I liked whipping your ass at one-on-one."

"I thought I whipped your ass," Guy said.

"Like fuck!" Doug said with a laugh. "I wish—" he stopped so that he might concentrate his attention on kicking at a pebble.

"You wish?"

"I wish, I don't know, sometimes it's hard to bring everything up," Doug said, avoiding Guy's direct gaze. "Everything you want to talk about, you know what I mean?"

"I'm not sure," Guy said. "If you need to talk, you can always call me. Or send me one of your little messages."

"Thanks."

They stood in a mutually unhappy silence, across a three-foot gulf their arms could not close. Guy disliked himself for being so civilly dismissive of the boy's appeals for help. Doug wanted to reveal himself, or wanted to want to. Of course he couldn't just do it. He needed that little nudge from Guy. He needed permission. It was perverse that Guy couldn't give it. But he couldn't.

They stood at an impasse, like telephone lovers reluctant to hang up before the other did. But each time Guy sounded a valedictory "well" or "okay," Doug would puff out a few more words, like a man blowing on a dying fire, determined to keep the last embers glowing. He did not want the words to die, to be left alone with Guy in silence. His incessant staring at his shoes and cracking of his knuckles gave far more eloquent testimony to his feelings than the words he was uttering.

"I should probably go," Doug finally said, as if he were trying to talk himself into it. "My parents will be wondering where I am. I hate it when they ask me questions."

"I thought they had a telescope."

"Yeah," Doug said, "but even with that they can't see everything."

"I should go too," Guy said.

"I want to play some more one-on-one with you," Doug said. "You're pretty good, for an old guy."

"You're pretty good, for a punk."

"I'm not a punk!"

Guy laughed. "No," he said, "you're not. But it was fun to call you one anyway."

"Maybe next week," Doug suggested.

"Let me know."

"I'll message you!" Doug said. He was drifting away; the space between them was widening, as if they were two ships that had rendezvoused at sea but were now setting out on their separate courses. "Or you can message me."

"If I can figure out how."

Doug was too busy dribbling to answer. He dribbled down the walkway to the gate; he dribbled up the street and into the night with a cursory wave, leaving Guy in the dark, listening to the receding slap-slap of the ball against the concrete, as if the tide were going out. Then he walked home.

iv. *The Bust*

FOR LUNCH, Ross sometimes cruised the arcades on Folsom. He'd catch a cab from his glass-and-steel office tower downtown, excited by the casual lies he told his secretary as he left the building—about meeting an old friend from college at a restaurant, or shopping for a gift for his wife; by the knowing, bored eyes of the cab driver in the rearview mirror; by the knowledge that he had about an hour to make something happen, to work out the kink between his legs. You took chances and didn't waste time. It was a bit like trying to score the go-ahead touchdown as the clock ran down.

He never felt out of place in his suit, even as he stepped up to the arcade's glass counter—filled with pink dildos and vibrators, and videocassettes in garish jackets—and bought the requisite tokens for the honeycomb of booths, sweetly aromatic with dried semen, in the rear. He did not feel out of place because the bulk of the workday, lunchtime traffic also wore suits, or khakis with nice shirts and expensive shoes. (Ross had learned early on, during one of his first visits, not to come on somebody's Kenneth Coles.) They were, in the main, men like him: fastidious, on deadline, serious about the business of anonymous concupiscence.

Really he preferred the working-class leavening provided by the bike messengers and manual laborers, many of whom were Latino or black or some mysterious, erotic racial amalgam. They tended to be younger, and if they were a little rough around the edges (wearers of Fruit of the Loom briefs rather than Calvin Klein boxers), they were also brimming with enthusiasm and the abandon without which good sex was impossible.

It had been a bike messenger, in fact—a shabby blond with luminous green eyes and a pair of tattoos, a dragon on his upper right arm and a tiny red heart on his left hip—who'd first rimmed Ross. After they'd eyed each other and squeezed into a booth, the biker implacably maneuvered their two bodies as if they were the crew of an early space capsule performing some esoteric experiment, until the trousers of Ross's Joseph Abboud suit had fallen all the way to the floor and Ross's buttocks were spread wide, giving access to the biker's hot, athletic tongue, which tirelessly probed and tickled even as Ross ejaculated with considerable violence against the side of the booth, sending a bit of goo toward the avid eye that blinked in the glory hole and getting some on the back of his tie.

Moments later, the biker jacked himself off onto the video screen, which, glutted with their combined cache of tokens, continued to play a scene of a naked woman holding a champagne flute while guy after guy shot all over her. Ross couldn't remember which of them had settled on that particular loop, but it didn't matter. Once he'd gotten off, none of it mattered. He and the bike messenger exchanged not a word as they straightened themselves up and briskly exited the booth, like football teammates, sweaty and determined, emerging from the locker room for the second half.

They would most likely never see each other again. That was certainly Ross's hope. And if they did by chance cross paths, Ross would ignore him, pretend that he did not see or recognize him. He never did it with the same person twice. It was not a conscious or deliberate policy, but it was policy all the same, and a shrewd one. No attachments, no sentimentality. Policy said: You have an hour, get it done, get out, get back in a cab and back to work, back to your phone messages and the brief you need to get out by 5 p.m. And when you return, as you know you will, find somebody else.

Emerging into the sunlight, climbing into a cab, was like waking from a dream. The arcade he'd left behind was no longer real; it evaporated from his consciousness like a sidewalk puddle in warm sunshine. The bike messenger no longer existed; nor, from other visits, the nineteen-year-old black kid who'd whipped an engrossing cock from his paint-spattered overalls, and the goateed buzzhead who'd wanted Ross to fuck him. They were gone, and he was once again in the office, returning his wife's call, waving to a partner who was passing by his half-open door.

There was, of course, a certain thrill in glimpsing a familiar face at the arcades: a face from a past encounter, or a face belonging to a colleague or an old acquaintance. In the latter case, mutual recognition as secret sharers led immediately to stability, since the alternative, as in a standoff between nuclear powers, was mutual assured destruction. The first time Ross recognized someone who recognized him, he was gripped by a fright he could not control by reason. But after that it happened fairly often, nearly to the point of becoming routine. There was something almost sociable about it; one might see anyone—even, one breezy April noontime, David Rice, Ross's first-ever male lover from the long-ago days before he'd married Katherine.

David was standing there in a buddy booth as if waiting when an unknowing Ross slipped into the adjoining booth and pushed the button that defogged the Plexiglas so the occupants of the booths could appraise each other. David's jeans were open and lowered to mid-thigh, and his hard cock was very much as Ross remembered it. Of course cocks were all basically the same; that was a lesson one learned from playing with a lot of them.

David looked more surprised to see Ross than Ross felt at seeing David, but it was David who suggested, through hand signs, that they meet up in Ross's booth. Ross nodded yes, feeling utterly calm though wondering, in a cool way, if by opening the door of his booth, he was somehow following the lead of the gatekeepers of Troy. David was, if anything, even sexier than he'd been ten years earlier, when they'd first hooked up, but he was also a potential short circuit, a crossing of life's wires. They fell into each other's arms anyway, and got into each other's clothes easily enough.

"I always wondered when you'd turn up," David said, out loud, into Ross's ear. His breath tickled. The sound of speech in such a place was like a roar in Ross's ears. He'd always maintained a scrupulous silence when going about his business with men. It was evident that David didn't, that he was something of a chatterer. He looked, in fact, as if he were waiting for some kind of reply from Ross, who had yet to say a word.

"I'm sorry," David said. "That didn't sound right. I didn't mean it to sound like that."

"I know," Ross said. The words sounded odd, tinny. He pressed his mouth against David's, ran a hand down the front of David's jeans, and felt an instant flush of relaxation—at doing rather than saying—while at the same moment the heat of arousal rose in him. They ground their bodies together, fondled each other, buttons and zippers opening, elastic waistbands yielding, more and more flesh exposed. All the while Ross kept his mouth busy with David's. David still tasted sweet and fresh: a little Crest, mixed now, in adulthood, with a little coffee.

"You really look good," David said a while later, when he'd managed to work his mouth free.

"You too," Ross whispered.

"Heard you had a kid," David said. The thought that he was doing some young father clearly excited him.

"Mmmmm," Ross grunted, moving his lips back to David's as if he were working on a caramel apple. Talk of any kind spoiled the spell, and talk about his family life in such a place was an unwelcome reminder that he had a family. He came to the arcades to forget them; while he was there, they didn't exist.

Eventually they were all but naked, their mouths running all over each other, up and down each other's torsos, tongues into armpits, around earlobes, over eyebrows, at the edges of nostrils, nibbling at nipples. They sucked each other with elaborate slowness, pulling at the balls, jiggling the base as they had learned to do with one another so many years before.

"We don't have to come," David said softly into his ears, as he held Ross. "Not if you don't want to."

"I want to," Ross said.

"So do I."

And they did, together, sensationally, raising a series of grunts and groans worthy of a gruesome murder in a second-rate movie. The din actually drew a knock at the door from some eager queen patiently awaiting news outside. A few minutes later, chatting briefly out on the sidewalk a discreet step or two away from the shop, they agreed to meet the next day, same time and place. But Ross knew even as he made the promise that he had no intention of keeping it. He recognized that little dart of eagerness in David's eyes, and he felt, inside himself, unwelcome stirrings of emotions that had long lay dormant. Unwanted feelings were like fires taking hold in dry forests; they had to be quelled at once, or else they would quickly become conflagrations.

When Ross reached his building, he went immediately to the men's room on the eleventh floor and, having locked himself in, took a quick inventory in the mirror. He saw that he'd sweated through his shirt, but if he wore his suitcoat, no one would notice. He smoothed his hair, brushed his teeth from the little kit he kept in his pocket, and hummed to himself as he unlocked the door and stepped back into the corridor, back to his office and his smiling secretary and the rest of the unsuspecting world he called home.

* * *

When, years later, Ross learned from his wife that David was ill and in the hospital, he nodded gravely while reassuring himself that he and David hadn't done anything to risk transmission. He would be fine. It occurred to him, too, that when the hapless David had died, the story of the two of them would die with him. Ross would go on knowing, of course, but he would be in sole earthly possession of the facts.

They were standing in the entryway. He nodded to Katherine and said, "I'm so sorry," and when she started to melt he took her in his arms as a father might do for a beleaguered daughter.

Of course David had gotten it. He had lived that sort of life, and if the papers were to be believed, nearly everyone who'd lived that sort of life now found himself in a similar predicament.

"Are you all right?" he asked after a discreet moment. Running his hands over her hair, he felt, for an instant, a flush of sentimental memory.

"I'm fine."

"I know it's hard."

"It doesn't seem fair," she said.

"I suppose not."

"I mean, why him?"

"Bad luck," he said with a shrug, ascribing the disease to misfortune instead of saying someone deserved it or should have known better, been more careful.

"Yes."

Of course Ross believed, in the privacy of his own thoughts, that David should have known better. He had not been careful; he had, in some sense, willed his unhappy fate. He had been reckless and taken risks in his search—a quixotic one, as Ross had explained to him years before, during their brief, hot intimacy—for love. Men did not, could not love one another. Sometimes they managed to cooperate, and sometimes they turned each other on. But sex was not love. As Katherine shuddered in his arms, he felt the desire for a man, some man, any man, welling up in him, like black, sticky oil bubbling up from a hole in the ground, and he was plotting what to do about it as they went into the kitchen and waited for Doug to come home.

That night, before Doug went to sleep, Ross paid a rare visit to his son's bedroom. The lights had been doused, and the boy was in bed, staring at the ceiling. The room smelled of sheets and pajamas laundered in Tide. Ross, having knocked and been given permission to enter, sat on the edge of the bed in the soft darkness, swallowing silently to steady himself. It was important that the boy see him as calm and authoritative. He could feel his son trembling with dread at his father's intimate presence. The boy's fear exhilarated and grieved him. It was an exercise in power, but power over others was so often ugly and hateful.

"Mom told you about David," he said.

"He's going to die."

"I don't know," Ross said truthfully.

"He has AIDS," Doug said. "He's going to die."

"I hope that doesn't happen," Ross said. "I know you care about him. I know he's a friend of yours."

"Do you care?"

"Of course I care."

"I thought you hated him."

"Of course I don't hate him," Ross said.

"He doesn't hate you."

"He told you that?"

Doug nodded.

"I've always liked him," Ross said stiffly. "We just . . . he and I never got to be proper friends, is all. And then our lives went separate ways after your mother and I got married."

"You mean he's gay."

"I suppose that's part of it," Ross conceded, marveling that the boy could speak of that fact unselfconsciously, could utter that sharp syllable without flinching. He couldn't help wondering if it was a good thing. Or if it meant something. "He wouldn't be where he is today if he weren't."

"You mean gay people deserve to get AIDS."

"No, that's not what I mean," Ross said. His patience surprised him, especially since Doug meant to provoke. The boy had certain precocious powers, and Ross admired but did not approve of them, particularly when aimed in his direction.

"What do you mean, then?"

"Well, it is a sexually transmitted disease," Ross said cautiously. "I'm sure they've taught you this in school. It has to do with what happens between two people. Two men."

"Straight people get it too," Doug pointed out.

"Not nearly as much," Ross said.

"You think God is punishing gay people. You think David deserves to die for being gay."

The sound of these hard words springing from Doug's young lips left Ross feeling exposed and naked and small. "Don't tell me what I think!" he said. "If you'll listen, I'll tell you. I've always liked David, and you know, your mother and he are close and I respect that. But we moved, and he moved, and your mother and I had you, and, you know, people drift apart over time. It happens. It isn't a crime."

"He asks how you are," Doug said. "Do you care how he is?"

"I've already said I do."

"He's sad," Doug said. "I think he wants to die."

"He didn't tell you that."

"No," Doug said. "I can just tell."

"Doug, he'll get better, you'll see, don't give up," Ross said, ashamed at the hollowness of his words. "He needs you not to give up. And when he feels better he'll be glad he didn't die and he'll know you helped him. He must have been happy to see you."

He could feel the boy blushing in the dark, and he swallowed his own disquiet in one thick gulp.

"I guess," Doug said, rolling onto his side and turning away from his father. "He didn't seem very happy to see anyone."

"How is he?" Katherine asked Ross when he'd returned to their bedroom. She was reading a book in the funnel of yellow light that fell from the lamp on her side of the bed.

"It's hard to tell," he said. "He keeps a lot to himself." He went into their bathroom. When he emerged five minutes later, ready for bed, she appeared still to be reading, but she looked flushed and preoccupied. He got into bed next to her and gently touched her hair.

"He's not even forty," she said in a halting voice.

He could not think of anything comforting to say, so he said nothing, hoping that his silence would somehow seem sympathetic to her and at the same time keep her from saying anything more. With rare exceptions, it was not human nature to keep talking into a void. The trick was not to be impolite about not responding.

Forty was the word that seemed to reverberate in the bedroom. Forty had always been unimaginable, a far shore beyond youth, but now they were in sight of it and would almost certainly achieve it. Except David. He would be forever in his thirties. For a moment Ross envied him his discovery of the secret of eternal youth: dying young. While she kept reading, tensely turning the pages, he settled back on his pillow and closed his eyes and was soon asleep.

When David finally died, Ross was calm about it. He made properly reassuring and supportive noises to Katherine and Doug, cooked them breakfast and sent them off to the memorial with a promise that he would walk the dog in the meantime. The family as a whole had been invited to the service, so he could have gone if he'd wanted to, but he suggested vaguely that it might be awkward, that it might not be what David would have wanted. Katherine and Doug did not argue with him.

As soon as they were gone, he found himself filled with random lust. He thought about going out to look for sex. He felt perversely drawn to Buena Vista Park, where there was always some action to be had and where, today, on the hilltop above the busy bushes, David's short life would be celebrated by a group that would include his wife and son.

The thought stimulated him violently—too violently. He had generally tried to avoid Buena Vista, telling himself it was dark and muddy and cold, with treacherous footing and dangerously deranged bums living in improvised lean-tos. He would think about the park or read about it on the Web and get himself so worked up that he would have to rush to one of his friendly arcades as soon as he could. They offered something like the rush of publicness he craved, without the corollary dangers. But it was those dangers that increasingly fanned the erotic flames in his imagination—until, on the day of David's memorial, he was like an overheating radiator, leaking from the seams.

It was all he could do not to pull out his car keys and start for the garage. He poured himself a glass of water and sat down until the urge to get in the car subsided. He kept picturing himself overtaking them, waving at them. They would think he'd changed his mind and was joining him, but halfway up the hill he would peel off, down the wooden stairs that had been cut into the steep hillside and its webbing of trails.

"How was the ceremony?" Ross asked Katherine when they'd returned home and Doug, after making arrangements by telephone, went off to meet a friend.

"Very nice," she said.

"Did they do the balloons?"

"It was just the right sort of spectacle, you know, playful and absurdly magnificent. Like David. He would have liked it."

She went off to the kitchen for a glass of water, and the dog followed her, hoping for a cracker. Ross stood there, still thinking about sex. Where he would go, what it would be like, what excuse he could give for going out. He tried to will away his inconvenient desires but did not succeed. He knew that once he was out looking for sex, he would at least stop thinking about everything else in his complicated life. Sex wasn't good for much, but if it could do that much for him—give him an hour or two of blind relief—then he wanted it.

"You're going out?" she said when she returned.

"Yes." He could simply have walked out of the house while she was in the kitchen, leaving a note of explanation, or nothing at all, but he didn't like to do it that way. Observing the formalities gave a kind of stability. "I've got a few little things to do that I didn't take care of earlier this week."

He could easily have been talking about office matters, and from the way she was nodding, she could easily appear to be understanding his vagueness in that way. They might well be using the shorthand of people who've known each other a very long time, people who were able to communicate richly and subtly with one another without, to outside eyes, seeming to be communicating anything at all.

"Back for dinner?"

"Oh yes!" he said. "Long before. Not much to take care of at all. Anything in particular you want?"

"Anything at all," she said. "I can't even bear the thought of microwaving something."

"I know how you feel," he said sympathetically, taking her hand for a shy moment. "I'll stop at the market on my way home."

Then he was out the door, down the steps to the car, in whose trunk he kept a pair of hiking boots, for just such expeditions as this. Ten minutes later, duly reshod, he stood in Buena Vista Park, where he ended up not having sex at all but walking around in a kind of trance, admiring the view and the trees and watching various combinations of men, scantily concealed by vegetation, go at each other in broad daylight. He looked into the sky for balloons but saw none, just the sun, settling on pillows of rose and plum as the air grew cool and smelled of fir and eucalyptus.

* * *

A tall figure drifted across the park's lawn toward the bench where Guy was sitting. He felt a twinge of apprehension. One's fellow man was generally harmless, if thoughtless, but Guy, because he'd not grown up in a big city, remained wary of being approached in poorly lit urban public spaces at night, even if the approaching person was merely walking a dog and wanted to make idle chat. But in a moment he recognized the figure and recognized, too, that the figure had recognized him.

"Rex," the figure called over his shoulder, in a deep yet tender voice. "Out of the sandbox!"

There was a rapid tinkling sound as the dog, invisible in the darkness, shook himself and the tags attached to the collar around his neck. In a moment Rex emerged from the ink, mane swaying around his neck like a furry hula-hoop, to sniff Guy's knee and dance away when Guy attempted to pet him.

"Hey."

"Hey," Guy said.

"You got my e-mail."

"I did," Guy said. "Here I am. You must live pretty close to this place."

"Why do you say that?"

"We keep meeting here," Guy said, "at your suggestion."

"Yeah, I guess I live pretty close," Doug admitted. "Down that way," he said, seeming to point uphill.

"Is it some kind of secret, where you live?"

"No," Doug said. He turned his head away as if he were addressing a nonexistent person sitting on his other side. Guy studied him in profile. The nape of his neck was smooth and vulnerably slender.

Guy noticed with regret that the hellos were scarcely out of their mouths before Doug began playing the male power games: being stoic and taciturn, carefully policing the line between chumminess and genuine intimacy, trying not to give anything away, though he was obviously dying to. But even across the studied distance between them, Guy could feel the warmth of him, smell his distinctive clean smell.

"Do you want some latte?" Doug offered Guy a sip from the tall paper cup he'd been holding in his right hand. "It's decaf."

"Thanks," Guy said, "but you don't want me drinking out of your cup, do you?"

"Sure I do."

"I have germs."

"Everyone has germs."

"Well, I do like coffee," Guy said. "And my shots are up to date. Okay, one swig."

He took a tentative chug from the cup, braced for a truly cloying mouthful. But Doug had sweetened the brew just enough to bring out its dark flavor.

"Thanks," Guy said, returning the cup to him and completing their obscure exchange. "Not bad."

"I only drink coffee when I'm nervous," Doug said.

"Yes, it's quite a nerve calmer, isn't it?"

"Yeah," Doug said. He was bouncing one knee up and down, as if trying to amuse a bored infant.

"You're nervous now?"

"Not really," he said, cracking one of his knuckles.

"Not really? I thought when you're nervous you drink coffee, and that's coffee you're drinking."

"Did I say that?"

"Moments ago."

"I guess I must be, then."

"So there must be a reason you're nervous."

"I guess."

"So what is it?"

"I'm not sure."

"Random anxiety?"

"I'm kind of a nervous person," he said. He patted Rex, and the dog responded by lolling his head back so that his square, stubby muzzle pointed straight into the starry night, like an antiaircraft battery. Doug leaned down and murmured something into one of Rex's soft, twitching ears.

"You don't seem like the nervous type."

"It's weird," he muttered in the general direction of the ground—a gesture magnified, Guy thought, by the simmering but unmentioned particulars of Doug's anxiety.

"What's weird?" Guy asked. He was trying to decide if Doug wanted to talk about a subject he'd yet to find the opening words for, or if the boy's mind had skipped off in some other direction, like a flat rock on water. He felt awkward and somehow craven, waiting there for a cue. He looked away, and thought about going home, getting into bed with clean teeth, watching television, reading until his eyelids grew heavy, drifting off to sleep in the dark cool peace of his room.

But Doug was radiating tension. He seemed to sense Guy's restiveness, and his tense throat-clearing established that he did not want Guy to go, that there was something he needed to talk about. They barely knew one another, yet they both seemed to sense that their lives were colliding in some way.

"I haven't talked to you in a while," Doug said. He made it sound as if their not talking was not only exceptional but Guy's doing—a blameworthy act of interruption and neglect—instead of the ordinary state of affairs between them. Their meetings were islands in a sea of separation, not the other way around, as Doug seemed to be implying, in an accusatory tone. "Not since Valentine's Day."

"It was weeks ago," Guy agreed.

"Yeah, I remember," Doug said. "So, did you, like hook up with anybody or anything?"

Guy smiled. "I spent most of the evening with you," he pointed out mildly.

"What's that supposed to mean?"

"Nothing," Guy said. "Nothing at all."

"It didn't sound like nothing."

"Don't get excited," Guy said.

"I'm not excited, I'm just stressed," Doug said, raising the cup of relaxing coffee to his lips and taking a long slug. All this in lieu

of apologizing, which implied responsibility, which was a burden
to be shunned whenever possible.

"I'm sorry," Guy said. He was about to encourage Doug to talk
about it, to bring forth his issues—something the boy had trouble
doing directly—but restrained himself. He was not Doug's psy-
chologist. Too often in the past had too many of Guy's friendships
been founded on the twin pillars of the friend's lust to confess and
Guy's sympathetic ear. And too many of them had later collapsed
when the confessions and the needs intensified, exhausting Guy's
sympathy. He was determined to break that pattern. Yet patterns
were hard to break, and the boy was trying to ask for help, and
pleas for help were magnetic. The moment for resisting the en-
treaty had passed some time ago. He would have to break the pattern some other time, possibly with someone else. For now, he was
caught.

"My dad—" Doug began, and stopped. "You don't want to hear
this," he said after a moment.

"Let me decide about that," Guy said.

"I don't think I can talk about it."

"You started to."

"I know *that*," Doug said.

The snippiness stung Guy a little, and he let the silence between
them stand.

"I really don't want to talk about it," Doug said. Guy could see
him watching from the corners of his eyes, so he shrugged. "I
mean, it's about my father and everything, and you don't even
know him. You've never even see him."

"Your father."

"He's a lawyer," Doug said.

Guy nodded. "Things don't sound so bad so far," he said.
"Many people are lawyers."

Doug made a face. "He's kind of this big, law-and-order, conservative type," he said. Without warning he gave a barking laugh,
a joyless yelp.

"That's no crime," Guy said.

"No, that's no crime," Doug agreed. "It's just so funny."

"That your father's a lawyer?"

"No, that's not funny," Doug agreed. "It's just, you know, you don't expect somebody like that to do anything wild or illegal."

"So your father's finally done something exciting?"

"Oh yeah," Doug said in a voice barely above a whisper. He looked away. Guy waited for him to continue with his report of excitingly unlawyerly, wild behavior, but he didn't. "And illegal," Doug finally added, as if not wanting to lose his audience.

"Come on," Guy said at last. "You're leaving me hanging here. Let's have it. Put me out of my misery."

"He got arrested," Doug managed to say.

"Arrested?" Guy said. This sounded disappointingly routine.

"Yeah," Doug confirmed in a mumble.

"For what? Drunk driving or something?"

The boy laughed mirthlessly. "Not even close."

"Embezzlement?" Guy suggested more daringly, his mind beginning to trace the ascending parabola of lawyerly sin.

"What's embezzlement?" Doug asked.

"Stealing money from your own firm or something," suggested Guy. He wasn't even sure that was illegal. It must happen all the time. Dennis would know. He was a lawyer. He would remember to ask Will to ask him.

"No, not that. At least that's not what he got arrested for."

"What did he get arrested for?"

"I'm not sure," Doug said. "Lewd conduct or something," he added, voice dropping to little more than a rush of air, like the last gasp from a balloon with an untied nipple. "On Sunday."

A long pause ensued. It was hard for Guy to imagine anyone's being arrested for lewd conduct in San Francisco, where lewd conduct was a way of life. But then, Guy supposed that the city's police, like politically aware police everywhere, periodically staged their little crackdowns on prostitution to let the citizenry know they were on the case, sending out attractive women officers to solicit johns—so often prominent and respectable married men (such as, apparently, Doug's luckless father), trolling the garish streets of the Tenderloin in their shiny Jaguars and Lexuses in pursuit of a few moments of fugitive joy—and then bust them.

"He got nabbed with a whore?" Guy said, surprise coarsening his language a bit. Suits, in his experience, did tend to be sleazier and more reckless than less expensively dressed persons, probably because they had to spend so many hours in what was, in effect, a uniform, with a tie knotted around their neck. All that good behavior made them crazy. Some of the best pure sex Guy had had was with guys dying to free their animal selves from all that worsted wool and silk, even if only for a few moments.

Still, Doug's father had to be in his middle forties at least, and Guy's picture of such a man uncoiling his wild self in the presence of a lipstick-smeared Tenderloin tart in bright-blue hot pants and ruby-red heels wasn't pretty. In episodes of middle-aged lust, dignity was so often the first casualty.

"A whore?" Doug said. "Who said anything about a whore?"

"I was just asking," Guy said. "I guess this isn't a story about your father and a whore, then."

"No, it isn't," Doug said. There was a definite whiff of sanctimony in his words, as if to rebuke Guy for letting his filthy imagination get away with him.

"Well, all right, we're not dealing with a prostitution question, then," Guy said. "What are we dealing with?"

"A men's room."

"A men's room?"

"That's what I said," Doug said.

"Just any old men's room?"

"No," Doug said, "a specific men's room."

"There are a lot of men's rooms in this town."

"I know that," Doug said in a flat voice, as if he were reading from the newspaper. It took a few moments for the meaning of this astounding revelation to soak through Guy's thick skull. "I'm talking about a men's room in Golden Gate Park."

"In Golden Gate Park?" Guy finally managed to say, as if there were anything remotely surprising about erotic antics in the park and people being nabbed at it. Most of the western half of the park consisted of homeless encampments, homosexual men in blue jeans and black boots cruising for sex, teenaged couples in parked cars, and, occasionally, police on dirt bikes, trying to scare people off or perhaps catch a few of the more blatant cases. The park was like a wayward province over which the government had lost control.

"Yeah."

"Did you say in a men's room?"

"That's what I said," Doug said.

Guy paused. "He was with a man, then?"

"I guess," Doug said with a snort. "Who else would be in a men's room? Except a cop, I mean. A guy cop."

"Your father's—?" Guy said. He couldn't say the word. What was the word? Doug's father was a married man, a father. There was no word, really. Doug and Guy were still sitting side by side on the bench, slightly hunched over and hands clasped between their knees, like second-string football players on the sidelines, watching the unfavorable progress of a big game. Words were failing them at last. "God."

"You think he's a fag," Doug said evenly. He glanced at Guy as Guy glanced at him, and he looked away. "Sorry."

"I didn't say that."

"You were thinking it," Doug murmured to his shoelaces. "Anyway, it's not a very nice word."

"I like it," Guy said. "I'm a fag, you know."

Guy could feel the boy getting ready to stand up and leave the scene of such unbearable frankness. It was one thing for Doug to know about Guy, quite another for him to hear Guy describe himself in a single rude syllable. He had called himself a fag, and how could a teenage boy be friends with a fag, even talk to one? Guy waited for Doug to rise.

But Doug failed to get to his feet. He just kept sitting there, Guy beside him. When the boy shifted his shoulder, Guy flinched involuntarily from a blow that did not arrive. Doug was merely finding a more comfortable position, and he gave a heavy sigh. They sat delicately pressed together, neither of them moving the smallest muscle. The motions of their breathing, rippling out to their joined shoulders as if from a stone thrown into a still pond, seemed, suddenly, engulfing.

"I shouldn't have said that," Doug finally said. "I shouldn't have said that word, I mean."

"Sometimes people say things they don't really mean when they're upset," Guy suggested.

"He's not, you know, gay or whatever," Doug said. "I mean, I know my dad, and he's not that."

"I know you do," Guy said easily.

"I mean, he's married and everything," Doug went on. "He's my father! So it's not like—"

"Don't worry about it."

"Who said I'm worrying about it?" Doug snapped.

Guy, stung again, said nothing.

"I don't know what's going on," Doug continued, trying to smooth over the hurt he had caused by pretending he hadn't caused it. "I mean, it's weird."

"I don't know," Guy said.

Rex, meantime, now sprawled on the basketball court, industriously dismembering an old tennis ball he'd rooted out of the bushes, as if he were a pig who'd found an especially choice truffle and decided to keep it for himself.

"Have you ever been arrested?" Doug asked Guy suddenly.

"I've gotten parking tickets. Does that count?"

"No. You don't get arrested for those."

"No," Guy agreed, "at least not the first few dozen. I guess if you don't pay now they come around with that boot and slap it on your wheel so you can't even drive. I don't even have a car, I just borrow Susannah's. But they're still irritating."

"I can't picture him in a men's room," Doug went on in a darkly dreamy voice, repulsed and fascinated, as if he were giving an eye-witness account of a gruesome auto accident. "Like, doing it or whatever. I mean, they always stink like shit. People piss and shit in there. Who'd want to do anything in there? It's gross."

"Did you ask him?"

"No, I couldn't ask him that stuff."

"Why not?"

"Because it's gross."

"You still want to know. You want to know *because* it's gross. I would. We want all the squalid details. It's human nature."

"Maybe your nature," Doug said, "not mine."

"Doug, I'm sorry," Guy said. He felt awkward and ill-equipped to deal with what was plainly a major crisis for this strange boy. With every phrase Doug's voice changed, from flipness to anger to bewilderment to horror to, finally, grief. He was like a man flipping through TV's five hundred channels and finding not one to suit his changeable mood.

In the midst of the flurry of words, Guy could feel that the boy was wanting to be held. As Doug leaned forward disconsolately, Guy let his gaze fall on the boy's broad back. But surreptitious gazing was as far as Guy could go. Grown gay men did not go around embracing teenage boys they barely knew, especially in dark parks, especially if the boy was as handsome and needy and vulnerable as Doug was. Noticing the boy's early beauty made Guy uncomfortable. He felt as if he were violating Doug, even as the boy was confiding and placing his trust in Guy.

"So what are your parents going to do?" Guy asked as gently as he could. "Have you talked to them?"

"I dunno," he said from between his knees. "I suppose they'll get divorced now."

"They told you that?"

"What else can they do?"

"I don't know," Guy said. "Maybe not get divorced. It's not the end of the world."

"How the hell would you know?" Doug said.

"I'm just saying, don't jump to conclusions," Guy said. "How's your mom holding up?"

"You don't even know her."

"No, I don't."

"She's all right, I guess," he said. "She's not crying or anything, if that's what you mean. She doesn't cry very often. I can't even remember the last time she cried. She's tough."

"And how are you?" Guy asked very gently.

"I'm fine," he said in a mangled voice. "Can't you tell? How should I be?"

"I don't know," Guy said.

"Have you ever had sex in a men's room?"

A lie stirred briefly on Guy's lips, followed by a damning hesitation. When he'd been in college, there had been a widely reported security sting in the men's rooms of certain university buildings, the places where furtive undergraduates, too young for bars, connected. The operation was mainly one of intimidation, shame being one of the great tools of social control. And the targets weren't the college boys but the lurkers and prowlers from beyond the university. But, just as porpoises sometimes became entangled in nets intended for deep-sea fish, a few luckless faculty and staff found themselves confronting stern men with badges. No one wanted deans and tenured professors having their names published in the school paper for public lasciviousness, but if they got caught, they tripped into action a mechanism of official disapproval that wasn't easily stopped.

Cities, while offering far greater possibilities, were less protective and less protected environments. As on the Serengeti, a version of natural selection obtained. It wasn't generally the young and the healthy that got caught, but the older and less acute of sight and hearing, the less agile, the naïve and uninformed, the out-of-towner. Or, rarely, the unlucky. Guy felt certain that Doug's father belonged to the last category. "Well," he said, "I've had sex in all sorts of places."

"Good sex?"

"Great sex."

"I can't see it."

"No?"

"I mean, it's not like there's a bed in there or something."

"No. Generally there isn't."

"Do people kiss?"

"Sometimes."

"That's gross," he said automatically. Guy could tell that Doug was trying to conjure an image of perverse tendernesses being exchanged in public squalor by men, one of whom was his father. It was a mighty task.

"I could never kiss a man," Doug said.

"No," Guy said. Of course Guy had once said the same thing, to himself and others, and had gone on saying it even when he'd begun to kiss men. Kissing another man—an extraordinary package of rough and smooth, hard and soft, tough and tender—had turned out to be far more exciting than getting into a man's pants, though that was exciting, too. The two together were sublime.

"Has some man tried to kiss you?" Guy asked.

"No!" he said.

"Because men can be pretty direct."

"I just—who would want, like, all those whiskers in your face? Girls have soft faces."

"That's true," Guy agreed.

"I like their curvy bodies. Men have hair on their bodies."

"True," Guy said.

"I'd be so grossed out by a hairy body!" Doug said. "Teresa's dad is like the hairiest guy I've ever seen."

"Teresa's your ex?"

"Yeah."

"And you got back together with her then dumped her again."

"She didn't like to swallow," Doug said. He reported this fact in a calculatedly calm tone that belied his eagerness to see Guy react to a leaking of sex news.

"How awful for you."

"She'd spit it out on the floor."

"That is very poor form," Guy agreed.

"Have you ever done that?"

"Done what?"

"Spit it on the floor. Or do you swallow it?"

For a moment Guy sat in stunned silence, trying to remember how this conversation had begun. Quietly enough, though with a whisper of unease. Now barriers were falling as if dynamited, boundaries were disappearing, questions were being openly asked: They were barely separated from each other. Guy could feel Doug's body heat and assumed Doug could feel his.

Prudence suggested that Doug's question should be discreetly punted away. Make a joke. Change the subject. Be honest and say, *That's a personal question I'm really not comfortable answering.*

Doug squirmed at his side. "You like blowing guys?"

"I thought we were discussing your sex life."

"Now we're discussing yours."

"I really don't have sex anymore," Guy said.

"Oh come on," Doug said. "You're not that old."

Guy shrugged. "It's getting cold," he said.

"What a cop-out!" Doug said. "I told you about my sex life and now you won't tell me about yours."

"I did tell you about mine," Guy said. "I told you I don't have one."

"I don't believe it."

Guy shrugged.

"It's not fair that I told you about mine and now you say you don't even have one."

"Did we have some kind of deal?"

"I thought we did, yeah. Well, sort of. Maybe. I don't know. I thought you did. You implied it."

"If there were anything to tell," Guy said, "of course I would tell you."

"It is cold," Doug said after a pause.

"Yes, nippy," Guy agreed.

"I should probably go."

"Me too."

"You want to see my house?" the boy asked suddenly.

"Now?"

"It's warmer than here."

"I should probably get home," Guy said, thinking of Doug's mother and what she would think about her teenaged son's hauling home a fag from the local unlighted park. Rex was now sitting like a sentry faced in the direction of the gate through which he knew he would soon depart. The dog was a model of patience, although Guy did notice that, as he and Doug continued to talk, Rex kept arranging and rearranging himself ever closer to the gate, as if to pull the invisible leash by which he controlled his master.

"My mom's down in L.A. with her sister for the night," he said. "I don't know where my dad is. He's not home."

"No," Guy agreed. His contacts hurt. He was tired and wanted to watch the empty news on television, wrapped in his cool, clean sheets. He did not trust this bold, unpredictable boy. He sensed strange, intense energy; he felt a trap were being laid for him.

But he heard himself say, "Okay."

* * *

There was an element of truth in the ravings of the Christian and right-wing cranks. Being gay was a choice: not of feeling, but of acknowledgment and acceptance. Ross Whitmore might well be homosexual, but he was not gay because he had never accepted his sexuality as part of himself. He stood apart from it; he held it at arm's length, like a pair of dirty socks he wished he could throw out but couldn't because he liked them too much.

For years he kept his cravings for men confined in a tight little closet, and his homosexual gratifications were entirely furtive and physical, his intimate connections with men purely a matter of body parts. He did not like to speak during sex; he certainly would never have exchanged names or numbers; he became addicted, finally, to the very anonymousness of his liaisons, the electric charge that rose from furtiveness.

He took greater and greater chances—longer and longer lunch hours spent at arcades, then whole weekend afternoons spent stalking Buena Vista Park, from which expeditions he would return home with sand in his shoes and foxtails sticking to his cuffs. He paid ten dollars for day privileges at the Y, where he spent shameless hours skulking from steam room to sauna to showers. At other times, when convenient, he haunted the men's rooms of Macy's and the Grand Hyatt and the Sheraton Palace, and of Golden Gate Park, where he was so indiscreet that he frightened off even seasoned players, men who for years had recognized his face. Was it really unexpected that one afternoon a cop would pop in and find him, alone, in flagrante delicto? He was relieved to be led off in cuffs, as if, after an exasperating wait, he'd finally gotten what he'd wanted and had been working for.

He could not tell anyone he'd been alone. That sounded too pathetic and desperate. If he had to go down on a morals charge, it would be a memorable one, even if he had to make it up. Men were competitive always, in the most improbable circumstances, competing not only against other men but against the ideal of manhood itself, competing to the end. A real man was always looking for it. A real man got as much as he wanted, whenever he wanted it; he was insatiable. The truth—that Ross was a fading middle-aged chap giving his spongy tool a dispirited wank at a lonely urinal in an isolated public toilet in a park, hoping to get caught—was unacceptable for purposes of moral dramatics.

So was the matter-of-factness of the cop, who, having fielded a complaint from some joggers, had approached in bored stealth, parking his dirt bike well away from the building and coming to the open door not along the asphalt path but by a more circuitous, and quieter, route that took him through some bushes where men sometimes got together. He found nothing in the shrubs, but inside he did find Ross, who, if he had heard the footsteps and seen the shadow, might have gotten it back in his pants in time and might have escaped with a blustery warning.

But there he was, and there was the officer, taking off his sunglasses to make sure of what he was seeing. When he said, "Sir, will you please come with me? You're under arrest," Ross felt a bubble pop in his heart. He wasn't sure if it hurt or relieved him, only that some longtime tension, like a chronic backache, was no longer there. The episode was remarkably quiet. Ross stood in the sunshine next to the officer's dirt bike while the officer radioed for a squad car to take the perpetrator to the station for booking. It was a warm, serene afternoon; the paths were full of joggers, bikers, strollers, roller bladers.

It wasn't at all the kind of scene he'd fantasized. He had pictured himself in some wild orgy with a bunch of guys as a squad of cops arrived on their little bikes, sirens wailing and lights flashing. There would be shouting and rough words and panic and maybe some scuffling. The air would smell of fear and contempt and shame; the police would be harsh, offended on behalf of the decent public. They would cuff everybody and shove them into one of those vans of ignominy. Media coverage. Live TV reports; stories in the papers; notification of families.

That was the scene as it should have been, and as he rode docilely to the station house in the back of the big Ford van, that was what it became in his mind.

* * *

The telephone rang, and it shook Katherine from the pleasant haze of Sunday afternoon that had gathered around her. The house was empty, the coffeepot full, the newspapers in a beckoning pile, the sun high in a blue spring sky. She was sitting on the deck perusing the business section when she heard the phone's insistent trills spilling out the casement windows over the kitchen sink, and she remembered, too late, that she'd left the handset inside. Cordless telephones had massively contributed to human laziness, including hers: She could not bestir herself to go in and answer.

She found herself staring, instead, at a hummingbird, a darting, glinting iridescence that appeared at the potted citrus plants Ross kept on the deck. There was a kumquat bush that never flowered, a Kaffir lime bush that never fruited, and a Meyer lemon bush that produced golfball-sized yellow globes short on acid. As the bird went about its business, hovering and lunging like a giant honeybee, the phone mercifully stopped ringing. Either the answering machine had picked up, or the would-be despoiler of her lovely afternoon had simply given up.

The uptick in blood pressure produced by the ringing telephone faded, and she settled back to peace. She loved the house most of all when only she was in it. If it was traitorous to think that, she didn't particularly care. She was discreet about her emotional treacheries. And it wasn't that she didn't care about, even love, the other members of her otherwise all-male household, including Doug's dog, Rex, whose greatest pleasure in life was lying at someone's feet. At the moment those feet were hers, and the dog had rather endearingly rested his muzzle on her right sandal—a gentle and, for a dog, civilized, reminder that she was to stay put, he didn't want her getting up and leaving him, certainly not for some task as trivial as answering the phone.

"Dear Rex," she said aloud. The dog fluttered his ears briefly at recognizing the familiar syllable. One of her corollary emotional treacheries was that, of all the males in the house, Rex was her favorite. The dog was emotionally open, unselfconscious about his needs and equally unselfconscious about giving in return the gifts he had to give: loyalty and affection. There weren't many people she knew, men or women, who could make the same claim. In fact there weren't any.

Of course she knew she had to make allowances for her son, who was thrashing around like a panicky dinosaur in the swamp of adolescence, as all boys his age did. One moment he was withdrawing to his room in sullen silence, the next he was bolting out the door with the barest of garbled explanations of where he might be going. She would, occasionally, if she were favorably positioned, demand that he tell her at least something about what he was up to, reassure her that his cell phone was charged and turned on so he could be reached in an emergency.

But those were the sorts of battles a mother had to pick carefully. When she stood to fight, she had to win, and the odd thing, she had come to realize, was that Doug wanted her to win, too. It was bad for everyone when children got the better of their parents, for that meant the toppling of the old order and its replacement by chaos. Children who succeeded in discrediting their parents had really succeeded in leaving themselves without guidance—a dismaying fact they were capable of recognizing only after they had brought it about.

Although Doug could not match Rex for emotional constancy, he was intermittently open with her, at least enough to keep the pipes that joined them from freezing up and cracking. He had let it be known, for instance, that he had some mysterious new friend, an older man he clearly meant her to think was his lover. That thought did not make her especially happy, but she didn't think it was likely, either. For one thing, Doug's innuendo had been a little too broad; if there really had been something going on, she assumed he would have been much more circumspect about it. It would have been no trouble at all for him never even to have mentioned this new friend to her.

For another, Guy was, whether Doug recognized it or not, clearly a successor to the late David Rice. It had been David who'd given Doug the emotional energy younger males seemed to crave from older men. Presumably Guy was a similar source of energy. She did not understand the need for or the nature of the transaction, and when Doug had been younger she'd secretly worried along with her husband that Doug's attachment to David was a predictor of Doug's own sexuality. But she felt now in her mother's bones that her son was not homosexual, not that she would have loved him less if it turned out he was.

If Rex had an emotional opposite, it wasn't his erratic teenage master, but the lord of the manor, Ross. Katherine had known when she married Ross that emotional openness and generosity were not, to say the least, his strong suits, but she had been too young and hopeful then to understand that time's passing would reinforce, not change, those basic dispositions. In the days of their courtship, she had been so impressed by Ross's polite intensity, the attention he constantly paid to her, that she didn't notice she was learning very little about him. He didn't say much about himself. He didn't laugh, either. Odd qualities in a beloved so often seemed endearing at first. It wasn't until the infatuation had worn off, and a pair were embarked together on the seas of real life, that they began to be disturbing.

Like all married couples, the Whitmores over the years had evolved a strategy for surviving the other's company. In their case, a central pillar of the strategy was an unobtrusive separation of their lives. They tended more and more to go their own ways, making sure not to inquire too closely what the other was up to, nor do anything that would cause inconvenience or embarrassment. She supposed he believed she had conducted a series of affairs, since that was what women in her position traditionally did, at least in French novels.

She did not know what she believed about what he might be up to. If anything. Ross was so bland in his closedness, so apparently lethargic, that it was hard for her to imagine his getting up to mischief. Yet on weekend afternoons he would often barrel out of the house with an energy and determination that startled her. Whatever he was up to, it meant a lot to him. That was fine with her. She was left with the coffee and the papers and the sunshine and the blissfully empty house—and, at her feet, a male creature who was content as she was to do practically nothing.

As in a horror film, the phone started ringing again. Woman home alone in a big house, she thought as, with a curse under her breath, she started for the door, Rex jumping up to be with her. Was it some psychopathic stalker, a madman who would hang up the instant she touched the handset? The machine had answered and begun its spiel by the time she pressed the button and said, "Hello?" There was an agonized beep as the interrupted machine bowed out of the connection. "Hello?" she said again, trying to sound less exasperated.

"Hi."

"Oh!" she said. "Is that you?"

"It is."

"I wasn't expecting you to call."

"Well, I wasn't expecting to call. I'm sorry, you were probably in the garden, reading the paper with Rex."

"As a matter of fact," she said, "I was."

"I thought so. Sorry. Are you sitting down?"

"I was. Why do you ask?"

"No particular reason. Can you spare half an hour?"

"I'm not sure I see what you're getting at," she said.

"I need you to run an errand for me. It should take about a half hour. Maybe a little more, not much."

"What is this about?"

"Can you meet me?"

"I think so," she said. She rang off after jotting the meeting place on the Post-It pad she kept next to the phone base.

She was wary. It was quite unlike her husband to suggest a meeting during one of his intervals of being inexplicably out of the house. When he went off by himself on weekend afternoons, to his office—as he usually claimed—or wherever he actually went, he made it clear that he would not be answering his telephone, even if he were sitting right there working at the computer or reading associates' memoranda. If he did call, it was only to announce that he would be home within the hour.

She was aware, as she went down to the garage, that their rendezvous point, Frederick and Stanyan, was several miles away from his firm's offices in the Financial District. Of course he'd taken his car when he went out, and a man in a car might drive here, there and everywhere, but she could not picture the corner, could not picture why he might want to meet at it. Possibly his car had a dead battery or a flat tire, but if that were the case, he should be calling Triple-A, not her.

As she backed carefully down the driveway, she found herself resenting men and their messes and their attitude that women's role was to clean them up. It began early, she saw now, with mothers tidying up little boys' rooms instead of demanding that they do it themselves. And yet, by doing the tidying up, were not the world's mothers asserting a claim and a power, filling a vacuum men had left open? It was evident to Katherine, if not to all women, that men were incapable of looking after themselves. They needed the regency of women. She did not like her role as regent but could not resist playing it.

When she pulled up to the appointed place, she noticed, first, a profusion of squad cars around a building she belatedly recognized as a police station. A police station! So Ross had been robbed, he'd been assaulted and thrown down in the mud by some thuggy crackhead, his alligator-skin wallet lifted, his watch too. Some patrolman had found him, lost and bewildered in the park, and brought him in. She was a burgher, and she trusted the police as defenders of decency, riders of white steeds and doers of good.

As to what her husband might have been doing in or near the park, she could not guess. But she would have her answer soon, because there he was, standing on the appointed corner like an overgrown schoolboy waiting sheepishly for his bus. He looked pale and drawn, like one of those heroic wretches she sometimes read about in the *Chronicle* who periodically got shot but managed to flag a cab to take them to the hospital, as if they were characters in a Shakespeare play, always able to deliver one more poignant speech before loss of blood carried them off.

"Thanks for coming," he said as he got into the car.

"Yes," she said expectantly.

"My own car's not far from here, actually," he said. "At Fulton and Funston. We just go up there and turn left." He pointed, and she began to drive.

"If your car's over there," she said, "how did you end up here?"

"The police gave me a ride, actually."

"I didn't know they did that."

"They do if they arrest you," he explained.

"Oh," she said, missing the point for a moment. She was preoccupied by the tangle of traffic at Oak and Fell. "I did see a lot of police cars around that building," she said when they began moving again.

"Yes, it's a police station," he said.

There was a brief pause.

"Are you telling me you were arrested?"

"I'm afraid so."

"And this happened where? In the park somewhere?"

"Yes," he said.

She waited for him to elaborate, but he did not.

"Might I ask what on earth caused you to be arrested in Golden Gate Park on a Sunday?"

He hesitated, examining his fingernails like a desperate student scanning a crib sheet. "It was nothing, really," he said.

"Nothing, really, except that they ran you into the station."

"Just to make a point. The DA doesn't prosecute these kinds of cases."

"*What* kinds of cases?"

"Public decency."

"You mean public indecency."

"Either way," he said.

"Are you saying you were arrested and taken into custody for an act of public indecency?" she asked.

"I'm saying the matter is closed," he said. "Go left here."

She was enraged to be automatically obeying him. She should have swerved the car like Mannix and gone right. Instead she honked at some poor wretch who was clearly lost, wobbling from lane to lane like a drunk while trying to study a map.

"That's all you have to say," she said evenly.

"I don't think this is the time and place to be talking about it," he said. Of course he was right, but she understood, too, that so far as he was concerned there never would be a time and place to talk about it. He had always been an artful fugitive of words. "The car's right there," he said, pointing. "You can let me out at the corner."

"You're coming home now?" she said, as he got out and stood at her car's open door.

"Sure," he said. "If that's what you want."

"It is what I want," she said.

"I understand," he said. "I'll meet you there."

"I'll follow you," she said.

"If you like," he said.

At home they repaired to Ross's study, a paneled, leathery room that had always reminded her of one of those English clubs that excluded women. She'd always felt uncomfortable in there, and at the same time she was thrilled to be violating an unspoken taboo.

"Doug's not here," Ross said with a shrug as he returned from the kitchen with two goblets of red wine. "Just Rex." The dog hurried into the room, just ahead of the closing door. Ross handed Katherine a goblet, but they did not toast one another. They each took a sip, then another, as if trying to ward off a chill.

"I think I'll sit down," Ross said, arranging himself at one end of a leather love seat that rested against a wall near his desk. If he were inviting her to sit next to him, it was an invitation she declined. She might sit behind the desk, or in the easy chair opposite the love seat, but she remained standing. It was awkward, but better awkward than too comfortable.

"Well, here we are," he said.

"Now are you going to tell me what really happened?"

"Do you really want to know?" he said with a bleak smile he directed mostly at the books behind her.

"I doubt it," she said. "But I think I have to."

"I think you're probably right," he said with a sigh. "I was with another man. In the men's room in the park, just near where I'd left the car. The police came in. I guess someone must have complained."

Her mind darted off like a startled rabbit. She'd known since she'd picked him up in front of the station house that it had to be bad, but she wasn't expecting something quite so low. Whatever else might be said of Ross, he had always been a model of propriety. He was a man who fussed about the right way to set the dinner table, to open a bottle of wine, to eat a bowl of soup, to write a thank-you letter. He was a catalog of the bourgeois niceties, and he was very convincing on their value in an uncouth world. He was the least vulgar man she had ever known.

Yet he had been arrested for public indecency, for—though he had not used the phrase—homosexual misconduct of some kind. He had been with another man; he had just said so. She had always known and never known. She had always trusted him not be stupid, not to get caught, not to let anyone, including her, see. She had trusted that he knew what he was doing, that he knew how to manage his life. Now there were words they could not avoid saying, images they could not avoid conjuring.

"I don't know what to say," she said.

"I don't either, really."

"I can't quite believe it."

"I can't, either," he said, as if they were talking about someone else, some unfortunate friend or relative who'd hugely, though predictably, fucked up.

"I suppose this means you slept with David," she said.

For the first time, he seemed surprised and a little off-guard. "David Rice?" he said. He coughed. "A few times. A long time ago. I always assumed you suspected as much."

"Why didn't you tell me?"

"I thought it would just hurt you," he said. "It was hardly anything at all, really."

"He was in love with you."

"No, he wasn't," Ross said. "Don't be silly."

"I could see it in the way he looked at you, the way he talked about you. The way he avoided you."

"Look," he said, "let's not get carried away."

"I suppose there have been others?"

"I really think it's pointless to go through this," he said.

"Do you have AIDS?"

"Katherine," he said, "no. Of course not."

"You're going to have to tell Doug," she said, emptying her wine goblet. "He has a right to know."

"He's just a boy," Ross said after a considerable pause. His tone carried an unmistakable note of pleading.

"This is not the sort of thing you can keep from him," she said. "He's not that young."

"I told you," he said, "that this whole thing isn't going anywhere. They don't prosecute this stuff. They don't put it in the papers. It's over and done with."

"I'm sorry," she said, "it isn't. And if you don't tell him, I will."

"It's my prerogative to decide what to tell my son and when," he said, assuming the formidable mantle of lawyerliness.

"Yes," she said, "and also mine. He's our son. He has a right to know what's going on in this family. Who his parents are. What the state of their marriage is."

"You're right," Ross said. "I'll talk to him. It'll be fine. He'll understand."

She didn't say anything. She went to the kitchen for more wine instead, and when she'd poured herself another goblet she stood at the window looking out at the deck and the garden, wondering when he would appear for his own refill, whether he would try to touch her, how she would react if—when—he did.

* * *

The Whitmores lived a few blocks uphill and around the corner from the park, on a quiet leafy street lined with late-model European automobiles and meticulously restored, turn-of-the-century houses, before one of which Doug and Guy came to a stop.

The windows in the front bay were dark, but along the side of the house a lone light was shining in an upstairs window. Guy thought he saw a shadow moving in the yellow glow.

"This is it," Doug said in a whisper, as if they were Cold War spies passing secrets in a deserted, rubble-strewn quarter of Berlin. "This is where I live."

"There's a light on," Guy said. He was determined not to whisper, but he couldn't bring himself to speak in full voice.

"I know," Doug whispered. "It can't be my mom. It must be my dad. Yeah, it has to be. That's the guest room, and that's where he's been sleeping."

Doug hesitated. "He must have just come home," he said. "He wasn't here when I left."

"It's getting late," Guy said again.

"Do you want to come in?"

"That's very nice of you," Guy said, "but I should probably be getting home. Susannah will wonder where I am."

"Maybe you'd like to meet my dad."

"I might," Guy said. "But I wonder if this is the best time."

"We're here, he's here," Doug said.

"He's under a lot of stress."

"You're afraid of him!" Doug said in a truncated yelp. "You're afraid he'll think there's something going on between us."

"There isn't," Guy said, "so, no, I'm not afraid of that."

"Maybe you've had sex with him," Doug said, "in some men's room somewhere. You're afraid you'll recognize him."

"I don't want you to be in an awkward position," Guy said.

"Me!" Doug said. "You don't care about me at all! What do you care if I'm in an awkward position?"

"I do care," Guy said, "and I don't want you to be."

"We can walk around the block," Doug said, although Rex had already stationed himself at the front door, calm in his canine certainty that someone would momentarily let him in. "By then he'll have gone to bed or something."

"Then what?"

"I can show you the house," Doug said, "part of it, anyway."

"I don't think this is a good time," Guy said. "I think I should go home and you should go inside and talk to your father."

"I don't want to."

"I can understand that," Guy said. "But you need to be with him. And he needs you."

"How do you know that?"

"I just do," Guy said.

"You think you know everything!" Doug burst out. "You don't know anything about my father or my family!"

"We're both tired," Guy said, "we need some sleep. Let me know what happens. E-mail me."

"Like you care," Doug said, spitting the words at the sidewalk, managing to look tall and crumpled up at the same time. Dimly Guy perceived that Doug's forlornness was both real and an act: a natural resource the boy was attempting to exploit to gain a desired end. The end was attention. Attention gave the illusion of filling some inner emptiness, as a candy bar might allay hunger pangs for a time, only to leave one hungrier than ever. A need for attention fed on itself, stimulated a craving for more attention.

"You'll be all right," Guy said.

Doug looked stricken. He snorted. "A lot you know about it," he said, trying to sneer. "I don't want to go in there," he added.

"You live there."

"I wish I didn't," he whispered.

"Your parents love you," Guy said. "Their problems don't change that. You're their son."

Doug said nothing. He was still staring at his shoelaces, as if salvation might be written in them. Guy glanced up again at the window and saw the shadow still moving there, a restless tremble behind the half-closed miniblinds, a man tumbling from the Olympian heights of fatherhood and partnership into a stony canyon of duplicity and disgrace. The disgrace, Guy wanted to explain to Doug, wasn't that Ross Whitmore was queer, but that he'd deceived the people

he loved—including the person he loved most: himself—in deny-
ing it. Secrets were an expensive luxury, and sooner or later the
bill for them arrived.

Better, Guy wanted to say to Doug, simply to bring it forth,
without shame or apology. That was the lesson of the father's life:
not to be corroded from the inside by a secret that need not have
been a secret. Not to build a life of towering respectability on an
untruth that was constantly in need of maintenance. Build, instead,
on the truth, even a truth one did not wish for.

"If we walk around the block," Doug suggested, "he might have
gone to bed by the time we get back."

Rex, standing at the door, clearly opposed this plan, but he was
outvoted by Guy's shrug of assent. He was fairly certain the light
would still be on when they returned in five or ten minutes, at
which time Doug, gambit having failed, would be obliged to face
his demon. But the boy was either lucky or knew more than he let
on, because by the time they'd completed their circumnavigation,
the Whitmores' house was entirely dark except for the porch light.

"You sure you don't want something to drink, water or something?" Doug offered. "There's usually a bottle of wine open."

"I'd be up all night peeing," Guy said. "But thanks."

They stood facing each other, close and hopeless, two people at
the fragile intersection of two universes, afraid to touch, because
they feared what the touching might lead to.

"Is there anything you want to tell me?" Guy murmured.

"I've spent the evening telling you all kinds of stuff."

"About him. Your family. How about you? Are you okay?"

"I'm fine," Doug said. "What are you saying?"

"I'm not saying anything," Guy said. "I'm asking."

"I'm not gay," Doug said. "I'm not like my dad. He's not gay, either," he added helplessly.

"I didn't say you are. Or he is."

"You're thinking it," Doug said. "I can tell. You think he's a
fag. You think I'm attracted to you."

"I'm concerned about you," Guy said.

"You don't care about me at all!" Doug said. "You're just trying
to manipulate me."

"I don't want to fight."

"You started it!" Doug said. He was shouting now in a hoarse whisper, but the strangled anger in his voice seemed to surprise him, and he subsided abruptly. He closed his eyes and after a moment swayed on his feet, like a sapling in a breeze. Guy nearly reached out to steady him, but the boy opened his eyes suddenly. They stared at one another without a word.

"I have to go," Guy said. "Good night, Doug."

"You're leaving?" an incredulous Doug said.

"It's late," Guy said. "We need our rest."

"I'm not tired!"

"Good night, Doug." Guy walked away quickly down the street.

"I'll e-mail you!" Doug called. He waved at Guy's receding shoulders, as if trying to spin him around, but Guy kept on walking, melting into the night shade.

"G'night," Doug said. He stood there for a long while, Rex patiently at his side, before finally giving up and going inside.

v. *The Kiss*

"THANKS for delivering me from my waifdom," Guy said to Dennis and Will as soon as they'd swung open the front door. Their matched set of shorthaired dachshunds, Hans and Franz, yipped excitedly at Guy's arrival, hurrying into the parlor as a kind of advance party, nipping playfully at each other and grabbing squeaky toys as they went. The dogs liked company and were scarcely suspicious—signs, Guy supposed with a certain degree of wistfulness, that they understood the world to be a place of unconditional love and affection and liver treats, in a way it never could be for people. Hans and Franz were glad to see whoever happened to show up. They expected to have a good time.

To watch Will and Dennis giving a little dinner party was to watch a ballet being performed without apparent effort. They were a well-trained duet, running through routines made familiar by years of repetition, aware at all times of where the other was and what he was up to. They hosted, they bantered, they pirouetted around one another in the kitchen, they sautéed, they stirred, they whispered private shorthand into each other's ears.

Even the occasional moments of friction seemed comfortable, as if they'd been there many times before, given and taken the same jabs over and over. Will and Dennis had achieved the elusive goal of all serious couplings: They had shaped themselves into a family. They lived in a universe of their own making, into which they sometimes invited an audience, such as Guy, who was alone on a weekend early in summer and was happy to sit there on a bar stool in their handsome kitchen, eating homemade chicken liver paté and Port du Salut cheese while they went about the business of making whatever it was that they were making and talking to him at the same time.

Part of the charm of Will and Dennis was that they didn't seem like a couple, but then the basic fact of coupledom was that its basic mechanism was never seen by other people. Couples were only truly couples when they were alone. Together in public, Dennis and Will were barely noticeable, just a pair of not-young men. They weren't much for public touching, and they seldom spoke.

Guy had always assumed that there just wasn't much for them to say to each other anymore, that they had worn each other out. He had no idea, because Will politely never told him, what they were like safe in the cocoon of their own home. Young people believed that love was sex and infatuation; older people knew it was trust and constancy, a long language of understandings and sharing.

According to Will's reports, they did sometimes fight, though Guy never understood entirely why. The grounds, as reported by Will, always seemed inadequate: One of them had failed to buy toothpaste, or had come in late, or made weak, bitter coffee. The real reason seemed to be a male inclination to combativeness. Like a pair of insecure nation-states uneasily sharing a border, they lived in a state of more or less constant readiness for strife. It was part of their private discourse. Disagreeing helped people define themselves; it helped preserve the sense of self from entirely vanishing in the vast reality of the couple.

Even as Will refreshed the platter of hors d'oeuvres, Guy was longing to ask him how they had done it, how they had managed to make a happy home in a world that never wanted them to succeed. Happy male couples were invisible several times over: unknown to the heterosexual world at large and scarcely more than a rumor in urban clusters of single queer men. They were nearly mythical, like leprechauns; there was no reason for them to exist, other than to furnish human satisfaction, and satisfaction was rarely a value of the larger human institutions.

In their presence, Guy was both relaxed and chastened. He felt more than usually single, the fact of their being together amplifying the fact of his aloneness. That they did not assert themselves as a pair made the effect of their alliance stronger. Like gravity, they were a powerful given. They did not refer to him as a waif. That was his word for himself, as if by making a joke of it he might disarm it as a source of social unease.

The house was a physical talisman of their long union. It was about them, and it belonged to them. Its charms were those of a bygone day—high ceilings, redwood moldings and rosettes, oak floors, high windows—rather than modern mechanical ones, though Will and Dennis had, at Will's insistence, installed a dishwasher: their first official act as owners.

Dennis denied Will's lighthearted accusations of being a Luddite, but, apart from the dishwasher, he did like to inveigh against gadgets and a contemporary tendency toward aggrandizement. These were signs, he liked to say, of boredom and decadence, selfishness propelled by too much money, people on Stairmasters at their loud neon gyms, watching CNN and the constant stream of ticker tape data from Wall Street on the electronic ribbon at the bottom of the screen. He professed to dislike e-mail and liked to tease Will about his voracious appetite for downloading smut from the Internet. The world, to Dennis, was a vulgar if amusing place, inhabited by entertainingly vile people who could be tolerated in small doses only.

"He thinks I'm entertainingly vile," Will said to Guy in a stagey whisper as Dennis thumped down the hallway to the closet that served as a kind of wine cellar.

"In the best sense!" Dennis said from the hallway.

"He hears awfully well," Guy suggested.

"Yes, he does, for an elderly gentleman, doesn't he?"

"Well, you know, people can't help what they are," Dennis said when he returned, laying an arm lightly around Will's shoulder for a moment, then removing it when he noticed the shadow of inadequacy flitting across Guy's face, "at least not very much. The trouble is that so few people make any effort to be better. They invest all their genius into defending their flaws."

"Here we go," Will said.

"Here we go where?" Dennis said.

"Speech! Speech! We haven't even opened the first bottle of wine yet and you're pontificating already."

"You're wrong!" Dennis said. "We *have* opened the first bottle of wine! Champagne, actually. It's waiting for us."

"Let's have some, then," Will said.

"By the way, there's a big Toyota Land Cruiser half-blocking your driveway," Guy reported as they ambled toward the wine, which was chilling in a sterling silver bucket on a pedestal in a corner of the dining room. While Guy and Will watched, Dennis popped the cork with the bottle still in the bucket, then wrapped the bottle in a towel, as if it were a newborn baby. They resumed their progress.

"A Land Cruiser?" Will asked Guy. "I wonder if it's that big gray one again. It must be."

"Property of a garageless yuppie fuck down the block," Dennis said agreeably. "Every day he drives it a mile and a half to his office in media gulch and the bogus little company he owns."

"I didn't know he owns a bogus little company," Will said.

"He does," Dennis said with a sigh. "He started it fifteen minutes ago and now it's worth trillions. He's the future. Dot-com this and digital that. I think he sells garbage bags online, or something equally indispensable."

"Should we have him towed?"

"Firebombed this time, I think," Dennis said. "Check the phone book. I'm sure the city has a special squad."

"We're so lucky to live here, aren't we," Will said, "in such a service-oriented city?"

"You were saying something interesting about people," Guy said to Dennis when they'd finally installed themselves in the front parlor and Dennis had poured out the champagne into lead crystal flutes. The tall bay windows gave onto a view of the city, just beginning to twinkle in the rosy twilight. Earlier, Will had made an exploratory foray into the garden but found it too chilly for human habitation despite the smoke and glow of the mesquite charcoal in the kettle grill, where a boned and butterflied leg of lamb was about to be removed from the cooking grate.

"I was saying something interesting? I was ragging on the garageless yuppie fuck again, as I recall," Dennis said.

"Do you think people are evil?"

"Well, I think the yuppie fuck might be, driving a behemoth like that around a crowded little town like this and blocking driveways. But no, as a rule, I don't think most people are evil," Dennis said, "and they certainly don't. The human capacity for self-pardon is virtually unlimited. It's our greatest natural resource. If only we could discover how to harness it! The problem isn't that people are evil but that they do evil and tell themselves they're doing good, which simply compounds the evil."

"He has it all figured out," Will said to Guy.

"And he likes to pretend he disagrees with me," Dennis said to Guy, "when in fact he agrees with every word."

"Is this true?"

"I don't know about every word," Will said. "He generates so many, it's hard to keep track of them."

"You see!" Dennis said triumphantly.

"He's a gloater," Will said to Guy.

Dennis pretended not to hear. "You seem interested in evil," he said to Guy. "It's not something we did, I hope! We haven't raised their rent, have we, Will?"

"Not yet," Will said with a smile. "Dennis is very uneasy about being a landlord," he explained to Guy. "Capitalism and class exploitation and all that. Vestige of a communist youth."

"Not a communist youth!" Dennis objected. "Socialist."

Will shrugged. "Big lefty sells out, gets law degree, hawks for corporations, makes pots of money."

"He's right, you know," Dennis said to Guy, not at all contritely. "We've joined the propertied classes, and I can't say I mind. But I don't like raising people's rent."

"That's good!" Guy said.

"We never planned to be landlords," Dennis went on.

"But we are," Will said.

"Yes, we are. It's funny how often you end up being or doing something you never intended to, and that's what your life becomes. We spend our youth trying to become something, and the rest of our lives trying to figure out how we became something else."

"*If* you're a brooder," Will added, "like some of us."

"Speaking of brooding," Dennis said, "Susannah's told us about your little friend."

"The boy," Will added. "The teenager."

"She's concerned about you."

"Really."

"That you're preoccupied and so forth."

"I haven't even talked to her much about him."

"Maybe that's why she's concerned."

"I wouldn't say he's my little friend," Guy said. "I wouldn't say he's my friend at all. I don't know if you can be friends with a sixteen-year-old boy."

"Sweet sixteen!" Will said.

"Steady!" Dennis said to him.

"Or seventeen," Guy said. "He might have had a birthday, I'm not sure. I don't keep track."

"Sixteen's a nice age," Will said.

"Will has this notion that adolescent boys are angels," Dennis said, snuffling with amusement, "as opposed to half-savage fiends, which is my suspicion. Of course, I lack the sentimental view."

"You're just not interested," Will said.

"That's true," Dennis agreed. "Certainly I'm not as interested as you are."

"You make it sound like I'm obsessed."

Dennis shrugged and smiled.

"So what's the news from the front?" Will asked.

"I'm not sure," Guy said. "He's a boy."

"We already know that," Will said.

"He perplexes me," Guy said.

"Oh," Will said.

"What he means, dear, is that boys are merely sketches of real people," Dennis said to Will. "They are plans and under construction, not the finished article. So you never really know what to expect. Is that right, Guy?"

"Exactly."

"No one's ever really finished," Will pointed out, "until they're dead. Anyway, maturity is overrated. Maturity means habits, and habits are dull."

"Habits are the foundation of civilization," Dennis said. "Habits mean stability and predictability."

"He certainly isn't predictable," Guy said. "Predictable is the last word I'd use to describe him."

"He sounds butch," Will said. "Doesn't he drive a little truck or something?"

"A nasty little truck," Guy said. "He spits, too."

"Well, if he doesn't know who he is—and it sounds as if he doesn't, and of course how could he, at that age?—then there's no way for you to know, either," Dennis said. "There's not a solid personality there yet to be known."

"It's exhausting business," Guy said.

"But you put up with it."

"He seeks me out."

"You don't have to respond."

"It would be cruel not to," Guy said, conscious—as he knew Dennis must also be conscious—that this was neither a complete nor a completely honest answer.

"Does he know about you?" Will asked.

"Oh yes."

"You've talked about it with him."

"Oh sure," Guy said. "Quite a bit. It doesn't seem to bother him, or he pretends that it doesn't. Or he just doesn't care, I'm not sure. It's hard to tell what he cares about."

"Other than himself," Dennis said.

"I think that's a little unfair," Will said. "You haven't even met the kid, you know."

"Guy is drawing a vivid portrait in my mind," Dennis said pleasantly, "of the narcissist as a young man. More wine?" He refilled the champagne glasses and resettled himself in the big easy chair with the green floral pattern. "I gather that he is handsome, or will be."

"I guess," Guy said. "I try not to notice."

"Your prurience is showing," Will said to Dennis.

"That may be," Dennis said smoothly, "but yours is waving its arms and turning red in the face. I'm curious about the erotic aspect, I admit. You used to live with someone, didn't you, Guy?"

Guy nodded, briefly reviewing the saga of Philip, the decade of his life gone. Any reference to Philip embarrassed him now. He wished he could erase Philip from his past. Philip would become the un-boyfriend, someone who had never existed. But Dennis knew he existed, and so the truth, for the moment, was unavoidable.

"But you're single now."

"I'm not unhappy being single."

"I don't doubt that you're not," Dennis said, subtly echoing Guy's double negative. "But you're available. At least he perceives you that way on some level."

"Are you saying he's queer?"

"Not at all," Dennis said. "I have no idea. You'd have a much better idea of that than I do."

"The thought has crossed my mind," Guy admitted.

"There you are," Dennis said. "That would explain a lot. But he's drawn to you beyond the question of sexuality. It has to do with adulthood, manhood, the state of his own family."

Guy shifted uneasily, trying to remember how much of the Whitmores' story he'd told Susannah and how much Susannah might have passed along to Will and Dennis.

"The state of his family isn't good," he said at last.

"And you're willing to listen to him talk about it," Dennis went on. "You're an adult who's willing to listen, who's outside the ambit of his family, whose life doesn't conform to the conventions he's seen—husband and wife and family and all that."

"No, it sure doesn't," Guy said. "I'm a divorced middle-aged queen with a roommate."

"He doesn't see you that way."

"Are you saying he's in love with Guy?" Will demanded.

"It's within the realm of possibility," Dennis said. "Let's enjoy our grilled leg of lamb, shall we? It should be about ready to come off the fire."

A few minutes later they reconvened over slices of pink meat, mint couscous, poached asparagus in a vinaigrette made with Greek vinegar, and a salad of blood oranges and goat's milk feta cheese. Dennis poured liberally from a bottle of zinfandel. There was a crusty baguette, too, and butter, and a bottle of Vittel.

"I can't have a love affair with him," Guy said.

"But you already are," Dennis said. "He's on your mind."

That was certainly true. Guy had taken steps to deflect Doug's attempts to contact him, but at the same time he was aware that taking evasive steps was proof of his own involvement. One did not bother to avoid someone who didn't matter. He was aware of hoping that Doug would find him anyway. Every time the telephone rang, he jumped a little, wondering if the caller were Doug and what he had in mind. Doug was young, but not too young to be one of those people who always had something to propose.

"I'm concerned about him, that's all," Guy managed to say.

"He's filling a space in your life," Dennis said, "just as you're filling some space in his."

"That's different from saying it's a love affair," Guy said.

"It could be," Dennis agreed.

"Dennis likes to see things in terms of love affairs," Will advised Guy. "It warms the cockles of his ancient heart."

"I do love warm cockles," Dennis agreed, "though not as much as young Will here does."

"I just feel that, you know, if he is queer or whatever, I have obligations," Guy said. "He's turned to me. He trusts me."

"Do you trust him?" Dennis asked.

"I don't know what you mean."

"He's just sixteen," Will reminded Dennis, who ignored him. "Is he honest with you?"

"I think he's trying to be," Guy said.

"Ah."

"That's the famous 'ah' you just heard," Will said to Guy.

"Does he tell you the truth?"

"In his own way," Guy said, squirming as he spoke, because he wasn't sure that was true, even if it meant anything. If there was one thing Doug wasn't, it was direct. His questions were loaded, his pronouncements rigged with double meanings and hidden escape hatches. He spoke with the self-protective caginess of the born politician, determined to seem to be telling people what they

wanted to hear while avoiding saying anything definite. Guy recognized the game, and at the same time understood that Doug
must be playing it from fear. It was a survival skill he had learned,
a way of shielding his vulnerable self in an uncertain environment.
    Imagining Doug's situation made Guy's heart ache. Things
were bad enough when the father's dark secret was safe. Now,
with word out, the mood at home must be more volatile. A man
who hated himself enough to take the risks Ross Whitmore had
taken would surely disdain a son who shared the inclination. It occurred to Guy, sitting there over his plate of couscous, that he had-
n't heard from Doug in quite a while. The boy's silence suddenly
seemed sinister, as did the steps Guy had taken to evade him. He
wondered if he'd been cold and ungenerous. Doug might need
him. Doug had nowhere else to turn.
    "Ah," Dennis said again, speculatively.
    "I'm not saying he's not honest," Guy continued, aware—and
aware that Dennis and Will were aware—that he was saying exactly that. But were they aware at the same time of the forgiveness
and pity welling up in Guy's heart? No boy would behave the way
Doug did unless he was unhappy and frightened. He was not the
first person to be frightened of the truth. Most of the adults Guy
knew had dedicated their moral lives to a program of evasion, denial, defensiveness and obfuscation of the painfully obvious, the
inevitable. If most people lived in a shadowy world of twilit truth,
why should Doug be held to a higher standard? And at such a
young age? One could not condemn the boy for acting in the way
he saw everyone around him acting, the way he'd been taught to
act.
    It was because Doug was young that the truth mattered and that
the habits of truth, though difficult to establish, were worth estab-
lishing. A sixteen-year-old was like molten lava, cooling and
hardening rapidly but still impressionable. He might still learn the
value of honesty, if honesty had value. Someone had to teach him,
and teaching required energy. It required fuel. Love was a powerful, dangerous fuel, like the liquid hydrogen used to propel rockets
into space. It could provide a tremendous boost; it could also cause
an annihilating conflagration. It was not a source of energy the

prudent teacher chose. But if it was a given, as it was so often, then the real choice was not whether to use it—whether to teach at all—but how.

"Forget honest," Will said. "He's underage."

Dennis handed him a napkin. "In case you start drooling," he explained in his most kindly, avuncular voice.

The fact of Doug's inadequate age should have chilled Guy's slightly fevered imagination, but it was beginning to have the opposite effect. He had always been attracted to people his own age or slightly older, and he had been mystified by the pantings of chicken hawks like Will, who seemed to lust for creatures who weren't yet entirely male, or complete, whose fine soft skin, hairless bodies and chins and wide eyes were unmistakably epicene.

He did not, in fact, approve of men who sought the company of youths, and he was uncomfortable to find himself apparently drifting in their direction. There was a glint of glee in Will's eye.

"He's not a child," Guy heard himself saying.

"I didn't say he was," Will said.

"Will, don't be mean," Dennis said. "I wonder if you would have handled things nearly as well if you found yourself in Guy's position."

"That's just it," Will said sadly. "I never do find myself in Guy's position."

"You're lucky," Guy said. "You just don't know it."

"Time to clear the table," Dennis said to Will. "We'll be in the parlor. You can bring the cheese plate in there when you've finished. Brandy too. Let's use those new snifters. And those pots de creme. Made with Key lime," Dennis said to Guy when they'd left Will to his domestic tasks. "Poor Will, he needs to settle down some. Kitchen tasks should help. The thought of youths gets him all worked up. He's become quite obsessed by your story," he said, as they sat in deep comfortable chairs in the parlor, "particularly because he knows so few details for certain."

"Obsessed?"

Dennis shrugged. "People are obsessive," he said. "It's how we know we're alive. I'm obsessed about coffee beans, for instance, and making espresso and checking to make sure the housecleaners aren't stealing anything. Quite an honorable list! Will is obsessed by young men. It seems perfectly natural, you know, but as it happens it's not an obsession I share."

"I'm not sure I do, either," Guy said.

"You don't have to account to me," Dennis said, "and I'm not criticizing. Will's interest, for instance, is harmless. He's like a dog chasing the neighborhood cats. He takes huge pleasure in the anticipation and occasional pursuit, but if he were ever actually in a position to catch one, he wouldn't know what to do."

"That's me," Guy said.

"You don't have to do anything," Dennis said.

"I don't know what I want to do," Guy said.

"It sounds as if you always make time for him," Dennis said.

"He doesn't ask for much," Guy said, noting how naturally and automatically he rose to Doug's defense.

"You must be getting something from him."

"He seems to need me."

Dennis nodded. "I heard about his father. A friend of mine works at that firm. Apparently—Ross, is that his name?—apparently he's resigned quietly, for personal reasons or one of the usual euphemisms. Quite a sad story. More gay self-destruction."

"I didn't know he'd resigned."

"No? I heard it just the other day, so it must be a fairly recent development. He would have no choice, really. The firm couldn't keep him on in light of the circumstances. 'Resigned' is a bit of a euphemism too, I think it's safe to assume. Does the boy know? About all the tawdry details?"

"I don't know about all of them," Guy said. "He knows what happened, though. He told me about it."

Dennis shook his gray head, clucking softly to himself. "You're in a peculiar spot," he said after a moment.

"I haven't heard from him in quite a while."

"No?"

"No. He started a fight the last time I saw him. He's on the tempestuous side. Likes to fight."

Dennis nodded. "It's what he's seen at home, most likely. Fighting equals intimacy. I'm familiar with the phenomenon!" he added with a small laugh. "Though not to that extent."

"I don't know if I've handled it right," Guy said.

"Handled what right?" Will said, bursting into the room pushing a cart laden with cheeses, grapes, sliced apples and pears, crackers, pots of coffee and tea, pots de creme, a svelte bottle of alembic brandy from Mendocino County, and three snifters of English cut lead crystal. "I think you should sleep with him," he added.

"Will," Dennis said. "Did you start the dishwasher?"

"I don't know how," Will said. "I mean it, Guy. There's a barrier and you have to break through it and that's the way."

"Why do I have to break through it?"

"Because you'll be miserable if you don't."

"Not that miserable," Guy said, but thinking about degrees of misery immediately made him feel more miserable.

"Pretty miserable. He's not that innocent, come on. Wasn't he out at bad-boy beach, checking out the nude guys?"

"He was walking his dog."

"One of the classic excuses!" Will cried. Dennis stagily covered his ears. "Guys like that always operate under cover."

"I'm not interested in guys like that," Guy said. "I've known enough of them. Avoiders of responsibility."

"Well, I'd try, at least," Will said. "To clear the air."

"You would not!" Dennis said. "You just like to think so."

"Dennis has advised me that if I ever get into this kind of trouble, he will not be making a trip down to the station house to post my bail," Will confided to Guy.

"I won't hear from him again anyway," Guy said.

"Don't sound so sad," Dennis said. "You've done what was right. You've behaved like a gentleman and an adult. If he's grown up in the kind of family it sounds like he has, you must have confused him. Some day he'll be glad he knew you, even a little."

"Will I be glad I knew him?" Guy wondered aloud. For the first time that evening, neither Will nor Dennis had any answer to make, to him or one another. They nibbled their cheese and fruit in a silence that finally broke into other subjects: mutual friends in disintegrating relationships, just emerging from disintegrating relationships, hoping to enter a relationship that wouldn't disintegrate. Questions of real property, seasonal produce, the minutiae of local politics in a city so awash in cash that there were no issues more urgent than the question of whether too much gilt had been used in refurbishing the city hall.

But while the desserts got eaten and the conversation coursed this way and that, far from the question of boys and a particular boy, Guy's mind remained fixed on that particular boy. The brandy flowed, the pots were devoured, the cheese and grapes engulfed, followed by more wine with the coffee and tea and a pack of Pepperidge Farm cookies, and he loomed larger in Guy's mind, as if in a dream, until he bestrode Guy's imagination like a colossus, crowding out other images, other thoughts, competing distractions.

Will and Dennis ended up on the couch together, shoulders pressing, Dennis's arm casually looped behind Will's shoulder. They were home and safe. Guy sat across from them, nibbling to ward off the faint chill that seemed to have settled on his part of the parlor. The evening was winding down. Will and Dennis were through nipping at each other. Soon, as Guy walked home alone through the cool and fragrant evening, they would be undressing, murmuring, cleaning their teeth, safe and secure in the heat and scent of the other. They were together, always would be, did not need or want the world to notice, did not much need the world at all. They were a couple, and couples made their own worlds.

By the time Guy finally left, Will and Dennis seemed scarcely to be aware of him. The goodnight hugs and kisses and blessings at the door seemed perfunctory. But, warmed by the wine, Guy walked home happily enough through the cool evening. His thoughts turned intermittently to Doug. He felt the boy out there, somewhere in the night: a presence, an imminence. But Guy had taken the precaution, some weeks ago, of changing his e-mail address and deleting his profile. That amounted to closing a door and locking it, soundlessly. Doug could still call, or come by. But Guy knew he would not run such a high risk of rejection, especially if he were aware that he could no longer reach Guy by Internet. A locked door, formerly unlocked, was a strong signal.

It might have been a stronger signal than Guy had meant to send. From time to time he had considered e-mailing Doug; he'd even drafted notes. But he hadn't been able to balance the tone between noncommittal and warm—to sound warmly noncommittal, as if he were a diplomat negotiating with an erratic foreign government—probably because he couldn't balance those conflicted feelings in his own heart. He thought about Doug often, and at the same time wanted nothing to do with him. He could not imagine satisfactory relations with the boy, and he was unhappy with himself for disappearing behind a barrier the boy could not breach. Having no relations with him was a species of unsatisfactory relations—an irony he noted without noting its deeper meaning: that the boy did not want satisfactory relations. Doug required, for the comfort of familiarity, some form of the many forms of misery the world had taught him was the stuff of life.

Although Doug was on his mind, Guy did not immediately recognize the dark figure huddled on the front steps of the building, jacket draped over his knees and wearing only a thin T-shirt against the damp night air. He was a momentarily exhausted skateboarder, a weary troubadour, a romantic wastrel, a runaway, someone smoking a joint, someone who'd just been dumped, someone waiting for someone else in the building. Guy was enough of an urbanite to be comfortable ignoring the figure except for the barest acknowledgment, a nod of the head, and proceeding into the building. He would have done just that, if the figure hadn't been blocking the entryway. When Guy tried gingerly to step around, the figure looked up and it was a boy and it was Doug.

A moment of awkward silence attested to their strained relations. Guy felt a strong urge to flee: inside if possible, down the street if necessary. Instead he said, "Hello."

"I've been waiting for you," Doug said.

"You look cold."

"I am. What time is it?" he asked. "Where were you? I thought you'd never show up."

"I didn't know I was expected," Guy said.

"I had to talk to you," Doug said. As always, his flair for melo-drama did not quite conceal an air of real urgency. "I tried to call but there was no answer. I was afraid you were avoiding me."

"I was having dinner with some friends," Guy explained. His keys were out now; just a quick motion and the door to the build-ing's foyer would be open. He concealed his hesitation by looking Doug square in the eye, which caused the boy to flinch and look away. A moment later, having mastered his fear, he returned the direct gaze. Guy couldn't help admiring his nerve. The kid was in way over his head, but he didn't give up.

"Would you like to come in, warm up for a minute?" Guy said.

"Um, sure, okay," Doug said, "if that's okay with you."

"Sure," Guy said. "I can make you some hot chocolate."

"That'd be great."

They trudged up the gloomy, musty staircase to the second-floor landing, where Guy produced another key and worked it in the lock. The door swung open. The apartment was dark and cool. Guy switched on some lights.

"Your place is clean," Doug said, looking around.

"You think so? It looks like it could use a good vacuuming."

Doug made an inaudible remark. Guy was already in the kitchen, where he set about scalding milk for the hot cocoa.

"Do you still have your roommate?"

"I do," Guy said. "Actually she still has me, since it's really her place. But she's not here. She went up to Yosemite for the week-end with some friends."

Guy could almost hear the gears grinding in Doug's head at this unexpected news.

"I guess you were surprised to see me," the boy said after a mo-ment. He was watching Guy spoon cocoa mix into a mug filled with scalded milk. "Were you?"

"Yes," Guy said.

"I told you I tried to call."

"There aren't any messages on the machine."

"I didn't leave any messages," Doug said. "I didn't want to leave messages on the machine. I hate those machines! I needed to see you."

"And here you are!" Guy said, presenting him the mug.

Doug cupped it in his hands for a moment before taking a cautious sip and emitting a small sigh of pleasure. "That's really good!" he said.

"Thanks," Guy said.

"You seem distant."

"Do I? I'm tired. And a little drunk."

"Sounds like a good party."

"Dinner."

"I didn't have dinner," Doug said to his shoes.

"Are you hungry?" Guy said. "I'm sure there's something here. Susannah always has leftovers lying around."

"I'm okay," Doug said, without conviction. Guy was already scrounging the refrigerator, where he came upon several congealed slices of mushroom-and-sausage pizza, and the remains of some pad Thai, including a large prawn, in a cardboard carton. In a moment, arranged on a paper plate, it was all in the microwave.

"Thanks," Doug said, as Guy took the paper plate and led Doug to the table. They sat at right angles. Guy drank some Calistoga while Doug inhaled the food.

"Better?" Guy asked.

"Yeah," Doug said. "That was good. Thanks," he said, looking away. He was looking around the darkened apartment—looking here, there and everywhere except at Guy.

"You haven't told me why you were calling," Guy said. "Or why you didn't have dinner."

"I wasn't hungry then!" Doug said.

"I understand," Guy said. He did not raise his voice, or in any other way react to Doug. He felt like a lion tamer, whip and chair in hand, confronting an unpredictable beast that had somehow gotten loose in his apartment. He would remain calm, remain adult.

"You don't understand," Doug said. "You can't."

"Why can't I?"

"You just can't!" Doug said.

"Try me."

Doug said nothing for such a long interval that Guy concluded he was thinking about something else, some new and vexing subject.

"I trust you," Doug said.

"Yes."

"My parents had this huge fight today," Doug said, barely audibly, "when my dad was moving out."

"I didn't know your dad was moving out."

"They were screaming and throwing things around," Doug said. "My mom called him an asshole, right to his face."

Guy was silent.

"They're getting divorced," Doug continued. "My dad's moved into this apartment. I think he has a boyfriend or something."

"What makes you think that?"

"I'm not sure," Doug said. "It's not as big as this place. You have two bedrooms, right?"

"Right."

"Yeah," Doug said. "It must be nice to have the place to yourself for a while."

"Would you like some cookies?" Guy said. "I think there's a pack of them here somewhere," he said, rummaging through the kitchen cabinets, which for him were largely terra incognita.

"You're probably tired," Doug said.

"Do I look tired?"

"I don't know," Doug said. For the first time he cracked a small smile. "What do you look like when you're tired?"

"Older."

"Then you don't look tired. How old are you again?"

"Let's not get into that," Guy said.

"You don't look that old," Doug muttered.

"We have mint chocolate chip," Guy said. "Is that okay?"

"Yeah, fine," Doug said. "What time is it?"

Guy consulted his watch. "Past my bedtime."

"Past midnight?"

"Just about."

Doug sighed.

"What's wrong?" Guy said. "Is that little truck of yours about to turn back into a pumpkin?"

"I don't have it anymore," Doug said. "I sold it."

This news was flabbergasting, and Guy was flabbergasted into speechlessness. Sixteen-year-old boys did not sell or otherwise voluntarily dispose of their dearly won motor vehicles.

"How did you get here?" Guy asked.

"I walked."

"That's a pretty long walk," Guy said.

Doug shrugged. "Twenty minutes. Thirty, maybe."

"Yes, I would think," said Guy, who was really thinking that it was late and chilly and difficult to get a cab and Susannah had taken the Toyota to the mountains and he could not, with a clear conscience, dispatch a teenage boy into the city night. He was thinking, too, that Doug had known all these things all along—had planned them, indeed was counting on them.

"I should probably go," Doug said. "You must want to get to bed, and I know I'm just a pest."

"Is your mother home?" Guy asked cautiously.

"I don't know, probably," Doug said. "Why?"

"Maybe she could come get you. Or a friend. Adam, is that his name? Is he around?"

"I'm not going back there!" Doug said in a burst of vehemence.

"But Doug—"

"I can't!" Doug said. "I can't go back there."

"What will you do?"

"I don't know," Doug said. "I could go to Adam's mom's. They're out of town but I have a key."

"How will you get *there?*"

The boy made a face. "Walk. Just like I walked here."

"When did you sell the truck?"

"Last week. I didn't want it anymore. They gave it to me," he went on, "they paid the insurance and the gas and everything. I just didn't want it anymore."

"How far is Adam's mom's?"

"Pacific Heights."

"That's at least an hour's walk from here."

Doug shrugged. "I wish I had Rex with me," he said. "But I need to figure out what I'm going to do first."

"You can't walk all the way over there."

"Sure I can," Doug said. "It's not that far."

"Not in the middle of the night."

"I like the middle of the night," Doug said. He was glancing in Guy's direction and blinking his eyes a good deal, as if the room were filled with irritating cigarette smoke.

"Yes, for sleeping," Guy said.

"Yeah, whatever," Doug said.

"I can't let you walk to Pacific Heights in the middle of the night," Guy said, ignoring Doug's remark. "I'm sorry."

"You can't stop me!" Doug said. "I'll do it if I want."

"You're right, I can't stop you," Guy agreed. "But I can call your mother and tell her you're here and need to be picked up."

"No!" Doug said. "Don't do that. She's tired. She's probably sleeping now. She takes sleeping pills. Lots of pills."

"I'm sure she'd be relieved to know where you are."

"Oh, she knows where I am," Doug said. "I left her a note telling her I was coming over here, to your place. I just didn't tell her where it was, exactly. She knows you're gay," he added.

"You put that in the note?"

"She knows we're close," he went on. Suddenly he yawned and rubbed his fists into his eyes. "I'm really beat," he said. He wandered to the couch and plopped down with a groan. "I like your couch," he said, "it's really comfortable. Does it fold out?"

"No."

"What do you do when you have guests?"

"We don't have guests."

"I'm a guest."

"We give them some leftovers to eat and send them on their way," Guy said. He spoke lightly but meant every word. Guests of the overnight sort were a plague, an invasion; they got into the peanut butter and left a trail of wet towels.

"Do your friends from out of town stay with you?" Doug was nothing if not persistent.

"I don't have friends from out of town," Guy said. "I barely have friends from in town."

"This feels like it should fold out," Doug said. "It's weird that it doesn't." He was squirming this way and that on the cushions, gradually reclining until he looked as if he were trying to sleep in a coach seat on a bad airline.

"You look uncomfortable," Guy said with some satisfaction. "I was going to suggest that you spend the night on the sofa, if you had to, but I can see it's impossible."

"I am comfortable," Doug insisted. He had closed his eyes and was trying to give the impression that, coddled on the aging cushions, he'd arrived at the frontiers of blissful sleep. He sprawled and sighed with stagey satisfaction.

"Maybe Will can give you a ride home," Guy said. "I'll call him. He's probably still up."

"Who's Will?"

"A friend," Guy said.

"I told you," Doug said calmly, "I don't want to go home."

"You have to go somewhere," Guy said.

"I like it right here," Doug said faintly. "I just need a blanket and a pillow."

"I'm sorry," Guy said. "I don't think that's a good idea."

Without warning Doug jumped to his feet. "I need to pee," he said, giving Guy an inquiring glance.

"Down the hall, on the right," Guy said.

Drawn by some tropism he could not acknowledge, he followed Doug and stood at the door the boy had left ajar, listening to a steady stream of piss reach the bowl, its roar like that of a small but vigorous waterfall. The roar gave way to a silence uninterrupted by a flush or a zip or the sound of a faucet being turned on, hands washed. Guy couldn't stop himself from picturing the boy standing there, just beyond an unlocked door and an open fly: standing there, waiting. He was waiting for Guy to slip into the bathroom; he was waiting for the talk to stop, and he didn't know another way to stop it.

Doug did not seem surprised to find him standing there when he emerged a long moment later, after a flush and a belch.

"It's all yours," he said.

"I don't have to go."

They stood there face to face. Doug looked down at the feet he was methodically shuffling. Then he looked up again, straight into Guy's eyes, as if making a dare. This time Guy looked away.

"I was thinking," Guy said, "that since Susannah isn't here and she took the car and you have to sleep somewhere tonight, maybe you should stay in her room. I know she wouldn't mind," he added.

"I should probably just leave," Doug said.

"I don't think that's a good idea."

"I'm in your way."

"Doug, you're not in my way," Guy said. "It's the middle of the night and we're both tired and you have to stay somewhere. I wouldn't feel right if you didn't."

"I don't know," Doug said.

"It's settled," Guy said. "Let's go to bed. I'm tired."

* * *

Somewhere in the middle of the night. Shapeless gray dark, a breeze rustling the window in its frame, a far-off foghorn at the Golden Gate, the occasional car speeding up the lonely street, Guy sleepless, wrestling with his pillows and his conscience, feeling the boy as sleepless as he, one wall away, waiting for the communion of flesh. Waiting for Guy to slip into his room, slip between the sheets next to him, slowly, gently envelop him.

Guy could feel what Doug was feeling: the self-awareness, dread, excitement, the fear of wanting something to happen, the fear of rejecting it and moments later regretting rejecting it, the fear that the course of one's life was about to change drastically, as if hijacked by events. The fear that one's life would not meet the expectations of parents, peers; would not be ordinary. That one would not only be different but would be perceived as different: far scarier than the mere fact of being different, which could be concealed and denied. But denial, secretiveness were costly. Being accepted was costly. Meeting expectations was costly. Everything was costly. The dawn of that recognition, its first reddish rays touching a young forehead, was the dawn of adulthood. Whatever you did or didn't do, you had to pay for it somehow.

Guy remembered the urgent terror of wanting. The confusion. Let a bolt of hot white fucking clear the air. That was one of the purposes of sex: to reveal people to themselves and each other, through desire. It was a kind of illumination, an intimate flare. So often it hastened the process of alienation. Once desire was satisfied, the way was clear for indifference, incompatibility, dislike, and all the other ways people knew to separate themselves from each other. Sex was a withering flame that dried, wrinkled, and consumed. That was a hard truth for the young to choke down. They needed sex and believed in its connective powers; they were deeply invested in the myth.

Guy was much less invested. There was a lot of sex that wasn't worth the bother, a lot of sex that brought more trouble than satisfaction. Yet he couldn't stop imagining Doug's belly, its taut fine skin strung between two slender hip bones, like a *timpano*. He imagined what it might be like to remember having touched that skin, that belly in heat. Sex was a thing best enjoyed in recollection. The acts themselves were generally a blur in the moment, the laying of the foundations of memory. They made sense, took shape, acquired their full dimension, only when they were over, showers taken, clothes donned, numbers exchanged, promises made, good-byes said.

It was rational to resist the lure of Doug's belly, but sometimes it was a bore to be rational. To be trustworthy and honest and in control, to be the adult. Sometimes living meant being irrational, giving in. Guy lay there in agony and with an erection, pillows clenched against his chest as if to soothe the grinding of uncertainty inside himself.

The walls danced with the gray shadows of tree branches outside the window, quivering in the night breeze. Like clouds, they assumed more familiar shapes in his mind, and began to act out little dramas. He saw a mother chastising her child; a boy playing stick with his dog; an army marching to war; students lining up for the final; a dentist grimly examining a wasteland of rotten teeth; people fleeing a plane crash. At the darkened door—which he'd left open as he always did, to let the air circulate, even at the risk of its being misinterpreted (Doug had shut Susannah's door tight when

he'd retired)—another shadow moved. There was a faint knock, repeated more loudly, accompanied by the hissing of breath.

"You there?" Doug whispered.

"Right here."

"Are you awake?"

"Wide."

"Am I waking you? I'm sorry."

"I was awake," Guy said.

"I can't sleep," Doug said. "The bed is weird."

"I can't sleep either," Guy said. "I don't know why."

"Maybe we should switch beds," Doug suggested.

"I like my bed," Guy said.

"Yeah, it's big."

"So is Susannah's. It's even bigger than mine."

"I don't like her pillows," Doug reported. "They're foamy or
something. They won't—I can't wrap them around my head."

"Maybe some warm milk," Guy said. He was sitting up in bed
now, reaching discreetly for the boxer shorts he'd dropped bedside
when he'd retired. He put them on and willed his hard-on to diminish. When he was presentable, he slipped from the sheets and
wrapped himself in his robe, conscious of the boy's eyes on his
body in the indistinct darkness. They moved in train to the kitchen,
where Guy scalded more milk in a saucepan, and they sipped it at
the table, like dowagers.

"It's good," Doug said.

"I'm drowsy already."

"I guess I should have told you," Doug said. He was looking this
way and that.

"Told me what?"

"I'm scared of the dark," he said, his voice at the edge of audi-
bility. "I know it sounds stupid."

Guy said nothing.

"Usually Rex sleeps with me," Doug went on. "He has this pad
right at the foot of the bed so I know he's there. It's weird that he's
not here tonight. I'm in this strange bed and all these strange
sounds and that tree keeps scratching its branches against the window. Did you know it does that?"

Guy nodded.

"It's creepy," Doug said. "I don't think I'm going to be able to sleep in there."

"Give the milk a chance."

Doug ignored him. "Maybe I should sleep on the sofa," he said. "Even if it isn't a foldout. At least I wouldn't have to listen to that stupid tree."

"I don't know if we have blankets for the sofa," Guy said.

"I can bring the comforter from her bed," Doug said. He lowered his voice and added, "Or I could stay with you."

Guy couldn't quite make out the last suggestion. "Sorry?"

"I said—oh, nothing. It's just that, you know, your bed's big and everything. I don't snore or anything."

Guy sat silent at the wolf's approach.

"I'm not a sissy," Doug went on. "I don't like the dark, is all. It's crazy. I'm sure I'll grow out of it."

"You're sure you don't snore."

"Positive."

"How do you know?"

"I just know!" Doug said. "Do you snore?"

"There has been the occasional complaint, yes," Guy said.

"My dad snores."

"I leave it up to you where you sleep," Guy said. "I'm going to bed. I can hardly keep my eyes open. I'll leave room for you. Good night. Turn out the lights when you decide what to do."

"Okay," Doug said.

A few minutes later Guy was aware of exaggeratedly careful footsteps on the soft plank floors, a tentative hand on the edge of the bed, the weight of another body hoisting itself onto the mattress beside him. In the dark and not speaking, Doug seemed warm and substantial. His presence gave simple pleasure. But Guy was still wide awake, despite the milk, and he was bone-hard between the legs. He felt as if his erection were throbbing audibly in the darkness. He kept his back to the boy.

He felt, in the shrinking envelope of air that separated them, a tingling like static electricity, the heavy imminence of storm. Every glancing contact between them carried a charge. He could hear

Doug breathing carefully next to him, trying so hard not to move that he disturbed them both.

"Doug," Guy said.

"I'm sorry!" the boy said. "I'm trying not to bother you."

"Stop trying so hard."

"I'm not tired," Doug said.

"I'm exhausted," Guy said hopelessly, because he knew he was quickly growing too tired to go to sleep. He rolled onto his back and folded his arms behind his head and gazed down his torso toward the fold of many folds in the comforter that rose above his hard-on.

"It must hurt when you, you know, like, get fucked or whatever," Doug said without preamble.

"I'm sorry?" Guy asked. Had the boy seen the fold for what it was? Guy shifted a knee into the air, creating a small tent over his lower body and giving his overheated dick space to breathe.

"I mean, I've, you know, used a finger or whatever and it was pretty uncomfortable," Doug continued. "Well, at first. Then it wasn't so bad. With Vaseline or whatever."

Doug, too, was on his back as he spoke, arms folded behind his head so that their elbows were nearly touching. Guy thought he saw the boy spread his legs slightly, but in the dimness it was hard to be sure. He was fairly certain Doug hadn't slipped out of his Joe Boxers. He felt the strain of wills—the dare that trembled on two sets of dry lips. He was tired, he was exhausted and curious, there was nowhere to go now, nowhere to hide.

"I suppose not," Guy managed to say.

"Do you ever use a finger?"

"I don't remember."

"That's so lame!" Doug said. "How could you not remember?"

"It's not the sort of thing I sit around remembering."

"That's a crock of shit, you totally remember," Doug said. "You've totally done it. I decided that maybe it's not so bad after all, getting fucked in the ass."

"Doug."

"I just can't see my dad with another guy's bone up his butt."

Guy groaned.

"You all right?" Doug asked. He had moved so that he was hovering above Guy and peering at him like an Arctic rescue dog.

"I'm fine," Guy whispered. "Thank you."

"You've fucked guys," he said in a conversational murmur.

Guy nodded.

"And they've fucked you."

"Oh yes," Guy said, almost inaudibly.

"Does it hurt?"

"No."

"'Cause you know what you're doing."

Guy nodded.

"Did it hurt your first time?"

"A little," Guy said, understating the matter. It had hurt quite a bit, and he'd bled. But his first time had been with Michael Donofrio, who had been careful, gentle and loving. Despite the pain, Guy had liked it. He felt in his eyes a wash of sentiment at the memory of a man who'd invested his passion in teaching Guy what to do and, in so doing, made their sex mutual across the large and complex gulf of differences between them. He wondered where Michael Donofrio was, whether he was still alive, still married. Had he ever been arrested for sporting with men? Had he crashed like Doug's father?

The strangest dreams were the dreams about being awake, about being absolutely confident that one had not yet fallen asleep, that what was happening, however astounding, was really happening. Guy had no recollection of having fallen asleep and had no sense of being in a dream. He could feel the boy's breath on his shoulder. He felt Doug's lips pressing against his own, Doug's tongue wrestling with his own, Doug's breath hot and urgent on Guy's cheek. The boy's hands ran up Guy's shirt and grappled with the top button of his shorts. In this quiet, empty apartment, bathed in night, Doug had made up his mind at last. Desire had burst into flame after an uncomfortably long smolder.

Guy surrendered. He moaned with pleasure and wrapped his arms around Doug to pull them tight together. He ran a hand down the small of Doug's back and under the loose waistband of his shorts. Squeezed the muscly globes of his ass; ran a finger in the crack and was rewarded with a groan and a twitch of the hips.

"You're snoring," a voice whispered in Guy's ear. Guy awoke with a jolt of surprise and embarrassment and understood that he'd been having a dream that had shaded away imperceptibly from his wakeful musings. He could feel the heat of Doug's mass at his side. That much was certainly real. So was Guy's priapism.

"Sorry," Guy whispered. He turned toward Doug and found the boy's face, mounted on a pedestal of cupped hand and forearm, scant inches away.

"It's okay," he whispered. His glance flickered momentarily downward. "I'm just not used to hearing somebody snore."

"It's because I'm on my back."

"Yeah, you are," he said. "Flat on your back."

The boy closed his eyelids halfway. He parted his lips slightly, giving them a single, moist sweep of the tongue.

"I'm sorry I started all those stupid fights," he said in a low voice, eyes now entirely closed.

"I know you've had a lot on your mind," Guy said.

"I've had a *lot* on my mind," Doug agreed. He seemed visibly relieved. He opened his eyes and gave Guy a dreamy glance, then closed them again. His mouth lay partly open. He ran his tongue over his lips. Guy noticed his head moving toward Doug's, as if the emergency brake hadn't been set in a truck parked on an incline. At the same time, Doug seemed to be moving toward him. Their mouths met with a dry, husky shock. Their lips made a neat seal.

Was Guy dreaming again? He laid a hand gently on the back of Doug's neck and waited for the pressing together of their bodies. He waited to awaken. But didn't. Doug tasted sweet and fleshy, and one of them—who?—issued a little moan. The boy did not pull away—not, at least, for a very long moment in which Guy felt himself melting into Doug at last. It was real. They were both awake; they opened their eyes and looked at one another. Then, ever so gently, Doug broke the kiss.

"What are you doing?" he said, still barely whispering, not, apparently, angry, or anything other than mildly curious, as if he did not quite understand what had just happened. Guy nuzzled his neck. Maybe Doug didn't want that; maybe he wanted to go back to kissing. They stared at each other for another moment. Guy closed his eyes and hoped Doug would do the same. Guy lifted his head so Doug could easily rejoin their lips, close the seal again, as if they were two spacecraft attempting a difficult docking maneuver. Guy did not want to hear any more words.

"You kissed me," Doug said.

Guy nodded.

"I can't believe you kissed me," Doug said. "Why did you do that?" he said. There was a thump as he fell away onto his back.

"It just happened."

"You made it happen."

"We wanted it to happen."

"I did not!" he said, with a nerve-shattering forcefulness that split the hot, close room.

"You were going to kiss me," Guy said.

"I was not!"

"You were thinking about it."

"That's bullshit. I could report you," Doug continued. "I could turn you in. You could be arrested for what you did."

"You're hard," Guy pointed out, staring down now at the unmistakable, cylindrical bulge angling up in Doug's loose shorts.

"I am not," Doug said feebly. He made no effort to turn his body to conceal what Guy had already seen. But it did not matter what Guy had seen, because it could not be true Doug wanted Guy, and therefore it was not true, and the fact that Doug had an erection could not be a true fact because it was unacceptable and therefore impossible.

"I know you think I'm gay," Doug said, staring at the ceiling, "but I'm not."

"How do you know I think that?"

"You kissed me!" he said. "You said you thought I wanted to. You think I'm gay."

"Shhh," Guy said. Doug emitted a miserable yelp, muffled by his forearm, which he appeared to be biting, like an anxious dog gnawing on a favorite bone.

"Why are you saying all these things?" Doug whimpered. "Why are you doing these things?"

Because, Guy thought, *the house is empty, you wanted to stay, you wanted to sleep in my bed, you want to as much as I do, we both want to seal the bond, how could this not be happening? Of course it's happening. It had to happen.*

"I'd better go," Doug said.

"Doug."

"I mean it," he said.

"We've been through this. There's no place for you to go. You wanted to stay here."

"I didn't think you'd be hitting on me!" he nearly shouted. "I trusted you and you're trying to use me!"

"You're the one who came knocking at my door."

"I couldn't sleep in there!" Doug shouted. "That's the only reason I came in here. I trusted you."

"Give me a break."

"You're misunderstanding everything," Doug said. "You think I'm attracted to you or something. You think I want to sleep with you. You think that's the reason I came in here."

"And isn't it?"

"You're pressuring me!" Doug wailed.

Guy was too shocked to say anything more. He wondered if Doug might be right. Maybe Guy had been deluded by his own feelings, like a driver blinded by his own reflected high beams as he passed through a blizzard.

"I can't have sex with you," Doug said. "You're a man! You're, like, twice as old as I am or something! I have to leave," he said, looking stricken as he spoke.

"You can't leave," Guy said again. "We've been through this."

"I'll leave if I want to."

"Doug."

"I'm not attracted to you."

"I'll tell you what," Guy said. "I'll leave."

"What are you talking about?"

"I'll go sleep in Susannah's room," Guy said. "You can stay here. I'll even leave you my pillows."

Guy hauled himself out of the bed. He felt like a wounded soldier desperately fleeing a battlefield rout, expecting to be machine gunned in the back.

"You're really leaving?" Doug called out.

"I really am. I'll see you in the morning."

Guy moved through the doorway toward Susannah's room. He could hear the thump-thump of Doug's feet in pursuit.

"Wait a minute!" Doug said.

At Susannah's door Guy stopped and turned. There Doug stood, on his face written the hope that Guy would apologize so they could go back to Guy's room together and finish what they'd started. If there were to be any apologizing, Guy knew, he would have to do it, because Doug couldn't: The boy's lashing out this time was too enormous for him to accept responsibility, or to try to make right. Guy would have to say the words Doug wasn't big enough to say, and the boy's accepting Guy's apology would be his way of acknowledging that he was sorry and Guy had been right.

"You don't have go in there," he said. "It's a crappy bed. You won't be able to sleep. Are you mad?"

"I'm not mad," Guy said, "just tired. I have to go to sleep, I'm exhausted. Good night, Doug."

Doug looked at Guy blankly, as if these words hadn't registered. Guy could have said almost anything to placate him—*I'm sorry, let's forget it, let's have a beer, take a walk, arm-wrestle*—but not that. Not *good night*.

"Good night," Guy said again. He stepped through the door and closed it carefully. Susannah's room was chilly—the window was open a crack—and he wasn't wearing a T-shirt. He shivered a little and felt a deep pain in his chest.

Of all the endings Guy had imagined to the evening, this had not been one of them. He wrapped himself in Susannah's thick comforter and tried to go to sleep but couldn't. After an interval of tossing and turning, he consulted the digital cube clock on its bedside table, thinking that it must be at least four in the morning. But it wasn't even two. Sleep would not take him. And when it finally did, he was too exhausted and rinsed out to notice.

He didn't know he'd slept at all until he woke with a start to find reddish morning sunlight gleaming through the miniblinds. He crept from Susannah's bed, swaddled himself in his bathrobe, which hung on the inside of the bathroom door, and made his gingerly way to his own room. Door ajar. Sunlight beginning to flare more brightly. The bedclothes tangled, the bed itself empty.

The apartment itself turned out to be empty, except for him. He looked in the kitchen, in the parlor, in the closets and on the deck, but there was no sign of Doug. It was as if he'd never arrived, had never been, was nothing more than a troublesome apparition in Guy's conscience. But there was a legal pad on the dining-room table, and someone had scrawled on the top page:

Guy,

> *Sorry to run out on you. Things got too weird last night. I couldn't sleep, so I took off. Don't worry, I'll be fine. I know how to take care of myself. I wish you hadn't come on to me. It screwed everything up. I told you I wasn't gay but you didn't pay any attention. I know this sounds harsh but it's true. Don't try to contact me, I don't know where I'll be. Maybe some day we'll be able to work things out, I don't know. I hope so.*

—Doug

Guy read the words calmly. He fixed himself a pot of coffee and some toast and sat down to read the newspaper, waiting for some feeling to wash through him. But there was none, other than relief. He made a brief tour of the apartment to see if anything had been stolen or gratuitously damaged—Doug being an attention seeker of the first order—but found nothing amiss. The unexpected guest had vanished in a puff of melodrama, taking with him his drumskin belly. Six hours before, thoughts of that belly—what it would be like to touch and kiss it, what lay above and below, what sounds its owner might make if properly touched and kissed and fondled—had kept Guy thrashing miserably in the sheets, wanting to make the return journey to his own bed, where Doug and his miraculous tummy lay waiting for a second chance.

Giving people second chances was poor policy because it assumed that a rough first time was a correctable fluke rather than the reflection of a deep truth. Guy did not know what Doug's deep truth was, except that it was plainly unpleasant. Easier to deal with the pragmatic issues at hand, such as the boy's flight. He could call the family home. He could call the police department's community-patrol officer, who rode around on a mountain bike. He might send Doug e-mail, or go out to look for him. The boy could be camped in the foyer, on the sidewalk in front of the building, in the little park halfway between their houses. Guy glanced out the window, saw nothing but smelled the fresh air, and let it go.

Doug would be fine. He'd said so himself. And there was no more business between them, really. The damnable question had come to a head and messily burst. Their entire relationship had been a march, really, toward that one little kiss and all the territory that had lain beyond. But the kiss had ruinously exploded, and that territory would not now be reconnoitered.

For that was the delicate way of human intimacy. Trying to create an intimate bond between two people was like trying to find the right angle for a space capsule to reenter the earth's atmosphere. Too steep an angle and the capsule would be incinerated. Too shallow an angle and the capsule would bounce off into space, lost forever. He and Doug had bounced into the void; the angle had been too shallow.

And, Guy thought, buttering some toasted Jewish rye and doctoring his cup of coffee with two sugars and a generous splash of half and half, it was just as well. In fact it was a relief. The world was full of *timpano* bellies; always would be. Narcissists and manipulators, too—often as part of the same package. The wise thing was to steer clear.

vi. *The Gate*

A UGUST AND HUMID, the wind strong in the south, the heavy gray air blooming into cottony anvil-shaped clouds over the hills. Every now and again a blue flash and rumble of distant thunder to the north. Erotic weather. A T-shirted Guy pedaled along in a pair of Spandex shorts, the bare skin of his forearms touched now and again by stray drops drifting down from the purple clouds scurrying overhead, vanguard of a truant tropical storm that had strayed north.

The weather felt like spring. It felt like summer back East, in the hay country. It felt, strangely, like Doug, who would always be evoked for Guy by summery, suggestive weather—the kind of weather that had prevailed on the day they'd met on the bluffs above the queer beach.

That meeting had been five years ago. They had not seen one another since the obscure spectacle in Guy's apartment more than four years ago. The long interval had been a peaceful one for Guy. He thought about Doug, but he did not regret the gulf that had opened between them. Guy wasn't sorry about the gulf because he'd created it, though he'd tried to do so unobtrusively.

And Doug had resisted, obtrusively. There had been notes in the mail from the boy, a flurry of hang-ups on the answering machine: all attempts to renew their dealings, to return to the point where events had spun so unpleasantly out of control and point them in a different direction. Guy read the letters, noting with dispassion their kaleidoscopic shifts in tone, from rue to pleading to scorn to fury, and finally to despairing self-pity. Then more rage, with its abuse carefully calculated—to the extent that an impassioned youth was capable of careful calculation—to wound but not to kill.

Doug was pushing every button he could find to push, setting bait right and left, but Guy, like a perversely indifferent fish, wouldn't nibble. His occasional responses—a card at Christmas, say, or on a birthday—were exercises in social correctness meant to honor a wider principle of civility, not to reestablish a rapport. And Guy was careful to phrase his comments so as not to stimulate Doug's lively sense of hopefulness.

But even Doug couldn't be too hopeful in the aftermath of their little disaster. He had gambled and lost, had misjudged the recoil of the emotional blast he'd set and sent himself spinning into limbo. Guy still thought about him, wondered what was happening in his life, but he was not curious, or foolish, enough to open the door. That would lead, sooner or later, to the same unhappy path they'd already explored. That was the nature of personalities. They fit together in ways that were apparent from the outset, and they would never fit together in any other way. They would never change.

Lessons of adulthood: change was unlikely, rescue of others all but impossible. Friendship had its limits and probably was an illusion as between people of widely different ages and outlooks. Wisdom resisted the temptation to bind the psychic wounds of strangers. It resisted the temptation to be drawn into the melodramas of others. Wisdom recognized that wounded people often used their woundedness as a kind of aphrodisiac and were expert at changing the subject, moving blame and abuse around like voltage on the power grid. Wisdom remained beyond their grasp.

Guy sailed along through Golden Gate Park, which smelled strongly of fresh-cut grass. Reminders of youth: mowing the family lawn; the damp turf of a Y-league football field on a cool and cloudy Saturday afternoon in October; hay in the nearby country on a Sunday morning in summer. He no longer remembered much of his own youth; it existed mainly as a set of smells that opened to flashes of feeling. Smells were a kind of time travel. For an instant one was sixteen again, filled with that hopeful energy. Then the flash faded, and the ordinary present returned, and one was glad not to be sixteen but somewhere on the deep, calm waters of one's adulthood.

He sailed past the infamous rest room where Doug's father had met his fate, penis in hand, in the shape of a bored police officer. Roller bladers and bikers and joggers whizzed by, a few of them now and then turning up the asphalt path toward the little cottage, where they could take care of some business. Guy pressed on, threading his way among the bare chests and Spandex, the whirring freewheels and rhythmic slaps of running shoes against the pavement. It was a relief to exit the park at last, leave the jostling human throng behind.

At the Golden Gate, crowds were thin. The weather was warm enough but too variably cloudy to draw the sun-worshipping masses to the beach. He rolled down the fire lane, tires popping on the gravel; he rounded the curve, passed the battery, dismounted, locked up where he always did. The layers of concrete lay deserted under the spitting sky. He drifted through the grass, high and tawny at the end of summer, to the promontory, which commanded a view of the coast for miles, and the never-ending, eerily silent traffic on the bridge. It was the place where Doug had first appeared, but now it was forlorn. On the boy beach he saw a scattering of towels, discreetly spaced. No movement. Muted, rhythmic roar of the surf.

Under the bridge passed a freighter, low in the water, bound for the orient with redwood logs or some other natural bounty, to return some weeks hence laden with televisions or small sedans. Guy watched the ship pass toward the gray shadows offshore, where other shadowy ships plied. Then he hiked down the narrow, twisting trails that wound back and forth across the face of the cliff until he was on the rocky platform just above the beach.

A tiny creek, trickling seaward from the headlands, spread into a muddy bog as it neared the edge of its journey. Guy cleared it in one spattering step. He exchanged provocative stares with an owl-faced boy in a goatee, then descended a stony escarpment to the beach, on whose sandy kelp-strewn carpet he made his way toward the foot of the bridge. The beach was mostly empty, except for the occasional body on a towel. A few bodies weren't on the sand at all, but stashed in the sconces formed by boulders where the beach met the cliff. One glimpsed a knee, a forearm, a foot; one glanced at the toenails as a marker of hygiene and vanity.

Fairly far down the beach a bouquet of limbs and appendages caught his attention. He could make out only a calf and foot and half of another. He could not precisely judge the condition of the toenails, though they looked a bit too shaggy to belong to a queer man. But he liked the hairy muscularity of the calf.

The incompleteness of the picture tantalized Guy, and he circled discreetly for a better view, approaching from behind and slightly upslope. The splendid calf, and its twin, were attached to the equally splendid body of a winsome young man, naked and flat on his back, eyes shielded by wraparound sunglasses. Beauty could be tiresome and monotonous, inconvenient and fearful, but even at its most bitter it never failed to compel. The boy's loveliness gave Guy a familiar twitch in the gut.

He continued circling, working toward a more head-on view, exercising the stealth of a photographer stalking a wary subject in the bush of Africa. The guy was very young, no older than his early twenties. Some hair on his belly, the lightest brush stroke between his nipples, the exquisitely creamy skin that was the evanescent glory of Caucasian youth. Experience suggested that such creatures flocked among themselves and were unlikely to be interested in someone like Guy, whose youthful charms now lay in a past measured by decades. He must be careful, he must be cautious, he must be noncommittal if discovered, he must be prepared to depart with apologies.

"Hi," the young man said, without moving his head or, in fact, anything other than his fullish lips.

Guy inhaled sharply. He felt as if he'd been slapped, not merely by the unexpected syllable but by the sense of recognition. He knew this man, this boy-man. It couldn't be. It was not possible. But it seemed to be.

"I saw you up on top of the cliff," the young man continued. He was smiling faintly now, and had lifted himself up on his elbows. The planar torso Guy remembered had given way to sleekly rounded pectorals. His legs were muscular and full, his shoulders broad. His face had come into focus, and the soft blurriness of adolescence was gone. And, of course, his dick, formidable and tender. He was a man, or nearly so. Guy felt weak in the knees. "I was hoping you'd be here. I've been coming here almost every day for the past couple of weeks. I figured you'd show up eventually."

"Doug?"

"So you do remember my name."

"Of course I remember your name," Guy said.

"I thought you might have forgotten," Doug said. "It's been a long time, you know."

"Yes," Guy said. "No, I haven't forgotten. I'm just—I'm sorry. I'm surprised, of course. What are you doing here?"

"I was hoping to catch some sun," Doug said. He removed the sunglasses from his face and gazed into the cloudy heavens. "It looks more like rain, though. I'm glad to see you."

"I'm sorry, I'm being rude," Guy said. "I didn't mean to be. I'm just surprised . . . I didn't really expect . . . "

"It's been a while," Doug said.

"Yes, you mentioned that."

"Years."

"I know."

"We met here, remember?"

"I do remember," Guy said. "Not exactly here. Up there." Guy was relieved to have an excuse to turn away from Doug so that he might indicate the spot where their paths had first crossed. The shock of Doug's unselfconscious nakedness, though delayed, had finally struck him.

"Right," Doug said. "I've been watching you come down the beach. I wasn't sure you were going to make it this far."

"What do you mean?"

"I thought you might see someone else you liked first."

"There's hardly anyone else here," Guy said, thinking of the owl-faced boy with the goatee.

"There's a few guys. Some of them are looking."

"How do you know that?"

"A couple of them hit on me," Doug said calmly.

"Oh."

"I dealt with it," Doug said. "I wasn't mean to them or anything. I just, you know, walked on by. You look uncomfortable," he added, his appraising eyes raking Guy.

"It's just unexpected—"

"I mean in those clothes."

"I've been biking," Guy said. "I'm a little sweaty."

"Maybe you should get out of them."

Guy was too surprised to say anything, and Doug laughed. "It is a nude beach, right?" he said. "Why don't you sit down and make yourself comfortable? I saved you a spot. Water?" He offered Guy a swig from his bottle of Crystal Geyser, which Guy accepted.

"Thanks."

"We haven't talked in a really long time."

"I didn't think you wanted to," Guy said. "Not after the way you left that night. It seemed pretty definitive."

"I tried to call you," Doug said. "You never answered the phone. I couldn't get your e-mail address. I guess you changed it or something. Maybe you changed service providers."

Guy was silent.

"I wrote you some letters. Did you get them?"

"I got them, yes."

"You never really answered them."

"I sent you a card now and then."

"You never said anything in those cards," Doug said. "They were just for politeness."

"That's very true," Guy said.

Doug looked him square in the eye. It was difficult not to look at his body, difficult to concentrate on the task at hand, which was resisting Doug's attempts to make him feel guilty. He did not feel guilty; he was not guilty.

"That really hurt me," Doug said. "It was like, you didn't take what I wrote seriously. Did you even read my letters?"

"Of course I read them."

"It really hurt me that you didn't respond," Doug said. "You never reached out to me at all."

"No, I didn't," Guy agreed. After a pause he added, "I didn't because I didn't want to."

Doug soaked up that meaning in silence.

"Reaching out would have been phony," Guy continued, "so I didn't. I had nothing to say. That's all there was to it."

"All there was to it?" Doug said, his voice rising to a hotter emotional register for the first time. "That's kind of hard to believe. I had lots to say. You must have too."

Guy shook his head. "Sorry," he said. "Just because you had things to say doesn't mean I did. I would have preferred that you hadn't written those letters. But I couldn't stop you. And when I did send you something, it wasn't in reply to something you'd written. It was because it would have been rude not to. Send you a birthday card, for instance, or a Christmas card. I'm sorry, maybe I'm silly that way. I wanted to acknowledge that you were out there without stirring up the pot again."

"Our friendship meant a lot to me," Doug said, drifting now toward a familiar sulkiness, which crossed his face like a cloud over the sun. "All I wanted was a dialogue, not stirring up the pot or whatever you call it."

"No," Guy said, "you did want to stir up the pot. Some of your letters were just wild attempts to get some sort of rise out of me. And what you wanted even beyond that was another chance, so you could pull the same stunt again."

Doug was silent, as he always was when slapped by the truth. Idly he pulled at himself.

"I'd had enough," Guy said, looking out to sea.

"I'm sorry you thought that I was pulling a stunt," Doug said. "I'm sorry you thought that little of me."

"It wasn't a question of thinking little of you," Guy said. "It was a matter of recognizing the pattern. This was the way we dealt with each other. I came to see that it would never change, and that it wasn't good for either one of us."

"That was a really bad time in my life," Doug said.

"Yes," Guy said. "Of course, that's no excuse. And it wasn't entirely your doing, anyway. It takes two people to make a mess like we made. I played my part. I decided I didn't want to play that part anymore."

"I know I didn't handle it right," Doug said. "I was shitty to you. I couldn't really blame you for blowing me off."

"You must be in college now," Guy said.

"Yeah," Doug said. He lay back flat and had, almost instantaneously it seemed, gotten completely hard. He was smiling mysteriously up into the heavens, touching himself as if unaware of what he was doing, and of the effect he was producing in Guy. "Man, your clothes reek," he said. "How can you stand to be in them?"

Without another word Guy peeled off his sweatshirt and T-shirt, undid the laces on his shoes, stripped off his socks, pulled his biking shorts off, aware the whole time that Doug was watching and studying. He did not want Doug to see his body, he did not want the field of their contest to be leveled in this way, nudity being perhaps the greatest democratic force in human affairs, but even more he did not want to be seen as shying away from a challenge. He was totally hard too, but acted as if it were nothing out of the ordinary. He squatted on the sand next to Doug, who was once again smiling skyward.

"Better," he said.

"Thanks."

"You've got a nice body. Gay men do."

"Gay men go to the gym," Guy said, "with cultish devotion."

"You ever done it out here?" he asked Guy.

"On the sand or among the rocks?"

"I always had a crush on you," Doug said. "I guess you knew."

Guy was silent.

"Did you have a crush on me?"

"You were so young," Guy said.

"I could see it in your eyes," Doug said. "I see it now." He looked directly into Guy's eyes with a gaze of appetite and longing, the elemental lasciviousness of youth. The young had little knowledge and no wisdom, but they did have lust: It was their way of engaging the world. And, for the moment, Guy was Doug's world.

Guy said nothing. He said nothing, did not move, as Doug moved closer to him, mouth half-open in anticipation. They closed their eyes; their faces drifted together; their mouths joined, just as they had once before; they grasped one another and groaned together. But this time neither of them panicked.

* * *

"Where's Rex?" Guy asked. It was slightly later, under a blowsy sky. Drizzle fell lightly on them; a cool salty breeze blew from the green water. Another ship was passing, and Guy wondered what its crew could see from the upper decks; he wondered whether they'd watched the whole show with their binoculars or a telescope; whether, in their pornographic transports, they could have begun to have perceived what was really going on, what was really at stake.

"Rex," Doug said. A smile flitted across his face. Then impassiveness. "You met Rex out here, didn't you?"

"When I met you."

"He got old," Doug said. "He got gray around the mouth and kind of blind. Deaf, too. He couldn't even hear the doorbell anymore. He was sad when I went away to school. My mom said he sat by the door for days, waiting for me to come back. He was glad to see me at Thanksgiving. I tried to explain to him where I'd been, but I don't think he heard me. I told him I wanted to take him back to school with me. He was old. He—I guess it was his hips or something. I don't know exactly. I wasn't there. One day he couldn't get up. He'd peed in the house and . . . you know. My mom had to take him in. Take him to the vet. I was in class," Doug went on, an awful tone of anger and self-recrimination creeping into his voice. "Anthropology. She called to tell me. When I came home the next time I scattered his ashes. I scattered them out here." He jerked his head upslope, toward the promontory where he and Guy had first met. "Up there. So he could see the bridge."

He paused with a choke, and Guy found to his surprise that he couldn't speak, either.

"I never got to say goodbye," Doug said after a little bit. "That was all I really wanted. I wanted to be with him so he wouldn't be afraid. I wanted him to know I loved him."

"He knew," Guy said.

"I guess," Doug said. "I feel like I let him down."

"Doug," Guy said gently, unable to say anything else.

"I wanted to call you up and tell you," Doug said, "because I knew you'd understand, but I just couldn't. I don't know why."

"I'm very sorry," Guy said.

"I loved him so much," Doug said. He took a deep breath and shuddered and lay back and reached out for Guy's hand. Guy permitted the contact for a long moment before gently disentangling himself. He noted with dark wonder that even in sorrow Doug was again hard, or perhaps he'd never gone soft. It had been a long time since Guy had lain with a such a very young man. Their powers of endurance and recuperation were miraculous—everything myth made them to be. Regarded purely as pieces of sexual machinery, they were marvels, like new cars, everything solid and tight and functional, eager to perform, with a bewitching smell.

"I'm glad you're here," Doug said, reaching out again for Guy as if Guy had not just delicately put him off. He was smiling now through the soggy mess under his eyes and on his cheeks. "I'm glad we're here together. There have been times I thought I'd never see you again. I've missed you. I've missed you a lot. I've thought about you all the time."

This was a cue for Guy to say the same thing in return. The whole scene was Doug's long-cherished fantasy, which, through luck and surreal persistence, he had brought to a kind of fruition.

"I've thought about you too," Guy allowed, measuring the words carefully. "Wondered how you were."

"My dad moved to Seattle," Doug said. "I don't really see him anymore. I go up there once a year. He sends me birthday cards and Christmas presents. I think he's got a boyfriend or something. He doesn't really tell me much. I don't blame him. If I were him I don't think I'd be saying much, either. My mom got remarried. After Rex died she sold the house and they bought a new place together. I stay with them when I'm in town, but I don't really like him. I haven't told her that. She's happy. That's what matters, right? I'd like a place of my own. Like yours. You still living in the same place?"

"The very same."

"Still with that roommate?"

"Still with her," Guy said.

"Oh," Doug said, hoping to seem nonchalant. "I thought you two were going to get married or something."

"We're not the marrying kind, apparently."

"Oh," Doug said. "Are you involved with anyone right now?" he asked after a lengthy pause.

"No," Guy said. It was the easiest possible answer to give, being true. He wasn't involved, had no plans to be involved, didn't want to be involved. He was happy where he was. Uninvolved.

"That's good," Doug murmured.

"It's good?"

"It's okay, I mean," Doug said. "I mean, it's not bad or anything, is it? You don't seem unhappy."

"I'm not."

"Because you never know when someone might come along."

"No, you don't."

"He could show up any time, any place. He could be someone you already know," Doug suggested.

"Let's hope not."

"Let's hope not?"

"I'm not looking for someone to come along," Guy said.

"Are you saying you're not looking?"

"That's what I'm saying."

"Wow," Doug said. He exhaled loudly. "I don't believe you."

Guy laughed. "Why not?"

"Because," Doug sputtered. "Just because. Everybody's looking! Everybody I know is looking, anyway. Nobody wants to be alone. You say you don't mind but that's because you are alone."

"I'm not really alone, though," Guy said. "I have friends, I even have sex sometimes. On the beach, when I can swing it."

He watched Doug's face blush and puff with embarrassment and frustration and determination.

"Are you gay, by the way?" Guy asked. Doug's hand was wandering along Guy's inner thigh; in a moment it reached its goal, and Doug began fondling them both in rhythm. The boy's eyes widened at the question, but he did not explode.

"Why do you ask?" he asked, with a slow smile.

"You seem pretty enthusiastic about some things you didn't seem so enthusiastic about when we last saw each other."

"So you think I am?"

Guy shrugged. "I guess I'm curious."

"I thought I might be when I went away to college," Doug said. "Queer, I mean. I was afraid I was. I guess you knew that. I didn't want to be. That's why I was so shitty to you. To prove to you that I wasn't. That way, if you believed I was straight, I could believe it too."

"I didn't believe you were straight, I'm sorry to say."

"I know. I could tell. That just made me crazier," Doug admitted. "I started wondering if you might be right. I couldn't stop thinking about you, I don't know why. Then I went to college and I had an affair with this guy and I found out . . . I wasn't."

"Bad affair?"

"No, it was good," Doug said. "He reminded me of you somehow. We cared about each other. But after about a week I knew men weren't for me. It didn't bother me, but it just wasn't the same as with girls. He was the only guy I was ever with."

"Until today."

Doug laughed. "It's weird, isn't it?" Doug said.

"What's weird?"

Doug lay back behind his sunglasses. "Now you remind me of him!" he said. "And I'm still in love with you, even though you're a guy. And older."

"I know," Guy said.

"So I guess I'm kind of bi," Doug said. "A little bi."

"That's cool."

"Isn't that what you always wanted?" Doug said.

"For you to be a little bi?"

"No," Doug said, "for our relationship to be reciprocal. For the feeling to be mutual."

"Is that what I wanted?" Guy said. "What did you want?"

"I don't know. Didn't you? I mean, aren't you?"

"Aren't I what?"

"You know," Doug said. "Your feelings and everything. You don't really talk about them, you dance around them. We just, I mean, come on, after that? You felt it too."

"I could never really figure out what I wanted," Guy said, gazing up at the clouds. "Or what I felt. Not just about you. I think it's been my biggest problem in life. Not being sure. Doubt is a punishable offense, I've realized. Things go better for people who know exactly what they want. They don't waste time wondering, they just go after it. I waste time wondering. I'm never really sure. I'm like Hamlet, a ditherer. And here I am," he said. He had gotten hard again under Doug's urgent ministrations. "Dithering. And enjoying it."

"Here we are, you mean," Doug said. "Dithering each other. And I have a girlfriend."

"Do you? Is she at this lovely beach with you today? Have you stashed her away somewhere?"

Doug flushed again but did not lose his cool. "She's down in L.A. for a few weeks," he explained calmly. Guy found himself admiring Doug's adult refusal to snap. "She's from there. I've told her about you. About what happened, you know, between us, back when I was in high school. She's cool with it."

"How do you know that?"

"She says so," Doug said. "I've talked to her about it a lot. She's helped me work through my feelings about the whole thing—how I, you know, how much you meant to me. Mean to me. She wants to meet you," he confided. "I've told her you're really cool, so don't let me down!"

"I don't see how I possibly could," Guy said, "since I have no idea what you mean."

Doug was sitting upright again. He embraced Guy, nuzzled his neck, stuck a tongue in his ear and very deliberately went down on him. Guy felt sixteen again, and sixty, and totally detached.

"You're pretty good at that," he murmured.

"Not as good as you." After a while Doug said: "So?"

"So what?"

"Do you want to come? You can come in my mouth."

"I don't want to right now," Guy said. Gently he pushed Doug's head away. "Thanks, though."

"Okay," Doug said. Since he had to transfer his sex energy somewhere, he transferred it to himself. "Do you want to meet her?" he asked while flogging away.

"I'm not sure," Guy said. "I can't see why I would."

"You'd like her," Doug said. He grunted; there was a distinct slurpy sound coming from his busy fist. "I think she'd like you."

"Maybe so."

"We could all have dinner or something."

"That would be very civilized," Guy said, "very grown-up." He was thinking of all the ways he might nicely say No; meanwhile, Doug masturbated.

"You sure you don't want to come?'"

"I already did," Guy pointed out.

"I sort of need to," Doug said.

"I understand," Guy said. "Go right ahead. I should probably start back, though. The sky is looking a little menacing, don't you think?"

"I haven't been paying much attention to the sky."

"I have. It's raining."

"Just sprinkles," Doug whispered. "Don't you want to come again?"

"I'm not twenty," Guy pointed out.

"I'm really close," Doug said, his voice transformed by a not-quite-perfected desire into something male and guttural. It wasn't a sound Guy associated with him at all. "I want you to fuck me," Doug continued. "I've never been fucked. I want you to do it to me. I want it to be you. It has to be you."

"A tale to share with your girlfriend later?" Guy asked, permitting himself a little jab. Asking the question helped conceal—though not much—a tide of lust rising inside him. That tide made him angry and sad; it threatened to wash away his control. "I don't have a rubber," he added. It happened to be true but it also pleasurably raised the stakes. Doug's Adam's apple worked.

"You don't?"

Guy shook his head.

"I thought gay guys always had rubbers with them."

"Not this one."

Doug frowned. "I don't either," he said. He paused for a moment, either to ponder the issue or give the appearance of pondering it. "That's okay," he said, voice parched. "We don't need one. I trust you."

"You trust me," Guy said. It was an arousing thing to say. The prospect was arousing. Doug lay supine on the sand, like a defeated city awaiting the invaders' sack with a mix of horror and ecstasy. They had already made love; there was no reason not to complete the final act. Doug was old enough to understand the risk of barebacking and, if he chose, assume it. Guy was not his keeper.

"Yeah."

"I don't have any lube, either."

"Jesus, I don't care!" Doug said. "Use spit."

"I don't think I can," Guy said, nevertheless.

"You don't have any spit? I have spit. Here." He produced some and, spitting it into his palm, offered it to Guy.

"I mean, I don't think I can fuck you."

"But you're hard," Doug said. "You want to."

"I do want to," Guy admitted. "But I don't want to more."

"That doesn't make sense."

"It does to me."

"I don't get it. I'm the one taking the risk."

"We're both taking a risk."

"But I'm clean!" Doug said. "Aren't you?"

"That's not the risk I mean," Guy said. "Not the only risk, anyway. If you don't already understand what I'm getting at, then I can't explain it. I just can't do that with you."

"I know you love me," Doug said. "We came together."

Guy was nodding, thinking about the green sea behind him, whether his bike was safe at the top of the cliff, whether he had enough water to make it home or would have to stop at a filling station along the way to replenish his plastic bottle. He thought about whether and when the rain would arrive in earnest: fairly soon, judging by the gusty winds that were beginning to blow. He stood at risk of getting soaked.

"That's not love," Guy said. He'd stopped nodding. "Coming together. That's sex. If it's even that. I'm not sure."

Doug stared at him without a word.

"Sex isn't love," Guy said, elaborating the point.

"I know that," Doug said. He was squirming with the discomfort of someone whose emotional and erotic experiences had taught him exactly the opposite: that sex and love were the same thing. Sex was love, an exchange of love, a salve on problems, a way of knowing, and of being known by, someone else; it was an event that deepened human understanding, bridged chasms, breached barriers, closed gaps, healed wounds, left people happy. It did do those things, sometimes. Far more often it did the opposite, quickening dislike, speeding dissolution, bursting bubbles of romantic fantasy, driving people away from each other. "I've—I've changed, you know," Doug went on. "I've learned a lot since the last time we talked."

Guy stifled a flash of impatience.

"You're much more muscular," he allowed politely.

Doug reddened down to the scattering of freckles on his broad shoulders. "I've been working out," he said. "But no, come on, that's not what I mean. I mean, I've thought a lot and everything. About things. About the way I behaved. The way I treated you. What happened between us that last night. I've talked about it a lot with Anna—she's my girlfriend. She's helped me not to be afraid of the memory. She's helped me see why I behaved badly."

Guy nodded but did not interrupt this convincingly delivered soliloquy, at once self-lacerating and full of self-pardon.

"I . . . what happened today, what just happened between us, should have happened then. That night," Doug said. He seemed to be gasping and swallowing a little. "That night I came to your room and got into bed with you. You remember."

"But it *didn't* happen," Guy pointed out. "That's the whole point, isn't it?"

"I *know* it didn't happen," Doug said, plainly exasperated. "I'm saying it should have happened."

"The fact that it didn't," Guy said, "says to me that it shouldn't have. It wasn't meant to be."

"What the hell does that mean?"

"It means that things worked out the way they were supposed to," Guy said. "It means that what happened was meant to happen, and what didn't happen, wasn't. And you can't make it happen now. Now isn't then. The circumstances have changed. We've changed."

"That's bullshit," Doug said. "It did happen, half an hour ago. It's happening now." He stroked Guy's dick for emphasis. "Look, I wasn't ready. I wasn't ready then. I was scared. I took it out on you. I've explained all this. I don't know what else I can say. I'm sorry. I shouldn't have blown up like that. I panicked. I couldn't help it. I didn't know what I was supposed to do. But it's different now. I'm different."

"You think you're ready."

"I am," Doug said. He smiled and raised his hips slightly. Guy smiled back and sighed. Thought of the act—that act, any act—wearied him. Their brief and intense erotic bout had satisfied his lingering curiosity about Doug's body: a young man's body, like so many others, athletic and well-proportioned. Guy was no longer curious. The thought of joining his body to Doug's did not make him tremble, as Doug was trembling, turning himself inside out with nervous energy. The boy's desire was sweet, really: a palpable hunger, lust for connection, a siren call, an invitation into the trackless swamps of the flesh. Guy was powerfully drawn, powerfully tempted by this boy in the sand, but he hesitated. He could not blind himself to the essential ridiculousness, the unseemliness of the situation. An awareness of unseemliness was a powerful, and maybe the only, antidote to lust.

"Do it," Doug whispered throatily. He was fingering his asshole now, just as Guy had seen it done so often in so many porn films. He wondered if Doug had picked up his technique from porn. Doug was touching him now, pushing him into position between his legs, as if Guy were some kind of inflatable sex dummy.

"No."

"No?"

"No. I can't. I told you." Guy rolled from Doug's hips and started shaking the sand from his shucked clothes. "It's not that you're not attractive," Guy went on. "You are. Very. It goes right through me. But being attracted to someone isn't the same thing as wanting to do something with that person. And I just don't want to do that with you."

"I might have a rubber after all," Doug said, rummaging through his backpack.

"With or without a rubber, it doesn't matter. I can't."

"But you're hard!"

"Temporary condition."

"I don't understand."

"I can't explain it."

"But I love you," Doug said. "I always have. And you love me. I know you do. You always have."

"Doug," Guy said. *I don't love you. Ignore those tears in my eyes.* "I'm too old for you. I've had my fill of this stuff. Beach sex, sand everywhere. Young horny guys. I've been there."

"You're just afraid!" Doug said.

"Maybe that's true," Guy said. "So what if I am?"

"You're afraid of happiness! You'd rather be lonely. You're running away! You're afraid! You're giving in to fear."

Guy shrugged. If it was true, he didn't care. Some fears were meant to be given in to. Others, to be fought. The trick was figuring out which was which. Doug's case wasn't a hard one.

"You'll be lonely!" Doug said again.

"I won't be lonely," Guy said. "I'm not alone. I have friends. I have a life I like."

"But you don't have anyone special!" Doug said. He was sitting up now, face flushed with passion and disbelief that a middle-aged man like Guy could not have someone special and, worse, purport not to be concerned about it, especially with someone like Doug seeming to offer himself for the role. He was also still hard.

"You don't need to worry about me, I'll be fine," Guy said mildly. "You really should be lavishing all this energy on your girlfriend."

"So that's what this is all about," Doug said. "Now I get it. It's Anna. You're jealous. That's why you don't want to meet her."

"It's none of my business."

"What do you mean, it's none of your business?" Doug sputtered. "It's totally your business."

"Your relationship with some girl?"

"I told you I told her all about you. She knows everything. She knows I'm here, and she knows why."

"You seem to be telling everyone everything about everyone else," Guy said. "I wonder why."

"I'm honest."

"Yes," Guy said in a tone of utter disbelief. It was impossible not to notice how often self-righteous young people passed off all sorts of double-dealing gossip as "honesty."

"You're just avoiding this whole thing any way you can and I've waited so long for us to be happy," Doug said, and now he was miserable and tears broke out on his face, coursing like trickles of rainwater down the smooth skin of his cheeks. "I don't understand why you're doing this," he said between sobs.

"Crying isn't going to make any difference," Guy said.

"I'll cry if I want to," Doug said. He cried a little longer, as if to prove that his sorrow were genuine and not some stunt, before bringing the show to a gentle stop.

"You don't love me," he said in a clear, cold voice.

Guy said nothing.

"You can tell me," Doug said. "I can take it."

"I don't want to talk about it."

"That's so male," Doug said. "Not wanting to talk about it. Repressing your feelings. It's not healthy."

"I'm sure not."

"I love you," Doug said. "It doesn't matter whether you love me or not. I don't care." He started weeping again, very softly, and he leaned forward to drape his arms around Guy's shoulders and bury his face in Guy's neck. They held that awkward pose for some time, until Doug looked up pleadingly into Guy's eyes.

"I'll always love you," he said.

"Doug," Guy said, patting Doug's hair, caressing his neck and his shoulders, taking a good whiff of his distinctive odor. "You'll be fine," he said. "Go back to your girl. Tell her you dumped me."

"But you're dumping me," Doug pointed out.

"That's not true," Guy lied. "But she doesn't need to know about all this anyway. Let yourself be happy with her. Forget about me. Move on."

"I don't want to forget about you. I don't want to move on."

"Of course you do. You just don't want to admit it."

Doug once again looked to be on the verge of tears.

"I don't feel right about this," he said.

"You will," Guy said. It was something he had to say. He knew that what Doug didn't feel right about was his failure to prevail. He had not succeeded in bending Guy to his will, in eliciting a declaration of Guy's love and then triumphantly rejecting him. These disruptions of the prerogatives of youth made him wretched. He had to live with defeat, and the worst sort of defeat: self-inflicted, against an adversary who declined to gloat or give any other reason for a liberating bitterness. Kindness was the best revenge. In offering sex Doug had gambled all his chips, and Guy had taken them and walked away from the table. The game was up.

"I hope you feel fine about it," Doug said ominously. He was fondling himself again, even as Guy donned his clothes.

"I do feel fine, thank you," Guy said. "It's getting chilly, don't you think? It looks like it's raining over in Marin."

Doug said nothing. There was cold challenge in his eyes, there was pain and pleading and disbelief and fury and hurt pride and determination and, under all that, genuine desire and genuine love. He did love Guy, but it was not a good thing. To be loved by Doug was a mortal threat. His was a ruinous love, a passion that scorched and withered, a love of power and games, triumph and defeat, sex among the wounded. It wasn't Guy's idea of love at all, really. They used the same words but spoke different languages, belonged to different species, inhabited different worlds. Doug's world was toxic to Guy; Guy was old enough to have learned that much. He didn't need to plunge into the poison one last time to make the definitive diagnosis.

Doug was working it, working it. Guy watched him pant and grunt and shoot halfway up his flat torso, as if in a porn film. Yes, it was still enjoyable to watch a youth squirt semen. The boy sagged desolately against a rock while Guy mopped him up, clinical in his gentle efficiency, like a nurse.

"Good-bye, Doug," he said, giving him a kiss on the forehead.

"You're leaving?"

"It's getting late, and I don't want to catch pneumonia."

"I've got a truck," Doug said.

"I thought you sold that thing."

"I got another one," Doug said. "It's up at the road. It's a pick-up. We can throw your bike in the back. We won't even have to take the front tire off."

"I don't have a flat tire this time," Guy said, unable to suppress a fond smile, "but thanks anyway."

"You don't need a flat," Doug said. "We can just put it back there and I'll give you a ride."

"I need the exercise."

"What if it starts raining before you get home?"

"If I don't get started, it will," Guy said. "Good-bye, Doug."

"I can't believe you're leaving me," Doug said.

"You'll be fine," Guy said. "You have a truck!"

With that he waved and started along the beach, retracing the steps he'd made only an hour earlier, still visible in the damp sand. He was resolute in refusing to look back at Doug, whose outraged and grieving gaze he could feel on his back. But when he reached the high outcropping at the top of the slippery stone stairs, he did permit himself a glance and saw, amid the nest of rocks, the boy still standing, glorious and fragile and unbearably naked. They exchanged slightly forlorn waves, like acquaintances passing on trains bound in different directions.

ABOUT THE AUTHOR

Paul Reidinger's first novel, *The Best Man,* was named one of the best novels of 1986 by the American Library Association's magazine, *Booklist.* His other novels include *Intimate Evil* and *Good Boys,* which novelist Paul Russell *(The Salt Point)* described as "brilliant . . . may well be to the late eighties and early nineties what *Dancer from the Dance* was to the seventies."

He lives in San Francisco.

Order Your Own Copy of
This Important Book for Your Personal Library!

THE CITY KID

_____ in hardbound at $39.95 (ISBN: 1-56023-168-8)

_____ in softbound at $16.95 (ISBN: 1-56023-169-6)

COST OF BOOKS_____

OUTSIDE USA/CANADA/
MEXICO: ADD 20%____

POSTAGE & HANDLING_____
(US: $4.00 for first book & $1.50
for each additional book)
Outside US: $5.00 for first book
& $2.00 for each additional book)

SUBTOTAL_____

in Canada: add 7% GST____

STATE TAX____
(NY, OH & MIN residents, please
add appropriate local sales tax)

FINAL TOTAL____
(If paying in Canadian funds,
convert using the current
exchange rate, UNESCO
coupons welcome.)

❑   **BILL ME LATER:** ($5 service charge will be added)
(Bill-me option is good on US/Canada/Mexico orders only;
not good to jobbers, wholesalers, or subscription agencies.)

❑ Check here if billing address is different from
shipping address and attach purchase order and
billing address information.

Signature_____

❑   **PAYMENT ENCLOSED: $**_____

❑   **PLEASE CHARGE TO MY CREDIT CARD.**

❑ Visa ❑ MasterCard ❑ AmEx ❑ Discover
❑ Diner's Club ❑ Eurocard ❑ JCB

Account # _____

Exp. Date_____

Signature_____

Prices in US dollars and subject to change without notice.

NAME_____

INSTITUTION_____

ADDRESS_____

CITY_____

STATE/ZIP_____

COUNTRY_____ COUNTY (NY residents only)_____

TEL_____ FAX_____

E-MAIL_____

May we use your e-mail address for confirmations and other types of information? ❑ Yes ❑ No
We appreciate receiving your e-mail address and fax number. Haworth would like to e-mail or fax special
discount offers to you, as a preferred customer. **We will never share, rent, or exchange your e-mail address
or fax number.** We regard such actions as an invasion of your privacy.

Order From Your Local Bookstore or Directly From
The Haworth Press, Inc.
10 Alice Street, Binghamton, New York 13904-1580 • USA
TELEPHONE: 1-800-HAWORTH (1-800-429-6784) / Outside US/Canada: (607) 722-5857
FAX: 1-800-895-0582 / Outside US/Canada: (607) 722-6362
E-mail: getinfo@haworthpressinc.com
PLEASE PHOTOCOPY THIS FORM FOR YOUR PERSONAL USE.
www.HaworthPress.com